THE PINK PONY
MURDER ON MACKINAC ISLAND

THE PINK PONY

MURDER ON MACKINAC ISLAND

A BURR LAFAYETTE MYSTERY

Charles Cutter

MISSION POINT PRESS

Published by Mission Point Press
2554 Chandler Rd.
Traverse City, MI 49686
(231) 421-9513
www.MissionPointPress.com

ISBN: 978-1-950659-63-0
Library of Congress Control Number: 2020910211

Manufactured in the United States of America
First Edition/First Printing

Cover design: John Wickham
Interior design and layout: Bob Deck

To
Bob and Yvonne

All happy families are alike; each unhappy family is unhappy in its own way.

Leo Tolstoy
Anna Karenina

CHAPTER ONE

The pink pony hung from chains and rocked back and forth in the wind. It was bubblegum pink and the size of a rocking horse. It hung above the door to the bar of the same name. This particular pink pony, like the ones before it, would soon disappear, but not before the night ended badly.

Just before 2 a.m., the bouncer threw one of the sailors out the front door by the collar of his pink shirt, the pink of his shirt and the pink pony an exact match. The rest stumbled out under their own power.

After the bar closed, the bartender surveyed the damage. The Christmas tree had tipped over and clung to the edge of the bar by duct tape, but the Christmas lights still twinkled. Lingerie dangled from its branches. She finished cleaning up, stepped out onto the sidewalk and stood underneath the pink pony. She reached up and pushed it once for luck.

An hour later, the chains swung in the wind. Just the chains. The pink rocking horse had loosed its moorings.

An hour after that, a man sat at the bar by himself. He had a quiet smile, his eyes were wide open, and his chin rested on his chest. The Christmas lights still twinkled, wrapped five times around his neck. Pulled tight and tied in a square knot, seaman-like.

* * *

The Pink Pony was on the ground floor of the Chippewa Hotel, across the lobby from the front desk. The Chippewa, circa 1902, a four-story, white frame, slightly ramshackle building of about sixty rooms, faced Main Street and backed up to the harbor. Not on a par with the Grand, but still one of Mackinac Island's finer hotels. The lobby had a thick, slightly worn, faded green carpet with red and yellow flowers the size of dinner plates. Purple floor-length draperies with climbing vines finished off the Victorian décor.

But the jewel of the Chippewa was The Pink Pony, which couldn't have been less Victorian. The bar itself ran along the west wall opposite the lobby, a nutty, polished white oak with long clean lines. The band played on a raised stage behind the bar, a pink pony painted on the wall behind the stage. Plate glass windows fronted Main Street with oak booths below them. There were booths along the east and south walls, vintage Mackinac race pictures above them, dueling twelve meters, a one-tonner flying a spinnaker, a J-35 pointing, its rail buried.

The bar was classy enough and stylish enough, but what made The Pink Pony was its location. Not because it was inside the Chippewa but because it was the closest bar to the docks. The sailors had made it famous.

* * *

The Port Huron-Mackinac had started on Saturday, just north of the Blue Water Bridge. Three hundred sailboats. Three hundred miles. From Port Huron to Mackinac Island, around the Cove Island buoy near the entrance to Georgian Bay, then west to the finish line between the red can and the committee boat at the eastern tip of the island. The fleet had been blessed with clear skies and a southeast wind that had backed to the west.

By Monday night, the lion's share of the boats were in, and the sailors made for the The Pink Pony. The bar smelled of cigarettes, spilled beer, suntan lotion and sweat. The Jelly Roll Blues Band, the finest cover band in Northern Michigan, had just finished *Son of a Son of a Sailor* for the third time. They promised to be back in fifteen minutes and walked offstage with their instruments, which showed good judgment, the patrons freelancing whenever they got the chance.

Jimmy Lyons, late thirties with deadly good looks, stood. He took advantage of the slightly less than deafening background noise and shouted, "A round for all the racers!" The sailors cheered. Jimmy shouted again, louder this time, "And for the racer chasers!" Another cheer, this one louder than the last. Jimmy waved a fistful of cash at the closest bartender, a fresh-faced, college-age girl with a ponytail the color of wet sand. Jimmy started toward the bar but knocked his chair backwards. It would have tipped over, but the bar was so crowded that the chair bumped into a sunburned fellow at the table behind him. Jimmy flashed a brilliant smile, made more so by his tan. "I am so sorry."

He dodged his way through the crowd and handed the money to the bartender. She looked over at the head bartender, a seen-it-all, auburn-haired beauty who, unremarkably, also had a ponytail, the style of the season. She nodded and the bartender reached down for a bottle of house whiskey, then poured shot after shot into plastic glasses. They'd learned their lesson long ago and had replaced glass with plastic before the fleet sailed in.

Jimmy downed one of the shots. He boosted himself over the bar, grabbed a fifth of whiskey, four of the plastic shot glasses and headed back to his table.

"That must have cost a fortune," said Murdo Halverson, later thirties, a thinnish man with jet-black hair that forever fell in his face. He had on a lime-green Lacoste and madras Bermuda shorts. He wore tortoise shell reading glasses and a nametag from the cocktail party at the Mackinac Island Yacht Club.

Jimmy poured a shot for himself and one for Murdo.

"If you were going to steal something, you might at least have stolen something better than Kessler's," Murdo said.

Like Jimmy and the rest of the sailors, Murdo had been up for the better part of three days and needed to get some sleep. He looked like he'd be ill at any moment. Jimmy looked like he could go on forever.

A well-oiled man in a blue Bayview Yacht Club hat reached across two tables and shook Jimmy's hand. "Congratulations. First is first. No matter how you get there."

Jimmy clenched his teeth, smiled back at the drunk, then turned and poured the shot down his throat. Murdo studied his shot but didn't drink it. Jimmy looked at Murdo, then drank Murdo's shot.

"What are you doing?" Murdo said.

"I've never seen you drink Kessler's," Anne Halverson said. She had black hair, darker than her husband's, an upturned nose, and green eyes the color of money.

Jimmy poured Anne her own shot. She drank it and shook her head. Her ponytail swung back and forth. "Smooth as silk," she said.

"You only won because of the protest," said Jane, Jimmy's long-suffering wife, if seven years qualified as long suffering. Tall, almost six feet, a leggy blonde, bustier than Anne. Pouty lips and her very own champagne-blond ponytail.

"You just don't like the name of my boat," Jimmy said, waving at some-one across the bar and jumping to his feet. "It's time for the tree."

"The tree?" Anne said.

"The Christmas tree. It's Christmas in July." Jimmy ducked out the door to the street.

"Now what?" Murdo said.

"The only thing to do is humor him," Jane said.

Jelly Roll started back up with *Cheeseburger in Paradise*.

"Damn this place," Murdo said.

Twenty minutes later, Jimmy burst back into the bar with a four-foot spruce duct taped to a makeshift Christmas tree stand. He set it on the bar next to the Labatt tap. The tree leaned but didn't tip over. He unwound a string of Christmas tree lights from his waist. They were C-9s, the old-fashioned kind. Big bulbs – red, green, blue, yellow and orange – the kind that didn't blink. He strung them around the tree and plugged them in. He took a second strand and wrapped them around his neck, like a necklace. The crowd cheered. Jimmy bowed and lost his balance. He righted himself, staggered back to his table and had another shot.

"That's the poorest excuse for a Christmas tree I have ever seen," Jane said.

"It is, isn't it," Jimmy said.

"Where'd you get it?" Anne said.

"Next to the fort," Jimmy said.

"God help us," Murdo said. He swept his lifeless hair off his forehead.

"Now it's time for the decorations," Jimmy said.

"We don't have any decorations," Anne said.

"Nonsense," Jimmy said. "How about your bra?"

"That's enough," Murdo said, his pointed nose now out of joint. "I think it's time to leave, Anne."

"Don't worry, darling. I'm not big enough to bounce." Anne slid her chair back, stood and bumped into a potted sailor, who scowled at her. "I'm so sorry," she said. She reached up underneath her top and took off her bra. He looked at her poking through her top and was all smiles. Her breasts brushed against the back of Jimmy's head on her way to the tree.

"That's quite enough, Anne," Murdo said.

"Darling, no one cares except you." She twisted her way through the tables to the Christmas tree and hung her white, lacy bra on the tree.

Jimmy stood and clapped. He waved, maybe at Anne, maybe at one of his crew. Jimmy knew everyone. "How about you, Jane-o?" He poured her a shot.

"What's it worth to you?" She looked at the shot but didn't drink it.

Jimmy leaned over to Murdo. "They all have a price."

"I heard that," Jane said.

"You were supposed to." He drank Jane's shot.

"My guess is half of what you've got," Murdo said.

"I've got a good lawyer," Jimmy said.

"So do I, baby," Jane said.

The band played *Son of a Son of a Sailor* for the fourth time. Everyone in the bar sprang to their feet.

Jane peeled off her bra, black, bigger than Anne's and every bit as lacy. She snapped it at Jimmy and kissed him on the lips. She twirled her bra like a lariat on her way to the tree and hung it next to Anne's.

Jimmy went back to the tree, took Anne and Jane by the hand, and danced with them.

Jimmy and the two braless women danced their way back to the table, hands over their heads, swaying to the music. It sounded like *Boat Drinks*, but it was hard to tell over the roar of the sailors, their wives, their girlfriends and a few stray islanders.

Anne planted a wet kiss squarely on Jimmy's lips, then sat.

"Stop it, Anne," Murdo said.

"It's a party," Jimmy said.

"She's my wife, and this has gone too far." He flipped his hair out of his face again.

"Nonsense," Jimmy said.

"You're drunk. And so are they."

Jimmy draped an arm over Murdo's shoulder. "That's the point." He looked over at the Christmas tree. Anne and Jane's bras had been joined by a dozen more. "We need something to go with them." He looked at Anne, who wound her way back to the tree.

She reached under her skirt, stepped out of her matching white panties and hung them on the tree.

Jane gave her a husband a withering look. Not to be outdone, she made her way back to the tree. She made a show of taking off her black panties and hung them on the tree.

Murdo groaned.

"Why don't you just go up to your cottage and go to bed," Jimmy said.

"Someone has to watch the three of you."

Jimmy looked at the tree. Weighted down with the flotsam and jetsam of lingerie, it had developed a dangerous list to port. He rushed to the bar. "Over here, Murdo. Help me prop it up."

Murdo followed Jimmy to the bar and righted the tree. "Thata boy!" Jimmy said. He duct-taped the tree to the bar.

Back at the table, Jimmy sat and plopped Anne on his lap. Her skirt climbed up her legs.

"It's time to go, Anne," Murdo said.

"The bar doesn't close for another hour," Jimmy said.

Anne wiggled on Jimmy's lap then untangled his Christmas light necklace. "You're going to strangle yourself," she said.

CHAPTER TWO

The porch swing hung from chains and rocked back and forth. Burr Lafayette pushed off from the porch with the big toe on his right foot. The nail on the big toe of his left foot had already started to turn black, and he was sure the toe was broken.

Was it just last night that I dropped that damned pony on my toe?

At the moment, though, his soon-to-be-lost toenail was the least of his worries. The throbbing began just above his eyebrows. Not a throbbing, a pounding. That's what it was. His head pounded like a pile driver keeping time with his heart. The eight aspirin and two quarts of water hadn't touched it.

Hiding behind sunglasses, Burr sat in the shade of the porch and rocked back and forth on the swing. The sun, reflecting off the water a hundred feet below, made his headache worse. "Damn that sun." He shut his eyes behind his sunglasses. "I never thought I'd say that," he said to Zeke, his aging Labrador retriever sprawled beside him.

"We're going to have to get ourselves straightened out before Eve and Jacob get here."

Burr rocked and rocked. Late forties. At one time he had been six feet. Still lean. Hawk nose, peeling. Straight, white teeth. Sky blue eyes. His eyebrows arched when he spoke. His hair was still the color of an acorn in autumn. He had a few gray hairs but pulled them out as soon as they came in.

Not quite a week ago, Burr had chartered *Scaramouche*, a Peterson 34. She was a fast boat with new sails, and the owner needed some legal work done, which Burr agreed to do for the use of the boat. He and his crew had won their class, and they made for The Pink Pony as soon as they tied up. He had drunk too much, and here he was on the porch of Windward with one of the top ten hangovers of his life.

The wind came up from the west, blew across his face and lulled him to sleep. Broken toe, pounding head and all.

His nap didn't last for long. The ding-a-ling of a bell sounded. Burr squinted through his sunglasses. The ding-a-ling of a bell on the handlebars of a bicycle, the old-fashioned kind with fat tires and a basket. The cyclist, a beefy man with white hair and a red face, puffed his way up the street, ever closer to Windward, where Burr Lafayette hid from the most beautiful day of the summer.

Burr watched the beefy man come closer to the cottage. To Burr's horror, he dismounted in front of the cottage. He leaned his shiny red Huffy against the hitching post and lumbered up the sidewalk. He wore the short-sleeve white shirt and blue slacks of the Mackinac Island Police Department.

"What fresh hell is this?" Burr said.

The cop stopped at the porch stairs. "Beg pardon?"

"Dorothy Parker."

"Who's she?"

"She's not from around here."

"I didn't think so." The cop huffed and puffed up the steps, then stopped to catch his breath. "That's a hike."

I hope he doesn't die on the porch.

"It's a long way up the East Bluff on a bike." At least the cop's complexion was fading from beet red to cherry tomato.

Maybe he isn't going to die after all.

The recovering policeman walked the length of the porch to Burr, Zeke, and the porch swing. "Chief Art Brandstatter." He stuck his hand out to Burr, who offered his own, reluctantly. The cop pumped Burr's hand, sending a brand-new pain up his arm and into his pounding head. Burr jerked his hand away.

"That's not very friendly," the cop said.

"I'm not feeling very friendly," Burr said. "No offense."

"None taken." The cop put his hands on his hips. "Come with me."

"Why would I do that?"

"Right now," the chief said.

"Officer Friendly, I'm afraid I don't even know why you're here."

"Sure you do. Now come along."

"No, I don't think I will."

"Mr. Lafayette, there is the matter of the missing pink pony."

Burr winced. "You'll have a heart attack if you get on that bike again," he said.

"It's all downhill to the Chippewa," Chief Brandstatter said.

"Why didn't you ride a horse?"

"Allergies. Come with me."

"Do I have to?"

"Only if you want to stay out of our little jail."

"Why would I go to jail?"

"Grand larceny." The cop smiled at him and lumbered back to his bicycle.

Burr slipped on his flip-flops and climbed on one of Windward's fat-tire bikes. He pedaled behind Chief Brandstatter along the row of Victorian cottages that lined the East Bluff. They coasted downhill, Zeke trotting next to Burr's bike. Burr winced every time his brakes squeaked. They turned west on Main Street, with St. Anne's Church, the Indian Dormitory and Mackinac Island Yacht Club all to starboard, the state-owned docks to port. Burr saw the flag flying in front of the harbormaster's building and smiled to himself.

Fort Mackinac, left over from the war of 1812 and now restored, looked down at them over Marquette Park. The fort a long, rambling, whitewashed wall in a rectangle, with blockhouses on the corners. Inside the walls, all the buildings any self-respecting fort would have: barracks, commissary, infirmary, cookhouse, guardhouse.

Burr dodged pedestrians and bikes, plus riders on horseback, horse-drawn carriages, drays – and their droppings. The sweet, ripe smell of horse manure turned his stomach, but even today he thought it preferable to the exhaust of Detroit, three hundred miles to the south.

At the Chippewa, the beefy cop stuck his left arm straight out and turned left. The opposing traffic ignored him. Brandstatter ding-a-linged and dodged his way to the sidewalk. He half climbed, half fell off his bike, then flipped the kickstand in place.

Burr coasted up and parked. He touched his temples with his fingertips and winced. He swept his hair back with his fingers. It curled as it broke over his collar, slightly longer than fashionable. He patted the crown of his head, feeling for the beginnings of a bald spot.

It might be a bit thinner.

He looked up at where the pink pony had hung just last night and how many martinis ago, the chains hanging from the ceiling.

"Damn it," the chief said as Zeke stood on three legs, his fourth above the rear tire of the chief's bike. "Make him stop that."

"I think he's just about done."

"Jesus, Mary, Joseph. When I'm done with you, I'm gonna arrest him, too." Brandstatter looked Burr square in the eyes. "Now where is it?'

"Where's what?"

Chief Brandstatter pointed up at the empty chains.

"I have no idea."

"Like hell you don't."

Burr looked back up at the dangling chains, then at Brandstatter. "Chief, I have no idea where it is."

Burr had stolen it last night and hoisted it up the flagpole at the marina, but he had no idea where it was now.

"You'd better have an idea, or you and that damned yellow dog can sit in my jail until you come up with one."

"Chief, I really don't know what you're talking about."

"Why don't we just go inside and straighten this out?"

He pulled on the door to the bar. "How can the Pony be locked at noon? That's a fire hazard." Brandstatter pulled on the door again, harder this time. "We'll just see about this," he said. "You come with me."

The chief rumbled up the sidewalk and into the lobby, Burr and Zeke followed him in. Burr slipped out of his flip-flops and wiggled his toes in the flowery carpet. His broken toe throbbed so he stopped wiggling that foot.

"Excuse me, sir, there are no dogs allowed in the hotel." Burr looked past the guests at a twentyish, strawberry blonde standing at the check counter, behind her, old-fashioned shelves with cubbyholes, some with keys in them.

"Zeke, sit." The aging Lab sat at Burr's left. Burr had a pretty good idea that a sitting dog wouldn't trump the Chippewa's no-dog policy, but he thought it was worth a try.

"Excuse me, sir. Sitting dogs aren't allowed either. There are no dogs allowed in the hotel. And shoes are required."

"I have shoes. I'm just not wearing them."

"Please, sir, your dog must go, and you must put your shoes on."

Burr looked over at Brandstatter, who was pulling on the door to the bar.

"I'm here on police business," Burr said.

"Really. I didn't know that khaki shorts and a polo shirt was the uniform of the day."

"I'm undercover."

Brandstatter walked up to the desk clerk. "Why are the doors locked?"

"It's closed right now."

"Why is it closed? It's lunch time."

"You'll have to ask Miss Hennessey," the desk clerk said.

"And where might she be?"

"I think she's looking for you."

"And why would that be?"

"Because The Pink Pony is locked."

"Look here. I'm here on police business. Unlock the door to the bar."

"That's why Miss Hennessey is looking for you."

Brandstatter pointed at her, then at the door. She bit her cheek, ducked under the counter and came up with a ring full of keys. Brandstatter followed and motioned for Burr to join them.

She unlocked the door, then turned to Burr. "I had no idea he was a police dog," she said, smiling.

Brandstatter opened the door and waved Burr and Zeke in. "Sit down right here," he said, pointing at a table. Burr sat. Sunlight poured in through the windows, lighting the larger than life pink pony painted on the wall behind the bar.

I can't get away from that stupid hobby horse.

He thought there was nothing more depressing than sitting in an empty bar. It had been cleaned, but it still smelled like flat beer and ashtrays.

I may be ill.

The chief sat down across from Burr. "We're going to sit here until you tell me where that damned horse is."

Burr and Brandstatter sat. Neither one of them said a word. Burr's head throbbed and his toe hurt. Just when the silence was getting to Brandstatter, the lobby door opened. In walked a woman with perhaps the most beautiful auburn ponytail Burr had ever seen, auburn with blond highlights. She had a longish nose, brown eyes and a few freckles. Jeans, a black tank top and tennis shoes. Maybe five-five. Curvy. All of thirty-five. Burr was pretty sure he'd seen her in the bar last night.

She walked over to their table. "Art, I've been looking all over for you."

"That's what I hear."

"You know what happened?"

"Carole," Brandstatter said, "why else would I be here?" He hitched up his pants. "I'm about to get to the bottom of it."

"Already?"

"No time like the present. How come the Pony's not open?"

She looked out the window, then back at Brandstatter. "Have you called St. Ignace yet?"

"I can handle the annual theft of the pink pony without the county mounties."

Carole walked over to the bar. "Come over here."

Brandstatter trundled over and looked behind the bar. "Jesus, Mary, Joseph. That changes the water on the minnies."

Burr looked over at the bar. There was the poor excuse for a Christmas tree hanging over the edge, lingerie still dangling from its limbs. He'd forgotten all about the tree.

Burr stood.

"Stop right there. Not one more step," Brandstatter said.

This has gotten out of hand.

"I'm sure we can straighten this out," Burr said.

"I wish we could. I surely wish we could." The chief hitched up his equipment belt, loaded with every tool in the arsenal of law enforcement, except a gun.

That thing must weight thirty pounds.

"Come over here. And don't touch a thing. Not one thing. And leave that poor excuse for a Labrador retriever right where he is."

The chief stood at the bar, next to the tree. "Stand right next to me and don't touch a thing."

Burr walked over to the bar. "We didn't have to come all this way for the pink pony."

"Apparently, we didn't." Brandstatter pointed behind the bar. "Look down there."

Burr bent over the bar and jumped, not quite out of his skin. The dead man sat on a chair, eyes wide open, smiling like he'd just heard a funny story. He had a necklace of Christmas lights wound five or six times around his neck and plugged in behind the bar. The lights were a nice touch, Burr thought, but they'd been wound a little too tight. The dead man's tongue hung out the side of his mouth and the joke was clearly on him.

Burr turned away from the dead man. The color ran out of his face. He was sure he was going to be ill.

"You don't look so good."

"I'm fine," Burr said, who wasn't.

"You look kinda green to me." He reached over the bar and grabbed a bottle of Fleischmann's gin. "How about a little hair of the dog?"

"I wouldn't drink Fleischmann's on a bet." Burr started for the door. "I think it's time for me to go."

"Not so fast. We have important police business."

"I don't," Burr said.

"You do unless you want to spend the rest of the summer in the hoosegow."

Burr kept walking.

"Did you hear what I said?"

"I did, and I've decided that I prefer jail. Zeke, come."

"How about you turn around and maybe I'll forget about that missing pony?"

Burr stopped.

"That's more like it."

Burr walked back to the bar.

"What we have here is a dead man," the police chief said.

That demonstrates a remarkable grasp of the obvious.

Brandstatter turned to Carole. "Why didn't you tell me right away?"

"That's why I've been trying to find you."

"What in the name of mercy happened?"

"I came in to open up. Both doors were locked just like they're supposed to be. This is what I found when I got here."

"Who closed last night?"

"Karen Vander Voort."

Brandstatter nodded. "Why don't you just leave us be while we get this sorted out. I'll take them keys."

"Shouldn't we call the police?"

"I am the police."

Heaven help us.

Carole handed Brandstatter the keys and left through the lobby door.

The chief reached for a glass, poured two fingers of the Fleischmann's and handed it to Burr. "This will help."

"I don't drink."

"Since when?"

"Since now."

The chief looked at Burr, then the two fingers of gin, then back at Burr. "Suit yourself," He set the glass on the bar. "I hear you do criminal work."

"I'm not a criminal lawyer," Burr said. "I'm a civil litigator. My practice is limited to appellate work." He looked at the two fingers of Fleischmann's. The thought of gin, even Bombay, sickened him.

Maybe a Red Eye will help.

Burr slid behind the bar. He found a towel and picked up a beer glass with it. He slunk past the dead man to the Labatt tap. One end of the lights was wrapped around the tap.

"Damn it all."

Carefully, very carefully he pushed the tap with the towel and drew himself half a glass.

"Cut that out," Brandstatter said. "You're corrupting state's evidence."

Burr held up the towel. He opened the refrigerator underneath the bar, took out a plastic jug of tomato juice and filled the rest of the glass with it.

"What in God's name is that?" the chief said.

"A Red Eye." Burr stirred the drink with one finger, then took a big swallow.

"Waste of good beer and tomato juice if you ask me." The chief squeezed behind the bar and looked over the dead man. "Any idea who he is?"

"He's got a yacht club name tag on. It says '*Murdo*,'" Burr studied the dead man. "What kind of name is that?"

"What kind of name is Burr?"

"Touché." Burr took another big swallow. His head was beginning to clear.

"Walk me through this," the chief said.

"I have no idea what to do," Burr said.

"Sure you do."

Burr finished his Red Eye.

That tastes like another.

"Chief Brandstatter, how long have you been in law enforcement?"

The chief puffed himself up like a rooster in a barnyard. "Thirty years."

"You've got thirty years on me," Burr said. "And how many murders have you investigated? Assuming this is a murder."

"This would be my first."

Burr grimaced. "I may have you there." He made himself another Red Eye, then disappeared under the bar.

"What are you doing?"

"Here it is," Burr said.

"Here's what?"

"Just what I was looking for." Burr held up a bottle of Worcestershire sauce. "Lea and Perrins. The only one worth using." He shook a quarter-of-an-inch into the new and improved Red Eye, stirred it with a finger and took a big swallow. "Much better."

"That's evidence," the chief said.

"What we have here," Burr said, feeling better yet, "are two absolute beginners. We need to get out of here and call someone who knows what they're doing."

"I know exactly what I'm doing."

Burr took a long pull on the Red Eye.

This has remarkable restorative powers.

His ability to think clearly had returned, and he was sure the two of them had better get out of there before they really ruined something. On top of that, Eve and Jacob were due at the ferry docks any time now, and there would be hell to pay if he managed to get involved in another murder.

"You don't even know who the dead man is."

"His name is Murdo."

"How do you know that's his name tag?"

Now the chief looked like the chicken on the chopping block. "Lafayette, I can't have a murder on Mackinac Island. Not on my watch."

"I'd say it's a bit late for that. We need to lock up the bar and get out of here." Burr looked down and saw the dead man staring at him. He jumped back a step and felt something crack under his flip-flop. He reached down and picked up a pair of tortoise shell glasses with a dangling bow. He held them between his thumb and forefinger.

"You're ruining evidence," Brandstatter said.

"My point exactly."

The chief bustled over to Burr and yanked the glasses out of Burr's hand. The bow broke off.

CHAPTER THREE

Burr stood in the shade and leaned against the wall of the warehouse on the Arnold Line dock.

The building housed the ticket office, waiting room, and the freight that had to be shipped over from the mainland, which was virtually everything. The building, white with green trim, had a sagging roof like a horse with a swayback.

Squinting through his sunglasses, Burr could see just enough to know when the ferry pulled in yet keep the glare from splitting his head in two. The Red Eyes had only worked as long as he was drinking them. Zeke lay at his feet, the dog's eyes locked on a mallard swimming just off the beach of the Chippewa.

Burr had finally persuaded the good chief to lock up the bar. He'd begged Brandstatter to call the Michigan State Police post in St. Ignace, but the chief insisted that "the situation," as he called it, should stay local and low key. After all, he said, it could have been an accident. Finally, Brandstatter relented and called the Mackinac County Sheriff's Department. The Homicide Division, such as it was, arrived by ferry from St. Ignace, the little Upper Peninsula town with the almost perfect harbor just across the Mackinac Bridge.

At last, the *Huron* pulled in, the sixty-foot, twin-hull catamaran with diesels that rumbled like a freight train. Two decks, white with green trim. After most of the fifty or so passengers from Mackinaw City disembarked – tourists of all shapes and sizes, Boy Scouts to serve at the fort, cottagers, islanders, workers – Jacob and Eve came down the gangway. Burr took off his sunglasses and hugged Eve.

She stared into his bloodshot eyes. "Was it that demon rum?"

"Gin."

Eve McGinty had been his longtime, long-suffering legal assistant at Fisher and Allen. When he'd resigned, he'd begged her not to quit, but she insisted on following him to East Lansing. She said she wanted a house with full sun so she could have a perennial garden. Burr thought there must be full sun somewhere in the Detroit area.

She was pretty. Late forties. Short with short brown hair. She favored gold hoop earrings which she tugged when she was nervous. A hint of crow's feet at the corners of brown eyes. The beginnings of a few wrinkles around the corners of a mouth full of perfect teeth. Burr knew she didn't like being older than he was, even if it was only a year.

"Let me get your bags," Burr said.

She pointed to a matching pair of Hartmanns. Eve had divorced well and looked every inch the cottager in a sleeveless yellow top, blue jean skirt and sandals.

"Jacob, where's your luggage?"

"For all I know it's at the bottom of Lake Michigan."

"This is Lake Huron."

"It's still a wretched lake."

Jacob, natty as always, wore a button-down blue and white pinstripe cotton shirt, linen pants, argyle socks, and oxblood Weejuns. He twirled one of the steel-wool curls on the side of his head. Jacob was wiry just like his hair. Short with a prominent nose. Not big, prominent. He had an olive complexion, but at the moment, it looked more like mashed potatoes.

Jacob Wertheim, the Wertheim in Lafayette and Wertheim, had also been a partner at Fisher and Allen. Despite Burr's objection, Jacob had insisted on following Burr to East Lansing.

When it came to legal research and appellate briefs, Jacob was without peer, which was exactly why Burr needed him. But Jacob had two of the worst qualities a litigator could have. He abhorred conflict and was deathly afraid of public speaking.

"Had I known I would have to take a ferry to get here, I never would have come."

"How did you think you'd get here?"

"I had the distinct impression that the Mackinac Bridge connected this infernal island to the mainland."

"The Mackinac Bridge connects the Lower Peninsula to the Upper Peninsula," Eve said.

"Most islands have bridges to them. Like Long Island."

"Or Belle Isle," Eve said.

"Had I known I would have to take a boat here, I never would have come," Jacob said again.

Burr put his sunglasses back on, which helped his headache but didn't do a thing to get them off the dock and up to the street. "Jacob, where's your luggage?"

"I'm too seasick to carry my own luggage."

Burr whistled at a dock porter. "Would you please take my friend's bags to that taxi?" The porter, a college-age young man with a bandito mustache, looked at him like he was crazy. Until Burr palmed him a ten.

"You two take the carriage. I'll follow you on my bike."

"What is that awful smell?" Jacob said.

"That's fudge," Eve said. "Mackinac Island is famous for its home-made fudge."

"And what's this on my shoe?"

Burr and Eve knew very well what it was. They looked at Jacob, who had turned a whiter shade of pale. Neither said a word.

"I know what it is. I know full well what it is." He lifted the foot and studied his shoe. "Damn it, Burr. It's horse manure." Jacob lost his balance and hopped on one leg.

This isn't going to end well.

Jacob stopped hopping, leaned over the dock and threw up into the lake. The duck swam over to investigate.

I'm not going to kill him until my headache goes away.

Eve boarded the carriage, followed by Jacob. Burr decided that there was no reason to pedal when he could ride, especially when it came to the hill up the East Bluff. Burr waited while a street sweeper towing a cart behind his bike pedaled by, then he threw his bike on the back of the carriage and climbed up front with the cabbie, an old man who needed a shave and a bath. Burr put Zeke between the two of them. Zeke always liked riding shotgun and didn't seem to mind sitting next to the driver.

The driver snapped the reins. "Git up," he said. "Git up, Gin. Git up, Tonic."

I just can't seem to get away from booze today.

The driver geed and hawed his horses up the hill to the row of Victorian cottages, minor mansions that made up the East Bluff, the poorer neighbors of the not so minor Victorians on the West Bluff, just past the Grand Hotel.

The cottages on both bluffs had been built at the turn of the century by the knights of commerce of their day, the barons of the Midwest from Detroit, Chicago, Cleveland, Cincinnati, and St. Louis. In the days before air conditioning, the prosperous fled the summer heat and humidity to Mackinac Island. That and the fact that, by the early 1900s, the British no longer posed a threat to the Upper Great Lakes. Then the U.S. Army abandoned the fort, and Mackinac Island transformed itself into the biggest tourist attraction in Michigan.

Burr looked down at the harbor, where the history of the island had begun.

Before all this, Mackinac Island was sacred to the Ojibwa, who believed that the island was home to Gitche Manitou. The Great Spirit. The island rose two hundred feet from Lake Huron, far and away the highest island in the Great Lakes. The Ojibwa had named it Mackinac – Great Turtle – which is just what the island looked like from a canoe.

Mackinac Island had long been a Native American fishing camp and trading center. The French explorer Jean Nicolet was the first European to discover the island. Later, John Jacob Astor made it the trading center for his fur empire. Now the island swells to ten thousand people in the summer, but by winter, only seven hundred year-round residents remain.

By the time the driver whoaed Gin and Tonic in front of Windward, Jacob's color, if not his spirits, had returned.

"What kind of place is this?" Jacob said.

"It's our summer retreat," Burr said. "For a month."

"A month? I can't stay here a month. I don't think I can make it through the day."

Eve climbed out of the taxi and took it all in. "This is magnificent. Look at this place. It's huge." Then she turned around. "And the view."

Burr jumped down from the taxi and landed on his broken toe.

"Damn it all," he said.

"What's wrong?" Eve said.

"I stubbed my toe." He thought it best not to bring up the missing pink pony and certainly not the dead man.

"How are you paying for this?" Eve said.

"Don't worry."

"It's always time to worry when you say not to worry," Jacob said, still in the carriage, still not sure if he was going to stay.

"Trade," Burr said. "We're trading for it."

"Trading what?" Eve asked.

"The owner needs some legal work done."

"You're trading my work product for this?" Jacob said.

"The boat, too," Burr said. "I won."

"This might be your idea of a vacation, but it's not mine." Jacob gripped the rail of the taxi. "If you want to live here for a month, you should pay for it. With cash."

"Burr has no cash," Eve said.

Burr had been head of the litigation department of Fisher and Allen, one of Detroit's best firms. He had been, perhaps, Detroit's best commercial litigator but had given it up, as well as his marriage – but not his son – over a client. A provocative client. A striking woman almost young enough to be his daughter. Over an affair that hadn't turned out. He'd been a fool and he knew it. After the year it had taken him to ruin the prior twenty, he moved to East Lansing and started an appellate practice. Complicated, esoteric litigation punctuated with the oral arguments that had made him famous in select legal circles. It had gone swimmingly except for the money part, which, of course, was the most important part.

But here they were, Burr fresh off a victory in the Port Huron-Mackinac and a month's worth of a five-bedroom cottage with a turret.

"There's no way we can afford to give up cash. Even for this." Eve started back to the taxi.

"Just look at those hollyhocks." Burr pointed to the garden in front of the porch.

"Don't hollyhock me, Burr Lafayette," Eve said, but she walked over to the four-foot-tall spires that had flowers like medallions. "They're so old-fashioned. They're beautiful … but they could use some help."

One down. One to go.

"Jacob, the Carp River is just over the bridge."

"I'm not going anywhere if I have to ride on a boat. And I don't fish for carp."

"The brookies are fat as a loaf of bread."

"They are?"

"They're always hungry, and you don't have to fish from a boat."

Jacob climbed down from the taxi.

Burr settled Eve in the Huron, the room right around the corner from his. Burr had taken the *Nicolet*, the master bedroom, complete with a turret. Burr loved turrets. The *Huron* looked south to the mainland and east to Lake Huron; the *Nicolet*, also south to the mainland but west to the bridge. The morning sun rose right into the paned windows of the Huron, lighting the room at 6 a.m. this time of year, which was exactly why Burr had taken the *Nicolet* instead. That, and the turret. Burr had deposited Jacob at the northwest corner in the *Astor*, with a view of hemlocks and not much else, which was just fine with Jacob, who didn't like a water view any more than he liked water.

* * *

Burr dozed on the porch swing in the late afternoon sun, Zeke napping at his feet. Eve, armed with garden clippers she found in the shed, had started on the garden on the east side of the cottage. Jacob was sulking in his room. Burr swung in a lazy back-and-forth arc, careful of his ever-blackening toenail.

This will do nicely.

Zeke-the-boy was to arrive tomorrow with the beautiful Grace, the former Mrs. Lafayette. As soon as his headache passed, all would be right in his world.

He heard the clop of horseshoes coming along the bluff. Then it stopped.

Alarmed but only slightly, he opened his left eye just as a woman climbed down from one of the Grand Hotel's finest covered carriages, black with a hint of red wine polished to a high gloss. It gleamed in the sunlight and hurt Burr's eyes.

"Stay right here, young man," the woman said to the driver, who wore the livery of the hotel: white pants, red jacket and a black top hat. "I shan't be long."

The woman marched up the walk, then stopped at the bottom of the porch. "Burr Lafayette," she said, not asking.

Who is this?

She looked like she was about seventy, but she had the hair of a younger woman, cut short, brown with blond highlights.

"Cat got your tongue?" She climbed the steps and walked over to him. "I knew your grandfather, Aaron."

She was a petite woman, maybe five-two. She wore a top with a floral print that went with her Papagallo wraparound skirt and navy espadrilles. Skin that had been out in the sun too long. A small mouth with thin lips. But her most striking feature was her eyes. Steely eyes that knew exactly what they wanted. One hundred percent Grosse Pointe, with an altogether commanding presence.

"He was the first one to figure out how to cut a square hole in metal."

Burr stood.

"Inventing the broach was something. In its day, that was really something." She looked over the water. "It was something in any day." She looked back at Burr. "Colonial Broach. A shame your father couldn't keep it going." She stuck a bony hand out. "Martha Halverson, Detroit Screw Machine Company." Martha Halverson took a seat on a green Adirondack chair next to the porch swing. "But that's not why I'm here."

"Somehow I didn't think so." He had no idea why Martha Halverson, clearly the matriarch of Detroit Screw Machine, had planted herself on his porch. But he was fairly certain he wasn't going to like it.

"Sit down. I need your help."

Burr returned to the porch swing. "I don't know how I could possibly help you."

"Shush and I'll tell you." She smoothed out an invisible wrinkle in her skirt. "My son has just been arrested for murder."

"That didn't take long," Burr said.

"I beg your pardon."

"I'm sorry, Mrs. Halverson, but I'm not a criminal lawyer."

"I know that, but you're a damn fine litigator. And you're here."

"I'm sorry, Mrs. Halverson. My practice is limited to appellate work."

She smoothed her skirt again. "Listen to me, young man. My son has just been arrested for murder. He's in that poor excuse for a jail downtown."

"What's your son's name?"

"Murdoch," she said. "Murdoch Halverson, but everyone calls him Murdo."

"I guess he's not the one who's dead."

"I beg your pardon," she said again.

"I'm sorry Mrs. Halverson, but I can't help you."

"Of course, you can."

"Is it possible that he did it?"

Martha Halverson gave him a murderous look. "My son might be a fool, but he's not a murderer." She jumped to her feet. "I can't stay here a moment longer. I have to get to the jail before this gets any worse." She dashed off the porch and jumped into the carriage. She leaned out the window of the carriage. "To the jail. Meet me there, Mr. Lafayette." The driver flicked the reins and off they went.

CHAPTER FOUR

Burr stumbled down the stairs at ten the next morning. He tripped over Jacob's luggage on his way to the kitchen, a white, airy room full of windows at the back of the cottage. Eve handed him a cup of coffee, sandy colored with too much cream, just the way he liked it. Sunlight streamed into the kitchen. A clear, crisp, Mackinac Island morning. What was left of it.

"How are you feeling?"

"Much better" he said. Burr felt as good as new, except for his toe.

"Seventeen hours of sleep will do that." Eve took in a deep breath. "He's at it again."

"It's recreational."

Eve opened the refrigerator, an ancient white machine with spindly legs and a black compressor on top.

"Poached?"

"On toast."

The swinging doors from the dining room swung open and in came Jacob, in pleated khaki shorts, a lemon-yellow Lacoste and sandals. A cloud of sweet smoke blew in with him.

"Nothing for me."

He stopped in the path of the doors, which swung back and hit him squarely in the back. "Damn this place. I'm getting off this blasted island this very moment." He sucked on the joint and held his breath.

"You just got here." Eve filled a frying pan with water and lit the stove.

"The stench of horse manure is overpowering."

"But there's no smog," Burr said.

Eve cracked two eggs into the now steaming water.

"There's plenty to do here. Zeke is coming today. I thought we could all ride bikes around the island."

"Why you named your son after a dog is beyond me."

"There's no greater honor than to be named after Zeke-the-dog. He's the best retriever I've ever had."

"It could be tough going through life as Zeke-the-boy," Eve said.

"Bicycles?" Jacob said. "Are you kidding?"

"There's the fort," Burr said, who knew immediately that he had said the wrong thing.

Jacob pushed open the swinging doors just as a tall, white-haired woman tried to enter.

"Watch where you're going, young man," she said.

"Aunt Kitty," Burr said.

"Come with me, Burr. Straight away."

"I'm just about to eat breakfast." Burr sat down at the table in the breakfast room that looked out on the east garden.

"Aaron Burr Lafayette, I can't believe you treated Martha that way. Your grandfather and her father were fast friends." Except for Zeke-the-boy, Aunt Kitty was Burr's only living relative. She was his grandfather's sister. A tall, thin, striking woman with a snow-white ponytail and fierce blue eyes just like Burr's. An aging beauty, she had become a lawyer when it was nearly impossible for women to go to law school.

Burr tried another tack. "I'm picking up Zeke in Mackinaw City this morning."

"Not today you're not. Put on a coat and tie and come with me."

"Grace will be waiting for me."

"I've already called her." Aunt Kitty turned on her heel. "Get dressed and get your bike." She turned to Jacob. "Unless I'm mistaken, that's a controlled substance."

Jacob disappeared through the swinging doors. Eve handed Burr his eggs.

* * *

Burr rummaged through his suitcase for the one tie he thought he might have packed. As far as ties were concerned, he had three rules. He always wore a tie when he went to court, when he went to a funeral and when he borrowed money. The corollary, never wear a tie on any other occasion, meant that he hadn't packed one for Mackinac Island. When he'd climbed aboard *Scar-*

amouche four days earlier, he never thought he'd be borrowing money, that anyone would die on him or, most of all, that he'd be going to court.

Eve popped in. "Looking for this?" She handed him his favorite tie, a silk foulard with blue diamonds on a red background. The tie he always wore on the first day of a trial.

"Where did that come from?"

"My suitcase."

"I can't believe you brought a tie."

"I thought you might need to borrow some money." She put her hands on her hips. "What have you gotten yourself into this time?"

"A favor for a friend of Aunt Kitty's." He tied a half Windsor and cinched it up around his neck. Like a noose.

* * *

Burr, Eve, and Aunt Kitty boarded the ferry to St. Ignace. Jacob refused to have anything to do with Burr's latest folly, as he called it. The three of them sat on the top deck, Burr's tie blowing in the wind.

"Just bail. That's all you have to do," Aunt Kitty said.

"I'm not a criminal lawyer."

"Tuck your tie into your shirt or you'll strangle yourself," Aunt Kitty said.

"This is my time with Zeke."

"We'll get to that. Just get Murdo out on bail."

The *Pontiac*, another Arnold Line sixty-foot catamaran, slowed and came off plane as it rounded the point and entered the harbor at St. Ignace. The first port of call in the Upper Peninsula after crossing the bridge, St. Ignace sat at the edge of an almost perfect harbor, sheltered from all points of the compass except east. St. Ignace had been a lumber and fishing port in times past but was barely bigger than a village. The county seat of Mackinac County, which included Mackinac Island, it serviced the island and what commerce remained in the south end of the U.P.

They walked the four blocks uphill to the century-old courthouse, a three-story, orange-brick municipal building. Martha Halverson met them on the steps. "You're late," she said.

Burr pulled his tie out of his shirt, pulled the sleeves down on his custom-tailored navy-blue blazer, hardly appropriate, but he'd been planning on cocktail parties, not court.

He opened the door for the three women. The floor had six-sided white tiles, each the size of a half dollar, laid in with black grout. A sheriff's deputy in brown shirt and tan slacks, and the biggest sidearm Burr had ever seen, led them to the courtroom toward the back of the building.

"You could hunt deer with that thing," Burr said,

"I have," the deputy said. "Stops 'em cold."

The deputy led them to the courtroom. "Five more minutes and you'd have had the public defender."

Murdoch Halverson sat at the defense table. A good-looking woman with raven hair sat in the gallery just behind him. Martha Halverson sat down next to her, then leaned over the railing.

"Murdo, this is Burr Lafayette. He's your lawyer."

He looked up at Burr, shook his head and flipped his jet-black hair out of his eyes. He was in handcuffs, which didn't really go with his lime-green Lacoste and madras Bermuda shorts, which looked like they'd been slept in.

"This is the most horrible thing that could possibly happen," the good-looking woman said. She had the greenest eyes Burr had ever seen. She offered her hand. "Anne Halverson," she said. "With an *e*"

Burr smiled and shook her hand. She had the look of the self-starved, well off. Thin but not emaciated. She had black hair, the same as her husband's. Burr thought that Anne and Murdo looked alike, not enough for brother and sister, but certainly a resemblance.

"Anne with an e," Burr said.

Eve and Aunt Kitty slid in next to Martha. Burr sat down to the right of Murdoch Halverson, who smelled of sweat and mildew. Across the aisle to Burr's right, the prosecutor. He had short brown hair and a nose that looked like it had been punched too many times. He was short and stocky and looked like he was in his mid-forties.

He's not fat. He's thick. Like a tree trunk.

Burr tap, tap, tapped the brand new Number 2 yellow pencil Eve had given him.

She thinks of everything.

The bailiff entered. He must be at least six-five, Burr thought. Shoulders the size of a door frame, but a bit of a belly. Black eyes, copper skin, black hair in a ponytail. His nose had been broken at least once, which made him look like a hawk. Burr squinted at his name tag. It read Henry Crow.

He's at least half Native American.

"All rise," Henry Crow said.

The judge entered from the back of the courtroom, mid-sixties, a big man with a full head of dark brown hair parted down the middle. He had on glasses with thick black frames. The judge made a show of arranging his silky black robe, then sat.

"Be seated," the bailiff said. "The court of the Honorable Takala Maki is now in session."

He's got to be a Finn.

The judge settled into his seat. "What is it this time, Mr. Karpinen?"

Another Finn. They probably go to the same church.

Karpinen stood. "Murder, Your Honor."

"Really?" The judge pointed his gavel at Murdo. "He looks more like a drunk driver than a murderer."

"Your Honor, on the night of July 17th, the defendant, Murdoch O. Halverson, 539 Windmill Pointe, Grosse Pointe Park, Michigan, was drinking with the deceased, James P. Lyons, the deceased's wife, and his own wife at The Pink Pony. The defendant and the deceased…"

Judge Maki raised his hand. "Gus, stop right there. Was this the night the race finished?"

"That was when the first boats got in."

"The Port Huron-Mackinac?"

"Yes, Your Honor."

"On the island?"

"Yes, Your Honor."

"Go on."

"The defendant and the deceased were seen arguing. At one point the defendant's wife sat on the deceased's lap. The defendant wrapped a string of Christmas tree lights around the deceased's neck."

"Augustus."

"Yes, Your Honor?" The prosecutor shifted his weight from one foot to the other.

"Who is the accused murderer?"

"He is," the prosecutor said, pointing at Murdo.

The judge scowled. "I know that. What is his name?"

"Halverson. Murdoch O. Halverson."

"And who is he supposed to have killed?"

"The deceased."

"What would his name be?"

"His name is, was, James P. Lyons."

"All right then. Enough of this defendant and deceased business. I can't keep track of them that way."

"Your Honor?"

"Use their names."

"Of course, Your Honor."

"In any event, the defendant ... " Judge Maki scowled again. "... Mr. Halverson, wrapped a string of Christmas lights around Mr. Lyons' neck."

"Christmas in July?" the judge said.

"I beg your pardon?"

"Never mind," the judge said.

"The next morning, when the bartender came in to open, she found Mr. Lyons' body. The lights were wrapped around his neck."

"Did anyone see him do it?"

"Mr. Halverson's fingerprints were on the lights."

"Anything else?"

"The defendant's nametag was on the deceased's shirt, and we found a pair of broken glasses that belonged to Mr. Halverson near the body."

Brandstatter must not have told him who broke the glasses.

"That's hardly conclusive," the judge said.

Burr thought this slightly encouraging.

"We believe Mr. Halverson was jealous of Mr. Lyons," Karpinen said.

"In what way?"

"We believe Mr. Halverson thought Mr. Lyons was having an affair with Mrs. Halverson. She had taken off her bra and panties and hung them on the Christmas tree. Right in front of everyone. Then she sat on Mr. Lyons' lap."

"Really?" The judge leaned toward the prosecutor. "Anything else?"

"One more thing, Your Honor. The defendant was seen leaving The Pink Pony at four in the morning. Two hours after it closed."

"What's the charge?"

"Open murder, Your Honor," Karpinen said. "The penalty box for good."

Burr stood. "Your Honor, this proceeding does not necessarily have to result in charging my client with a crime."

"I'll decide the purpose of this hearing, counselor." The judge pointed his gavel at him. "What did you say your name was?"

"Burr Lafayette, Your Honor."

"Mr. Halverson, please stand," Judge Maki said. Murdo stood, as did Burr. "Counselor, I didn't ask you to stand."

"May I have a word, Your Honor?"

The judge pointed at him with his gavel. "No, you may not." He sighed, then relented. "I suppose you might as well."

"Your Honor, there's not nearly enough evidence to charge my client with murder. It's not even clear that my client had a grievance with Mr. Lyons, let alone murdered him."

"Mr. Lafayette," the judge said, still pointing, "Are you aware of the standard for arraignment?"

"I am, Your Honor."

"Then you must agree that the prosecutor has presented far more than necessary. And you must surely agree that there is probable cause. In fact, the prosecutor has presented far more than the law requires."

"Your Honor, this is nothing more than an alphabet soup of possibilities, not probabilities."

"Mr. Lafayette, approach the bench."

Murdo sat. Burr slipped out from behind the defense table and walked to the bench. The prosecutor followed, walking with a limp, his left leg stiff at the knee. "Not you, Gus. This is between me and Mr. Lafayette."

Karpinen limped back to his table.

Burr stood squarely in front of Judge Maki, braced for the pointing gavel. "Mr. Lafayette, I note you are wearing a very expensive blue blazer. A blue blazer that might be worn to a fancy cocktail party."

"Your Honor?"

Judge Maki shushed him with a finger to his lips. "And what must be a fifty-dollar tie." Burr looked down at his favorite tie. "Now then, Mr. Lafayette, moving down, your khakis are acceptable, but turning to your feet, I see you are wearing Topsiders, which are not appropriate in my courtroom."

"Your Honor," Burr said.

"Mr. Lafayette, lift your pant legs."

"Your Honor?"

"Your pant legs." Burr lifted them. "Just as I thought. Just what I saw while you were sitting." The judge pointed at his ankles. "Where are your socks, Mr. Lafayette?"

"My socks?"

"You heard what I said."

"I'm not wearing socks, Your Honor."

"I can see that."

"Your Honor, I was pressed into service at the last minute, and I don't have any with me."

"How can that be?"

"I don't wear socks between April and November, except when I'm in court."

"You're in court now."

"Yes, but I hadn't planned on it."

"Why no socks?"

Burr bent his knees in the hope that his pants would cover his bare ankles. "They make my feet sweat."

The judge pointed at Burr's ankles, then at Burr. "If I ever have the misfortune to see you in my courtroom again, you will be wearing socks or I will jail you for contempt."

This has gotten way out of hand.

Burr nodded and started back to the defense table.

"I'd say you're going to need your penalty killers," Karpinen said as Burr passed him on his way to the defense table. Burr sat.

Judge Maki took off his glasses and inspected them. He set them down, put them back on, then pointed at Murdo. "Stand up, Mr. Halverson," Judge Maki said. Murdo and Burr both stood. "You two don't have to stand there, side by each, but suit yourself. This court finds that there is probable cause to find that sometime in the early morning of July 18th murdered James Lyons. How do you plead?"

Murdo's lip quivered.

"How do you plead?" The judge pointed at Murdo.

"Not guilty, Your Honor," Burr said.

"Just because the two of you are standing side by each doesn't mean you can speak for him," the Finnish judge said. "I'd like to hear from the defendant."

"He's not the defendant yet," Burr said.

"He's about to be," the judge said. "How do you plead?"

"Not guilty," Murdo said.

"All right, then," Judge Maki said. "Murdoch O. Halverson, you are charged with open murder. You are hereby remanded to the Mackinac County Jail. The preliminary exam will be two weeks from today." The judge banged his gavel.

"Your Honor," Burr said.

"We're all done, counselor."

"Not quite, Your Honor."

"How so?"

"Bail."

"Bail? For murder?" Judge Maki said.

"Your Honor, even if there were a scintilla of evidence that my client committed a crime, which there isn't, he is still entitled to ask for bail."

"All right, then." Judge Maki scratched his chin. "Bail is set at two million dollars."

"That's far too much."

"Don't tell me how much is too much," the judge said.

Martha Halverson jumped to her feet. "We'll take it."

"You'll what?" Judge Maki said.

"Apparently, we accept," Burr said.

"I object, Your Honor." Karpinen stood and limped to the bench. "This man is a murderer."

"Overruled," Judge Maki pointed his gavel at the bailiff. "Get the money, Henry," the judge said on his way out.

* * *

Aunt Kitty had arranged for a car. Burr took charge of lunch and took them all to Lehto's US-2 Pasties, a square little one-story, white with green trim. They sat around a Formica table with faded blue and not so faded yellow boomerangs. Burr thought Lehto's was the very definition of modest.

The waitress seated them next to the window with a grand view of US-2, a two-lane highway that begins in St. Ignace and ends at the Pacific.

Lehto's US-2 Pasties served one thing and one thing only. Burr ordered them all pasties, which arrived in short order.

"This is the most vile thing I have ever seen," Anne said." She pushed her plate as far away from her as she could.

Burr cut into his pasty and a small cube of rutabaga slid out of the crust. He stabbed it with his fork and held it up in triumph. "Genuine pasties always have rutabaga."

"I can't imagine why you would you bring us to a place that only serves these awful things," Anne said.

"This is an Upper Peninsula delicacy." Burr chewed the rutabaga slowly.

"Why is it named after what a stripper covers herself with?" Anne said.

"This is a pasty with a short *A*, not a pasty with a long *A*." No one at the table blushed, but then Anne, at least, was no stranger to provocative lingerie.

"This area, north of here, actually, was settled by Cornish miners. Their wives took meat, onions and root vegetables – potatoes, carrots, rutabaga, and once in a while the odd turnip – vegetables that would keep all winter – mixed them all up and baked them in a flour crust. They wrapped them in oiled paper, and their husbands took them down in the copper mines for lunch."

Burr cringed when Murdo put gravy on his pasty, but he didn't have the heart to tell him that only Trolls – Michiganders who lived in the Lower Peninsula – put gravy on their pasties.

"Until this awfulness happened, I had never been on this side of the bridge. I wish I'd never come," Anne said.

"This is precisely why we're here. The Yoopers have their own way of doing things. It's like a sandlot baseball game." Burr chewed a turnip. Rutabagas and turnips in the same pasty were really something. "And the rules favor the neighborhood kids."

"Thank you for representing my son. I'm so grateful that he's out of jail," Martha Halverson said.

"The bail didn't have to have been that much. I'm sure Burr could have gotten it reduced," Aunt Kitty said.

"Thank you, Mr. Lafayette," Murdo said. He still looked like he'd slept in his clothes, but at least the handcuffs were off.

"I thought you'd get the charges dismissed." Anne looked at her pasty but made no effort to retrieve her plate.

"The standard for an arraignment is low. It's only probable cause, and the judge has great latitude. Murdo could have been charged on much less."

"What do we do now?" Anne said.

"Now we finish lunch," Burr said.

"What about Murdo?" Anne said.

"The preliminary exam is in two weeks. The standard is the same as it was at the arraignment, so I expect Murdo will be bound over for trial."

"Can you get the charges dismissed?" Martha said.

"Mrs. Halverson, I'm not a criminal lawyer. You have plenty of time and apparently plenty of money to hire the very best criminal lawyer you can find."

"We want you."

Burr considered mentioning the missing pink pony, Chief Brandstatter, the Christmas tree and his introduction to Jimmy Lyons, but since this was his last hurrah, he decided against it.

"Murdo was with me the entire night," Anne said.

"I doubt that will help at the preliminary exam," Burr said.

"Why not?" Anne said.

It was Aunt Kitty's turn. "Because the evidentiary standard is so low. The standard is not 'beyond a reasonable doubt' like it is for a conviction."

"If I were your lawyer, I wouldn't bring it up," Burr said.

Murdo looked up from his pasty. He had gravy on his chin, which Anne wiped off with her napkin.

"The defense strategy is almost always to see what evidence the prosecutor has, without giving away your own arguments."

"You mean there will be a trial?" Murdo said.

"I'm afraid so. Unless there's evidence to the contrary," Burr said.

"There is," Anne said. "Murdo was with me the entire evening."

"You're his wife. A wife will say anything," Burr said.

"But it's true."

"It may be true, but I doubt it will be enough for Judge Maki. At the trial, the jury has to find guilt beyond a reasonable doubt. They may well believe you."

"I said it was true."

"Then you and Murdo have nothing to worry about."

* * *

After lunch, Burr drove them all back to the ferry. Eve and the Halversons sat in the cabin. Aunt Kitty motioned to Burr, who led him to the upper deck.

Once the ferry cleared the harbor, the captain opened up the diesels. Burr felt them pulse under him, in time with his throbbing toe. An east wind had blown up a chop on Lake Huron that slapped against the hull and sprayed into Burr's face.

"How about if we get out of the wind?" Burr said.

"We'll be in the lee of the island any minute now."

"We'll both be soaked by then."

"There it is," she said.

"There is what?"

"The Grand."

Burr had no idea why the Grand Hotel had anything to do with anything. He'd seen the hotel from the water, stayed there, eaten there, drank too much there. A four-story hotel with a porch that stretched six-hundred feet. The longest outdoor porch in the world. One of the finest views in Michigan, perhaps anywhere. Built in 1887 by the Illinois-Michigan Railroad to give its passengers a destination. Esther Williams made a movie in the Grand's outdoor pool. Christopher Reeve had starred in *Somewhere in Time*.

"Count seven down from the Grand." A row of Victorian cottages, mansions really, ran along the West Bluff north of the hotel. The ritziest of the old money.

"That's Aerie, the Halversons' cottage," Aunt Kitty said.

Aerie was four stories and had three turrets, white with royal blue trim and a royal blue roof.

"I'm not a criminal lawyer." Burr wiped the spray from his face.

"You might consider Martha's checkbook." Aunt Kitty handed him her handkerchief.

CHAPTER FIVE

Burr insisted that Aunt Kitty stay the night. The next morning the two of them biked to the harbor, Zeke leading the way. Aunt Kitty boarded the *Huron* and left for Mackinaw City, then on to Cottage Number 59 on Harbor Point. Burr and Zeke-the-dog waited for Grace and Zeke-the-boy. Two ferries later, Grace and their son walked onto the dock.

Grace had shoulder-length black hair, soft gray eyes and a sad smile. An altogether beautiful, if melancholy, woman.

She had never forgiven him for their breakup or for leaving Fisher and Allen. He knew he'd been a fool to leave Grace, and he was fairly certain that Humpty Dumpty couldn't be put back together again.

"Be careful with him," she said.

"I will, Mom," Zeke-the-boy said, a tow-headed nine-year-old whose eyes matched his father's.

"Yes, Grace," Burr said. He tried to kiss her goodbye, but she turned aside.

"Don't let him out of your sight." Grace boarded the ferry.

Later that afternoon, Burr and the two Zekes stopped at the Dwight Good Springs, a trickle of a spring, unsafe to drink, and the umpteenth time they'd stopped to rest on their bike ride around the island. Zeke-the-boy had insisted on riding his own bike around the island for the first time ever. Burr hoped they'd make it back to Windward by dark.

The narrow blacktop that circles the island, M-185 is the only state road in Michigan that prohibits cars, trucks, and everything else with an engine. It runs eight miles along the shore, at the base of hundred-foot limestone bluffs with cedars and spruce growing out of the rock. Every summer, Burr had pedaled Zeke around the island, first in a basket, then on the back of a bicycle built for two. Now, for the first time, Zeke was pedaling on his own. Until he wasn't.

Zeke-the-boy climbed off his bike and let it fall. "I can't go any farther."

Just as Burr was about to encourage Zeke about the virtue of persistence, a carriage from the Grand stopped next to them. The passenger door swung open.

"You look like you could use a ride," said Anne with an *e* Halverson.

"We're just taking a little break," Burr said.

"A ride would be great," Zeke-the-boy said.

"We're almost home."

"Climb in. You must be hungry," Anne said.

The driver hoisted the bike onto the luggage rack. Zeke-the-boy climbed in. The carriage set off, Burr and Zeke-the-dog following. Anne took them to the Village Inn, just off Main Street. The owner was a Harvard lawyer. Burr didn't hold that against him because he let Zeke-the-dog lay under the table.

"Burr, you simply must help us. Murdo's lawyer doesn't know what he's doing."

"I'm sorry, but I don't do criminal work."

"He won't let me testify at the preliminary exam."

"I wouldn't either."

The waitress arrived. "I'll have a hamburger, fries and a chocolate shake," Zeke said.

The waitress turned to Anne. "Ma'am?"

Zeke leaned over to Burr. "She's going to order food that tastes like dirt."

"What was that?" Anne said.

"Nothing," Burr said.

"Spinach salad. And iced tea," she said.

"Told you," Zeke said.

"And you, sir?"

"Same as him. And a Labatt."

"And he's going to cancel the preliminary exam." Anne placed her napkin on her lap, but neither Lafayette followed suit.

"Murdo is going to be tried for murder, with or without a preliminary exam," Burr said.

"It's so unfair. We're trying to get pregnant, and then this happens."

I'm not sure I needed to know that.

"You could help us. You just don't want to."

The food arrived. Burr passed a french fry to Zeke-the-dog.

* * *

Burr and the two Zekes spent the better part of the next week exploring the island. In Burr's case, re-exploring. They toured both forts, the battlefield, Skull Cave, the haunted museum. They made the rounds of every store that stocked treasures to catch the eye of a nine-year-old. They took the ferry from the island to Mackinaw City and then to St. Ignace just for fun. The island was famous for its homemade fudge, and Zeke-the-boy was infamous for his sweet tooth. They spent so much time at Ryba's Fudge that Burr swore off fudge for life.

Not a word from the Halversons and not a thought about them from Burr.

A week later, he delivered his sole heir back to the beautiful Grace, Burr and the two Zekes exhausted.

* * *

Burr rocked gently on the porch swing. He pushed off with his broken toe, almost better now except for the nail, black as night.

Two weeks into the longest vacation he'd had since college, Burr wasn't sure if Jacob could last. He wasn't sure Eve would ever leave.

Burr thought he had just enough credit to make it two more weeks, maybe Labor Day if he was lucky. He was going to swing on the porch swing and watch the freighters pass through the straits, upbound and down-bound, empty or full. He didn't care which.

He drifted off to sleep.

* * *

"Mr. Lafayette. Mr. Lafayette." Burr ignored the voice until a finger poked him. "Wake up, Mr. Lafayette." Burr opened his eyes. Scooter. It was Scooter.

Scooter rented the first floor of Burr's building in downtown East Lansing. Burr had bought the six-story former Masonic Temple when he'd moved to East Lansing from Detroit. He had the building redone when he was still flush with cash. He put his office and living quarters on the top floor. The bottom floors were to be a restaurant and retail, offices above, but it hadn't quite worked out that way. Scooter rented the first floor for Michelangelo's, a quite good northern Italian bistro, even though he was a skinny WASP with a pasty complexion. Unfortunately, Scooter was just about it for the rent roll and was chronically late with the rent, which meant that Burr ate more than his fill of "free" Italian food.

"Wake up, Mr. Lafayette." Scooter poked him again.

Burr shooed Scooter's hand off his shoulder. "What on earth are you doing here?"

Scooter handed Burr a certified letter, return receipt requested. Burr studied the envelope, then set it next to him on the porch swing.

"Aren't you going to open it?" Scooter said.

Burr scratched Zeke behind his left ear, the Lab's favorite place. "In the entire history of the universe, I have never received a certified letter that brought me one iota of good news. They're always bad. Dunning letters, defaults, tax liens. Regular mail isn't any good, either, except for the occasional check."

"Aren't you going to open it?" Scooter said again. He started wringing his hands.

"No, Scooter. I don't think I will."

"But I signed for it." Scooter added pacing to the hand wringing.

"I wish you wouldn't have."

"Don't you want to know what's inside?"

"It can't be good." Burr scratched Zeke's left ear again.

If dogs could purr, Zeke would.

"It's from the City of East Lansing. The city shut down your building, Mr. Lafayette."

"Did you open the letter?"

"I would never do that, but the elevator doesn't work right. It's never worked right. In fact, the inspector got stuck in it."

"Which floor?"

"Between four and five."

"That's where it sticks," Burr said.

"You knew that?"

"It doesn't matter. There's no tenants above the second floor," Burr said.

"Your office and apartment are on the top floor."

"I take the stairs," Burr said. He didn't trust elevators. "Scooter, stop wringing your hands and sit down."

"The fire department had to come."

Burr grinned.

"The city closed the building.

"They can't do that."

"Which means my restaurant is closed."

"Your restaurant is on the first floor."

"I can't pay the rent if Michelangelo's is closed."

"You don't pay the rent when it's open."

Scooter tore open the letter, handed it to Burr and left.

*　*　*

Burr, his nap ruined, stewed for the better part of an hour. Then he changed into khaki slacks with a crease like the blade of a knife and a button-down pinpoint oxford with enough starch to pass for a two-by-four. He bicycled on Anne's Tablet Trail, the semi-secret path through the woods to the fort, then took Frog Alley across the island to the West Bluff. Lake Huron washed against the beach a hundred feet below.

Burr parked his bike in front of the cottage Aunt Kitty had pointed out from the ferry.

Martha answered. "Why, Mr. Lafayette. What can I do for you?"

"I wonder if we might speak a moment," he said, ready to eat crow. "May I come in?"

"Yes, of course. Well, no, I think not. It's so pleasant today … let's sit on the porch." She walked past him to a corner of the porch with a set of white wicker furniture.

The two of them sat in silence. Burr looked down at the lake, the bridge and Lake Michigan beyond. In a truly rare moment for Burr, he didn't know what to say. Martha finally broke the silence. "What is it that you want, Mr. Lafayette?"

"It's about the case."

"Yes?"

"There may be more to it than you might think."

"How so?"

"There's a peculiar way of life here on the island, and more so in the

U.P. I think you'd be well advised to have a lawyer who is familiar with the people and the way things are done here."

"You said that when we had lunch."

Anne came out to the porch. "Burr Lafayette, I thought I heard your voice." Anne sat down with them.

"Burr thinks we should hire local counsel, Anne dear. I was about to tell him that we hired the family's lawyers."

"They haven't listened to a word I've said."

"Where is Murdo?"

"Detroit. He's fiddling with his silly screw machines. That's all he thinks about," Anne said.

"Murdo should never, ever have done business with that awful Jimmy Lyons," Martha said. She turned to Burr. "Mr. Lafayette, you said yourself you aren't a criminal lawyer."

"That's true, but I know the island and I know the U.P."

"I'm sure our lawyers can handle this," Martha said.

"I tried to hire Mr. Lafayette, but he turned me down," Anne said.

That was before Scooter and the elevator.

Anne put her hand on her mother-in-law's arm. "Let's hire him."

Martha looked at Anne's hand on her arm, then at Burr. "How much do you need, Mr. Lafayette?"

"Ten thousand," he said. "To start."

* * *

On his way back to Windward, Burr stopped at the Iroquois, a four-story, white frame hotel on the beach. He knew the chef, and he left with three fresh whitefish filets. Just as he was about to climb back on his bike, a very old man on a very old bike pulled up alongside him.

"Afternoon, Mr. Lafayette."

"Willard, you're just the man I was looking for." Burr didn't know Willard's last name. In fact, he wasn't sure that Willard had a last name. Willard was the Windermere's dock porter and unquestionably the oldest dock porter on the island. He was at least eighty, skinny, with wispy, white hair. He still carried suitcases in the basket of his bicycle.

Right across the street from the Iroquois, the Windermere, a three-story yellow house that had been converted to a bed and breakfast long ago, was the very place where he had courted Grace.

"Willard, you're just the man I was looking for," he said again.

"Whatcha need, Mr. Lafayette?"

"Do you still have that typewriter?"

"Yep."

"I wonder if I might borrow it."

"What for?"

"I'm working on a case."

"It wouldn't be that murder at the Pony, would it?"

Everyone here knows everything about everybody.

"Nasty business," Willard said.

"I guess so."

"Let me get you that typewriter. Then I've got to go." He disappeared inside the big yellow house, then reappeared with his old-fashioned Remington with inky letters on metal rods that struck the paper.

Eve isn't going to like this.

Willard set the typewriter next to the whitefish in Burr's basket. "I got to get going. Guests coming in over at Shepler's." The old dock porter got on his bike and wobbled off.

* * *

"This is some of the most delicious fish I've ever eaten," Jacob said.

"It's whitefish. A very large minnow," Eve said.

The three of them were sitting at one end of the massive oak table in Windward's dining room. A soft summer breeze drifted in along with the fading summer sun. Zeke, ever on the lookout for a handout, camped at Burr's feet.

Jacob chewed slowly. "It's so moist."

"What's gone wrong?" Eve said.

Burr ignored her, though she looked radiant in a yellow sleeveless dress, even if she did have a bit of a farmer's tan on her upper arms.

Gardening will do that.

"The dutchess potatoes are a fine pairing with the whitefish," Jacob said.

"It must be a big problem," Eve said.

"Stop it, Eve. Burr has the makings of a fine chef." Jacob had his napkin stuck in his pink silk Hawaiian shirt with palm trees. "I think I may be actually beginning to like it here."

"Burr?"

"Yes, Eve."

"The whitefish is exquisite, but what's gone wrong?"

"Actually, there is one thing."

Jacob chewed ever so slowly on a green bean. "I love french-cut beans. What did you season them with?"

"Dill," Burr said.

"It's the elevator, isn't it," Eve said, not asking.

How does she know?

"The city closed the Leaning Tower of Lafayette, didn't they?"

Burr nodded. He'd named it Lafayette Towers, but the Leaning Tower of Lafayette had stuck.

Eve finished her wine and poured herself another.

"I'll get it fixed," Burr said.

"With what?"

Burr squirmed in his seat. He felt like a fifth-grader caught chewing gum in class. "We have a new case."

"We?" Eve drank her wine, not sipping. "How much to fix the elevator?"

"About ten," Burr said.

"Ten what?"

"Ten large."

"Ten thousand dollars?"

"It's an advance."

"It must be some case."

Burr poured himself another glass, too.

"Did you put olive oil on the beans?" Jacob said.

"Extra virgin."

"I thought so."

"He hasn't heard a word you've said." Eve took a big swallow of wine. "What kind of case is it?"

"Murder," Burr said, "more or less."

Jacob finally caught up with them. He stuttered. His hands shook, spilling some beans to the floor. Zeke, no fan of vegetables, ignored them.

"You know nothing about criminal law," Jacob said.

"I didn't last time, either."

"I should have gotten back on the ferry before I got involved in the garden," Eve said, mostly to herself.

Burr retreated to the kitchen. He came back holding pie. "Cherry," he said. "Fresh cherries from the Leelanau Peninsula." He set the browned beauty on the table and cut Jacob a healthy slice.

CHAPTER SIX

"All rise," Henry Crow said.

They all stood.

"The court of the Honorable Takala Maki is now in session."

Judge Maki made his entrance.

"You may be seated," Henry said.

They all sat, Karpinen at the prosecutor's table. Burr, Murdo, and Jacob at the defense table. Martha Halverson, Anne, and Eve behind them. The gallery was overflowing, but then a murder in Mackinac County was big news, probably the only news.

Judge Maki looked over the courtroom. "We are here today for the preliminary examination of Murdoch O. Halverson in order to determine if there is sufficient evidence to bind him over for trial for the murder of James P. Lyons."

The judge motioned for Burr to come forward. Burr stood in front of the judge. "Mr. Lafayette, are you wearing socks?" he said under his breath.

"Yes, Your Honor."

"You may be seated."

We're off to a good start.

The judge looked at the prosecutor. "Mr. Karpinen, you may proceed."

The Mackinac County prosecutor stood. He had on a tan suit with a white shirt and solid blue tie.

A bit pedestrian.

"Your Honor," Karpinen said, "in the early morning hours of Tuesday, July 18th, Mr. James P. Lyons of 5 Kingswood Circle, Birmingham, Michigan, was murdered in The Pink Pony."

"The Pink Pony," the judge said, as if he hadn't heard it at the arraignment.

"Your Honor, The Pink Pony is a bar inside the Chippewa Hotel on Mackinac Island."

"I know where it is."

The gallery snickered. There was hardly a soul within a hundred miles who didn't know where The Pink Pony was.

Judge Maki rapped his gavel. "Quiet." Back to the prosecutor, "You may continue."

"Subsequently, Murdoch O. Halverson, of 539 Windmill Pointe Drive, Grosse Pointe Park, Michigan, was arraigned on an open murder charge. We are here today to show that sufficient evidence exists to charge Mr. Halverson with open murder."

There's a clicking sound when Karpinen speaks.

"Your Honor…" Another click.

The judge cut him off. "What is that sound?"

"Nothing, Your Honor."

"Stop the nothing sounds."

"Yes, Your Honor." More clicking.

"Come up here," the judge said.

Karpinen limped up to the judge. "Yes, Your Honor?"

"Open your mouth. Open your mouth and look at me."

"I beg your pardon."

"Open your mouth." Karpinen opened his mouth. The judge leaned forward and looked in.

What's going on?

Judge Maki sat back in his chair. "Gus, where's your bridge?"

"My bridge?"

The judge wagged his gavel at Karpinen's mouth.

"My bridge," Karpinen said. "It's in my pocket."

"Put the damn thing in your mouth. That clicking is driving me crazy."

The prosecutor fished around his shirt pocket, took out a three-tooth bridge and put it in his mouth.

"The prosecution calls Police Chief Arthur Brandstatter."

The clicking's gone.

Karpinen limped to the right of the witness stand.

He still can't bend his left leg.

The chief waddled to the witness stand and the bailiff swore him in. Brandstatter beamed. Karpinen turned to Brandstatter, but his head didn't move quite right. It looked like he couldn't turn his head unless he turned his whole body with it.

This guy is really dinged up.

"Mr. Brandstatter."

"Chief Brandstatter."

Karpinen ignored him. "You were the first person on the crime scene, is that correct?"

Burr now stood. "Objection, Your Honor. The prosecution hasn't established that a crime was committed."

Judge Maki sighed. "Mr. Lafayette, isn't it a little early in the day for this?"

"Your Honor, it hasn't been established that a crime was committed," Burr said again.

The judge looked up at the ceiling, then at the prosecutor. "Sustained. Please rephrase the question."

"Chief Brandstatter, please tell us when you arrived at The Pink Pony and what you found."

Brandstatter cleared his throat. "I got there about noon on July 18th. The bar was locked, which it shouldn't be at that time of day. Not in July. So I go in the hotel and I have the desk clerk let me in through the lobby door. At first, I can't see anything 'cause it's bright sunlight outside and dark there inside the bar. And it smells, you know, how a bar smells. Like beer and cigarettes. I don't see anything, not at first. 'Cause it's dark."

Karpinen rolled his eyes without moving his head. "Please get to the point."

Brandstatter glared at Karpinen. "I am trying to describe the crime scene."

"Objection," Burr said.

"Overruled. Get on with it, Art," the judge said.

More throat clearing from the Mackinac Island Chief of Police. "At first I don't see anything 'cause it's dark. Then my eyes get used to it. And I still don't see anything. The bar's empty. Nothing. Well, nothing except a sawed-off Christmas tree tipped over the bar with Christmas lights and women's underwear on it. So, I'm thinking this is some kind of a prank, which wouldn't be that unusual. It being race week and all. And, of course, the pink pony is missing again, the one that hangs outside the bar."

Karpinen nodded.

He can't turn his head, but he can nod.

"Happens every year. Some drunken sailor steals the hobby horse. But it always gets returned. Not this year, though. Not so far." Brandstatter glared at Burr. Burr grinned back.

"Please, chief," Judge Maki said.

"As I was saying, I decide I'll go have another look-see. So I go back over to the bar. Still nothing. Except that tree full of underwear." The chief paused. "But then I see something glowing behind the bar. And I see him."

"Finally," Judge Maki said under his breath.

"What's that?" Brandstatter said.

"Nothing. Nothing at all. Please continue."

"There he is. Sitting in a chair behind the bar, right underneath the Labatt's tap. Dead as a doornail. That's not the half of it. He's sitting there with Christmas lights wound all around his neck. Like a necklace."

"Really," Karpinen said.

"Yes, sir. He's lit up like a Christmas tree. He's got a whole string of Christmas lights wrapped tight around his neck. Like a noose, except this noose is lit up. C-9's they were. The big, old-fashioned ones. The kind that don't blink. He's bent over at the neck, with them lights wrapped tight. The cord's wrapped tight around the tap, and it's plugged in. He's got the defendant's name tag on his shirt, and I found Mr. Halverson's glasses right underneath the body," Brandstatter said, pleased with himself.

Nothing about me so far.

"How did you know he was dead?" Karpinen said.

"His eyes are all bulged out and he's white as a ghost."

"We have a body. At last. Anything further, Mr. Karpinen?" the judge said.

"No, Your Honor." The prosecutor limped back to his table.

"Your witness," Judge Maki said.

Burr walked up to the portly policeman. He pulled down the cuffs of his baby blue, button-down, pinpoint oxford, which did not need pulling down. He straightened his red foulard tie with blue diamonds, which did not need straightening. He unbuttoned the jacket of his thousand-dollar charcoal suit, slightly threadbare. "Chief Brandstatter, were you the first person at the scene of the death?"

"You mean the murder?"

"It hasn't been determined that there has been a murder."

"Well, if you ask me ..."

"I didn't ask you," Burr said.

The chief bit his lip.

"Let's start over," Burr said. "Were you the first person to find Mr. Lyons' body?"

"Not exactly," Brandstatter said.

"Either you were the first person to find to find Mr. Lyons' body or you weren't," Burr said. "Which is it?"

"I was the first law enforcement officer to find the body."

"Who was the first person to find the body?"

"That would be Carole Hennessey," Brandstatter said.

"And who is Carole Hennessey?"

"Head bartender at The Pink Pony."

"Did she tell you that she found the body?"

"No," the chief said, smiling again. "I found it on my own."

Burr had him now, but Brandstatter didn't know it. "Chief, where was she when you found the body?"

"She was looking for me," Brandstatter said.

"If she was looking for you, then there was a period of time after she found the body, but before you found the body, when no one was there?"

"I suppose so." The chief's smile faded slightly.

"So, there was a period of time when someone could have tampered with the evidence."

"No," the chief said, confident again.

"Why not?"

"Because the bar was locked. That's what got me going in the first place."

"Then how did you get in?"

"I got a key from the desk clerk."

"So, Chief Brandstatter, someone else had a key to the bar?"

"Of course they did. How else would I get in?"

"Chief, if you got in, couldn't someone else have gotten in?" Burr paused. "Before you?"

"No," Chief Brandstatter said.

"Did you check to see how many sets of keys there were and who had them?"

"No," Chief Brandstatter said.

"Chief, for all you know, someone may well have been in The Pink Pony after Mr. Lyons died and before Ms. Hennessey found the body and started looking for you."

"Impossible," Chief Brandstatter said, finally understanding where Burr had taken him.

"After not determining who may have had access to The Pink Pony and when they might have had access, you then searched the bar and examined the body. Is that right?"

"That's right."

"Did you wear gloves?"

"Gloves?"

"Yes, gloves. Things that you put on your hands." Burr held his hands out in front of him and spread his fingers.

"No." Brandstatter wiggled in his chair.

"You corrupted the scene by moving and possibly removing evidence, and you contaminated it with your own fingerprints?"

"Objection, Your Honor!" Karpinen jumped up as best he could. "High sticking. Counsel is attacking the witness."

I get it. He's a hockey player. That's why he's so dinged up.

"Your Honor, I am merely trying to determine the caliber of the investigation of the first responder."

"Overruled." Judge Maki waved his gavel at him. "But you may not attack the witness, counselor."

"Yes, Your Honor." Burr pressed the attack. "Chief Brandstatter, how many so-called murders have you investigated?"

"One," Brandstatter said.

"Meaning this one?"

"I suppose."

"So, this is your first one."

"People don't die on Mackinac Island like this."

"Your Honor." Burr pointed at Brandstatter. "I submit that the crime scene was contaminated, and the investigation was botched ab initio."

"I beg your pardon," Judge Maki said.

"*From the outset,*" Burr said.

"I know what it means, Mr. Lafayette. And for the record, if you continue with your attitude, I will cite you for contempt, ex cathedra."

Touche'.

Brandstatter leaned over the railing and hissed at Burr. "I know damn well you're the one who stole the pink pony, and as soon as I have a little more proof, I'm going to arrest you for grand larceny."

Burr leaned toward Brandstatter and hissed back at him. "In Michigan, grand larceny starts at a thousand dollars. If that hobby horse is worth fifty dollars, I'll eat it."

"You want me to tell him you were there with me drinking beer and tomato juice?"

"I don't care. It just makes you look even more inept."

Judge Maki leaned toward the other two leaners. "What's that?"

"We're exchanging pleasantries," Burr said.

Brandstatter erupted. "This drunk stole the pink pony."

"What did you say?" the judge said.

"I move the witness' outburst be stricken from the record," Burr said.

"Objection," Karpinen said.

"Stop it. All of you," Judge Maki said. "Strike the last exchange from the record." Judge Maki wagged his gavel and pointed it at Burr and Brandstatter. "If the two of you have other business to attend to, do it outside of my courtroom." He pointed his gavel at Karpinen. "That goes for you, too."

"Yes, Your Honor," all three of them said, more or less in unison.

"Anything further, Mr. Lafayette?"

"No, Your Honor."

"You are excused, Chief Brandstatter." The chief climbed down and started waddling back to the gallery. Burr turned his back to the judge just as Brandstatter passed him. He held his hands as if he were holding the reins of a horse and whinnied softly at the chief.

"Call your next witness, Mr. Karpinen."

"Yes, Your Honor. The prosecution calls Dr. Winifred Burgdorfer."

A tall, rail-thin relic of a woman collapsed into the witness stand. She had her snow-white hair pulled back in a bun so severe it stretched out the wrinkles in her face. She had a long, narrow face and paper-thin lips.

She looks like Willard's older sister.

After the swearing in, Karpinen began. "Dr. Burgdorfer, you are the medical examiner for Mackinac County. Is that correct?"

"It is," Dr. Burgdorfer said in a husky alto.

"Would you please tell us your credentials."

Judge Maki waved his gavel. "Get on with it, Gus. We all know Winnie."

Karpinen nodded. "Dr. Burgdorfer, did you perform an autopsy on the deceased?"

Judge Maki looked down his nose at Karpinen.

"On Mr. Lyons," Karpinen said.

"I did."

"And what was the cause of death?"

"Asphyxiation."

"Asphyxiation?"

"His airway was cut off and he couldn't breathe." She put her hands around her neck. "He was strangled."

"How did this occur?"

"When I examined him, he had a string of Christmas tree lights wrapped around his neck."

"What exactly killed Mr. Lyons?" Karpinen said.

Dr. Burgdorfer leaned forward. Burr realized that she wasn't wearing glasses. *Extraordinary.*

"The string of lights, of course."

"Nothing further," Karpinen said.

"Now we have a cause of death," Judge Maki said

It was Burr's turn. "Dr. Burgdorfer, when you performed the autopsy, did you do the customary blood tests?"

"I did." She smiled a not very nice smile at Burr.

Burr smiled a nice smile back. "And did you measure the alcohol content in Mr. Lyon's blood?"

"I did."

"And what did you find?"

"It was .21."

".21. That's high, isn't it?"

"Objection," Karpinen said. "Calls for an opinion."

"Sustained," Judge Maki said.

"Dr. Burgdorfer, what is deemed to be legally drunk in this state?" Burr said.

"Legally drunk is .08."

"So, Mr. Lyons was drunk." Burr smiled.

"Quite." She smiled back at him.

"Objection. Counsel is flirting with the witness."

"Come on, Gus," Judge Maki said. "It's refreshing that they get along so nicely.

Not for long.

Burr continued smiling. "Is it possible that Mr. Lyons was so drunk that he literally drank himself to death?"

"No."

"Is it possible that Mr. Lyons could have committed suicide?"

"No, it's not."

"Why not?"

Dr. Burgdorfer stopped smiling. "Because he would have had to wrap the lights around his neck, plug them in, and then hang himself. Which he did not do."

"Isn't it possible that he accidentally killed himself?"

"I hardly think so," she said, no trace of a smile.

"Isn't it possible that Mr. Lyons wrapped the Christmas lights around his own neck?"

"No, it's not."

"A moment ago, you said he could have," Burr said.

"That's not what I said."

"Come on, Dr. Burgdorfer," Burr said, not smiling. "Were you there that night?"

The good doctor sat up, ramrod straight. "Of course not."

"You don't know how the lights got wrapped around Mr. Lyons' neck. Do you?"

"Objection," Karpinen said. "Counsel is badgering the witness."

"Mr. Lafayette, there is no jury here. Just me. Stop with the theatrics." He pointed his gavel at him. "Do I make myself clear?"

"Your Honor, I merely asked a question."

"Then merely ask it politely."

Burr turned away. He knew he had the old woman, but he also knew it didn't matter. So far, Karpinen had a dead man and a cause of death. "I have no further questions, Your Honor."

CHAPTER SEVEN

"The state calls Karen Vander Voort," Karpinen said.

A sandy-haired young woman with a ponytail glided to the witness stand. She had a nutty-brown tan, a long face and orthodontist's dream teeth, white as the ice surrounding Mackinac Island from January to April.

She must be Dutch.

Burr had a vague recollection of her from the now infamous night.

Henry Crow swore her in and Karpinen started in. "Miss Vander Voort, please tell us where you were and what you were doing the night of July 17th and during the early morning hours of July 18th, the morning Mr. Lyons was murdered."

Burr started to stand.

"…died," Karpinen said.

"Bartending at The Pink Pony. I was the closer."

Karpinen limped back to the prosecutor's table and picked up a photograph, which he showed to Karen Vander Voort. "Was this man at The Pink Pony the night of July 17th?" he said.

"Yes."

"Your Honor, the prosecution introduces this photograph of Mr. James Lyons as People's Exhibit One."

Burr stood. "May I examine the photograph?"

"If you must," Judge Maki said.

Karpinen handed Burr the photograph. A handsome devil, Burr thought. Jimmy certainly looked better alive than dead. "No objection."

"Remarkable," Judge Maki said. "Proceed, Mr. Karpinen."

"Let the record show that Ms. Vander Voort has identified Mr. James P. Lyons as being at The Pink Pony on the night of July 17th," Karpinen said.

"For Pete's sake, Gus, get on with it," Judge Maki said.

"Was Mr. Lyons one of your customers that night?" Karpinen said.

"I made the drinks for his table, and when he came up to the bar, I poured a round of shots for everyone."

"Who was he with?"

"He was sitting with him," she said, pointing at Murdo. "And her," she said, pointing at Anne.

"Your Honor, please let the record show that Miss Vander Voort is pointing at the defendant, Murdoch Halverson, and his wife, Anne Halverson."

Judge Maki nodded at Karpinen.

"Was there anyone else at the table?" Karpinen said.

"Yes, there was another woman. Mr. Lyons' wife."

"Objection, Your Honor. Speculation," Burr said.

"Sustained."

"Was there another woman at the table?"

"Yes."

Karpinen turned to the gallery, his neck and trunk together, then back to the witness. "Ms. Vander Voort, do you see her here in the courtroom?"

"No."

Burr turned to Murdo. "Was it Jimmy's wife?" he said, sotto voce.

Murdo nodded.

"Was she the one with the black…"

Murdo nodded again.

Judge Maki banged his gavel. "Mr. Lafayette, the proceedings are up here," he said, not so sotto voce.

"Yes, Your Honor."

Why isn't she here?

"When was the first time you remember seeing Mr. Lyons?"

"He came up to the bar and bought shots for everyone. It cost him a fortune. Then he stole a fifth of whiskey from behind the bar."

Karpinen clicked his bridge.

Burr cringed.

"Miss Vander Voort, please tell us about the Christmas tree."

"The Christmas tree," she said.

"Yes, the Christmas tree."

Just like you practiced.

"About midnight or so, Mr. Lyons came up to the bar with a tree, a little one. It was nailed to some boards, and he put it on top of the bar. Then he wrapped a string of lights around it, the big, old-fashioned kind. He plugged them in and they lit up. Christmas in July." She smiled.

Karpinen looked at Murdo, then Burr. Finally, he said, "Were there any other Christmas lights?"

"There was another string. Mr. Lyons had them around his neck," she said. Karpinen nodded at her.

"Objection, Your Honor," Burr said. "It is patently obvious that the prosecutor has coached the witness and has gone so far as to tell her what to say."

"Overruled."

"Miss Vander Voort, please tell us what happened next. In your own words, of course."

Of course.

"A little while later, Mrs. Halverson came up to the tree. She took off her bra and put it on the tree."

"She what?" Judge Maki said, almost falling out of his chair.

"She took off her bra from under her blouse and put it on the tree," Karen Vander Voort said again.

"Then what happened?" Judge Maki said, clearly aroused.

"Then a bunch of the women did the same thing," she said.

"Did what?" Judge Maki said.

"They took their bras off and put them on the tree. There must have been two dozen."

"Then what happened?" Now there were beads of sweat on Maki's forehead. *This has to stop.*

Burr stood. "Respectfully, Your Honor, I believe it is the prosecutor who is supposed to be asking the questions."

The judge gave Burr a withering look.

"Continue, Mr. Karpinen," he said.

"Miss Vander Voort," Karpinen said, "did Mrs. Halverson put anything else on the tree?"

"A little later, she came back up to the tree. She took off her panties up there and put them on the tree."

"My heavens." The judge took off his glasses, wiped his forehead with the sleeve of his robe, then put his glasses back on.

Burr thought Maki might keel over on the spot.

This is a disaster.

Burr stood. "I object, Your Honor."

Judge Maki wiped the sweat off his forehead again. "Mr. Karpinen, no more of this. Please."

Karpinen smiled knowingly at the judge, then turned to the witness. "Miss Vander Voort, were you able to see what went on at Mr. Lyons' table?"

"At first, they were having a good time. Then Mr. Lyons' wife got mad and left."

Burr jumped to his feet. "I object, Your Honor. The witness has no way of knowing if the other woman was Mr. Lyons' wife."

"I can clear that up," Karpinen said.

I'm sure you can.

"Proceed."

"Miss Vander Voort, what made you think the other woman was Mr. Lyons' wife?"

"She had a wedding ring on, and Mr. Halverson said something about her getting half his money."

Burr jumped again. "Your Honor, not only is this speculation, it's hearsay."

Judge Maki took off his glasses and glared at Burr. "Counsel, I don't think it matters a hoot right now who the other woman was. Overruled." He turned to Karpinen. "Continue."

"Do you know why the other woman was mad?"

"I think she was mad at Mrs. Halverson."

"Why was she mad?"

"Because she was flirting with Mr. Lyons. It looked to me like she was jealous."

"Objection, Your Honor. The witness doesn't know what the other woman was thinking. And it hasn't even been established that the other woman was Mrs. Lyons."

"Your Honor, she is testifying about what she saw, not what Mrs. Lyons thought," Karpinen said. He turned to Burr and grinned, stiff neck and all.

"Overruled," Judge Maki said. "Mr. Lafayette, you surely know the rules of evidence better than that."

The old fool is letting Karpinen get away with murder.

"Was Mr. Halverson angry with Mr. Lyons?" Karpinen said. "No. Let me rephrase the question." Karpinen cleared his throat, then he coughed.

I hope he swallows his bridge.

"In your opinion, did it look like Mr. Halverson was angry with Mr. Lyons?"

"Yes."

"Thank you, Miss Vander Voort. I have no further questions."

"Now we have a motive," the judge said, mostly to himself.

"I hardly think so," Burr said, not to himself.

"What's that?" the judge said.

"Nothing, Your Honor," Burr said.

"I didn't think so."

Burr walked up to the comely witness. "Miss Vander Voort, you said you were bartending that night and you were the closer. What does the closer do?"

"The closer makes sure the bar is pretty well cleaned up, makes sure there's no one left in the bar or the kitchen and makes sure all the doors are locked."

"And was all this as it should have been?"

"Yes."

"Miss Vander Voort, back to your bartending that night. What were the four of them drinking that night?"

"Drinking?"

"Yes, drinking. The Halversons and the Lyonses." Burr put his hands in his pockets.

"I don't remember."

"What color shirt was Mr. Lyons wearing?"

"I don't remember."

"And Mr. Halverson?"

"I don't know."

"Mrs. Halverson?"

The comely witness was coming slightly undone.

"Miss Vander Voort, isn't it possible, perhaps likely, that Mr. Halverson was up at the bar and dropped his glasses there?"

"I don't know. I don't really remember."

"You remember the color of Mrs. Halverson's panties, but you don't remember anything about Mr. Halverson's glasses. Your memory is some- what selective, isn't it?"

Karpinen struggled to his feet. "Counsel is badgering the witness."

I like it when he has to stand up.

"On the contrary, Your Honor. The Pink Pony was nothing if not a mob scene that night. I am merely trying to find out what the witness remembers, which seems to be only what Mr. Karpinen has coached her to remember."

"That's quite enough, Mr. Lafayette." He wagged his gavel at Burr. "You may continue. Without the commentary."

"Miss Vander Voort, did you see Mr. Halverson strike Mr. Lyons?"

"No."

"Did you see him push him?" Burr said.

"I don't remember."

"You don't remember?"

"She already said she didn't remember," Karpinen said.

He didn't stand up this time.

"Did you see Mr. Halverson even touch Mr. Lyons?"

"I did hear Mr. Lyons tell Mr. Halverson to calm down."

"That wasn't my question," Burr said in his most paternal voice, not that paternal was his strong suit. "You don't really remember very much, do you?"

"Objection," Karpinen said, standing.

That got him up.

"Stop it, Mr. Lafayette. Stop it right there," Judge Maki said.

"I remember that Mrs. Halverson had a lacy white bra and lacy white panties. She took them off and hung them on the Christmas tree. Then she sat on Mr. Lyons' lap."

Judge Maki's glasses fell off his face. "I beg your pardon?"

"Your Honor, that is a nonresponsive answer. I move that it be stricken from the record."

"On the contrary, Mr. Lafayette." Judge Maki fumbled with his glasses and put them back on. "I think this shows that Miss Vander Voort had a very good idea of what was going on at Mr. Lyons' table."

Just when I had her.

"I have no further questions, Your Honor." Burr walked back to the defense table and sat.

"Your next witness, Mr. Karpinen," Judge Maki said.

"Thank you, Your Honor. The state calls Patrick Gurvin."

A tan young man in his twenties made his way to the witness stand. He had a full head of brown hair, brown eyes to go with it, a square jaw and a Roman nose, also peeling. A good-looking young man, Burr thought.

The bailiff swore in the witness.

"Mr. Gurvin, can you tell us where you were during the early morning hours of July 18th?"

"I was on the beach behind the Chippewa."

Burr knew exactly where he meant, a strip of beach next to the Arnold ferry docks. Where Zeke had watched the mallard.

"Do you remember what time it was?"

"Sometime after two in the morning."

"How do you know that?"

"Because I had been at the bar at the Murray and it closed at two. I went over to the beach after that."

"What did you see while you were on the beach?" Karpinen said.

As if he doesn't know.

"There's a door in the back of the hotel, on the beach side." He shifted in his chair. "Anyway, I saw the door being opened."

Here it comes.

"Then I saw a man's head peek out, like he was sneaking."

"Objection, Your Honor," Burr said.

"Nonsense," Judge Maki said. "Continue," he said to Gurvin.

I didn't know that 'nonsense' was a legal term.

"Where was I?" Gurvin said. "Oh yeah, I saw this guy's head peek out the door and look around. Then he came out. He looked around again. Then he snuck along the side of the building and disappeared around the corner."

"Do you see him in the courtroom today?"

"Yes," Gurvin said.

"And who is it?"

"Him," Patrick Gurvin said, pointing at Murdo.

"Your Honor, for the record, please have the court take notice that Mr. Gurvin has identified the defendant, Murdoch Halverson."

"So noted," Judge Maki said.

"How do you know it was him?"

"There was a light on in the kitchen when he opened the door. His hair kind of fell over his forehead. And he took his hand and pushed it out of his eyes. Just like that," he said pointing at Murdo, who had unfortunately chosen that particular moment to do just that.

"Damn it all," Burr said.

"What's that?" Judge Maki said.

"Nothing, Your Honor." Whatever his shortcomings, Judge Maki was not hard of hearing.

"Are you sure it was Mr. Halverson that you saw?" Karpinen said.

"Yes," Patrick Gurvin said.

"No further questions, Your Honor."

It was Burr's turn. "Mr. Gurvin, did you have anything alcoholic to drink at the Murray on the night in question?"

"Yes."

"What would that be."

"Beer."

"What kind of beer?

"Stroh's," the young man said.

"How many did you have?"

"I don't know," Gurvin said.

"Why don't you know?"

"We were drinking pitchers."

"Pitchers," Burr said.

This could be promising.

"How many pitchers?"

"Seven or eight. I don't really remember."

"And how many of you were there?"

"Five for a while. Then three."

"Seven or eight pitchers. That's a lot of beer."

"We were there for a long time."

"How old are you, Mr. Gurvin?"

"Twenty-one," he said.

He doesn't seem too sure of himself.

"May I see your driver's license, Mr. Gurvin?"

Karpinen staggered to his feet. "Objection, Your Honor. Irrelevant."

"I will show the relevance, Your Honor," Burr said.

"Proceed, Mr. Lafayette. I'm getting hungry."

"Yes, Your Honor," Burr said, but he didn't care if Maki was hungry. Gurvin handed Burr his driver's license, reluctantly. Burr made a show of studying it. "Mr. Gurvin, it says here that you were born on July 24th. Is that right?"

"Yes."

"And today is August 3rd. So that would make you twenty-one."

"Yes."

"But on the day in question, July 18th, you were twenty." Burr looked down at the driver's license, then up at Patrick Gurvin. "Isn't that right?"

"I don't remember."

"What do you mean you don't remember?"

"I don't remember."

"How can you possibly not remember how old you were two weeks ago? You were twenty, for God's sake."

"Don't talk like that in my courtroom," Judge Maki said.

"Yes, Your Honor," Burr said.

"I object. Mr. Gurvin's age is totally irrelevant," Karpinen said.

"I'm about to show the relevance, Your Honor."

"Be quick about it."

"Mr. Gurvin, you testified that you were drinking Stroh's at the Murray on the night of July 17th."

"Yes."

"And at the time you were underage."

"I was almost twenty-one."

Burr ignored him.

"Mr. Gurvin, you testified that between three and five of you drank seven or eight pictures of beer at a time when you were not of drinking age. You were quite likely drunk, and yet you remember precisely what you saw."

"We were at the Murray a long time."

Karpinen stood. "Your Honor, this is about murder, not underage drinking. If we're here to try minors in possession, the line of defendants would stretch to the ferry docks."

"My point, Your Honor, is that the witness' testimony is unreliable. Not only was he quite possibly drunk, his character is in question."

"So noted," Judge Maki said. "Anything else?"

Burr thought Judge Maki was starting to look hungry.

Maybe I should finish.

"Mr. Gurvin, were you with anyone that night or during the early morning hours of the next day on the beach?"

"Yes," he said, smiling.

"Who was it?"

"A girl," Gurvin said.

"A girl," Burr said.

"Yes."

"Did she see anything?"

"Objection."

"Do you think she saw anything?"

"I don't think so."

"Why is that Mr. Gurvin?"

"Well, she was on her back."

"Which way was she looking?"

"I think mostly her eyes were closed."

Burr moved in for the kill. "Were you on top?"

"Yes."

"Did you have your pants on?"

"Yes."

Burr gave the boy a scathing look.

"Technically. They were around my ankles."

Judge Maki slammed down his gavel. "That's quite enough, Mr. Lafayette. Mr. Gurvin, you are excused."

Patrick Gurvin loped off. Burr sat down.

If this is all Karpinen has, I just might get this dismissed.

Until Karpinen called his last witness.

"The people call Emil Conti," Karpinen said. A short, slight man in his fifties walked to the witness stand. He had longish hair, brown with a little gray, combed straight back. It didn't do much to cover his bald spot, but it curled at his collar and made him look younger than he was.

He had big yellow teeth, coffee-colored eyes with bushy eyebrows. He wore a brown suit, beige shirt and a tan tie with a floral print. But it was Emil Conti's nose that fascinated Burr. Big and brown, with giant nostrils. All in all, Burr thought, he looked like a rodent. A handsome rodent.

"Mr. Conti, please tell us your occupation."

"I am a detective with the Mackinac County Sheriff's Department."

"Do you have any special duties?"

"Homicide."

"Did you investigate the homicide at The Pink Pony?"

"Objection," Burr said.

"I withdraw the question, Your Honor." Karpinen gave Burr an annoyed look.

"You're playing a man short," Burr said under his breath.

"Detective Conti, did you investigate the death of Mr. Lyons?"

"I did."

"Please tell us what you did and what you found."

Emil Conti, the handsome rat, talked with his hands – pointing, wringing, waving. "First, I sealed off the area, the entire inside of The Pink Pony. Then I examined Mr. Lyons. He appeared to have been strangled with Christmas lights. They were wrapped around his neck, tight, and then wrapped around the Labatt tap and plugged in."

"Did you find anything else?"

"A name tag, the paper kind with a sticky back, was on Mr. Lyons' shirt. Right here. It said *Murdo*." Conti pointed to the breast pocket of his jacket. "And underneath the body, a pair of tortoise-shell reading glasses that belonged to the defendant."

"Did you find anything else?"

"There was a stubby Christmas tree on the bar with ladies'…"

"Never mind that," Judge Maki said.

"The lab found the defendant's fingerprints on the lights." He touched his fingertips together.

"Did you find anything else?"

Here it comes.

"I interviewed a number of people who knew Jimmy Lyons. They all said he was having an affair with Mrs. Halverson."

That should just about do it. I may as well object.

"Objection," Burr said.

"Stop it, counselor," Judge Maki said. "At this rate I'll never have lunch."

Burr had a reply but thought it best to keep his thoughts to himself. For once.

"Mr. Conti, in your opinion, do you believe that Mr. Lyons' death was accidental?"

"No."

"Do you believe he was murdered?"

"Yes."

"By whom?"

Emil Conti pointed at Murdo. "By the defendant, Murdoch Halverson." Conti pointed at Murdoch like he was shooting him with a pistol.

"I have no further questions, Your Honor," Karpinen said. He and his stiff leg struggled back to the prosecution's table. "He shoots. He scores," he said to Burr, softly but with malice.

"Mr. Lafayette," Judge Maki said.

We have a motive. Strike three.

Burr drummed his fingers. It was painfully clear where this was headed. Now there was a dead man with a name tag and a motive. On top of that, Judge Maki was hungry.

"Mr. Lafayette, are you still with us?"

Burr stood. "The defense has no questions, Your Honor."

"Thank heavens for small favors. You are excused, Mr. Conti." The judge looked at his watch, then at Burr. "You may call your first witness."

"We have no witnesses," Burr said.

"Will wonders never cease," Judge Maki said, mostly to himself.

Karpinen stood.

"Sit down, Gus. You're all done."

Karpinen sat.

"The court finds there is sufficient evidence to bind the defendant over on a charge of open murder." He banged down his gavel.

Burr bolted to his feet. "Your Honor, there is still bail…"

"You sit down, too."

Burr sat.

"Don't any of you follow me to Aggie's. It's meatloaf day and I don't want to see any of you anywhere near the gravy. Bail is continued." The hungry judge slammed down his gavel, opened the door behind him and slammed it on the way out.

CHAPTER EIGHT

The unhappy group, also hungry, found the closest restaurant to the courthouse, aptly named the Lilac. There were a few brown flowers clinging to what had once been shrubs but were now small trees. Burr thought a pair of clippers would do wonders for the view. The smell of sauerkraut and kielbasa hung over the restaurant like a fog.

Burr looked across the table at Murdo, who was reading the menu with tortoise shell glasses that matched the ones found next to Jimmy Lyon's body.

He's going to need different glasses for the trial.

Burr studied the menu. It looked like he could order anything he wanted as long as it had either sauerkraut or kielbasa in it.

The waitress, a thin, gray-haired woman with wire-rimmed glasses, came over to their table.

Those glasses would be perfect for Murdo.

Martha shooed her off. "Mr. Lafayette, your performance this morning was totally unacceptable."

I knew this was coming.

"You didn't lift a finger to get the charges against poor Murdo dropped."

I just wanted to have lunch first.

Burr put down his menu. "All Karpinen had to do to get a murder charge was show that there was probable cause that a crime was committed. The standard is very low."

The three Halversons stared at him.

"All he had to show was that it was more likely than not that a crime was committed. It's a much lower standard than what's required to convict."

"Which is beyond a reasonable doubt," Jacob said.

I have at least one ally.

"You should have called me. Murdo was with me the whole time," Anne said.

"Respectfully, I think your credibility might have been called into question."

"I beg your pardon."

"With the Christmas tree and the lap."

"How dare you," Anne said.

Jacob shrunk in his chair. Eve rolled her eyes.

"And we have no reason to let Karpinen know what we have on our side," Burr said.

"The judge doesn't like you," Anne said.

"You're right, but now that Murdo's been bound over for trial, it doesn't matter. We're on our way to circuit court and a new judge."

"I think we should have kept the family lawyers," Martha said.

"Now what do we do?" Murdo said.

"Now we have lunch," Burr said.

* * *

Burr swung on the porch swing, a glass of Kim Crawford in his hand, Zeke at his feet. Burr only drank Sauvignon Blanc in the summer, only before cocktail hour, and the only Sauvignon Blanc he ever drank was Kim Crawford. There were more expensive Sauvignon Blancs than Kim Crawford, but none of them had the same sparkling, grapefruity taste. He had three more cases in the pantry, charged to his account at Doud's. Surely enough for the rest of the season.

Burr took the bottle out of the ice bucket and refilled his glass. He admired the curves of the bottle.

If there is a Kim Crawford, she's a leggy blonde with a ponytail.

He sipped the wine, careful not to kill the whole bottle at once. It was going to have to last until cocktail hour. An hour later, Burr was napping on the swing, his glass empty and the dead soldier turned upside down in the ice bucket.

He woke to a tap, tap, tap on his shoulder. There before him stood a leggy blonde with an exquisite champagne ponytail.

Kim Crawford in the flesh.

He stood and offered his hand. "Burr Lafayette."

She ignored his outstretched hand. "I know who you are."

"And you are?"

"I thought you did a reasonably adequate job at the preliminary exam, but you're going off in the wrong direction for the wrong reasons."

"I didn't see you there," he said.

"I was in the back."

Mid-thirties, almost six feet. Blood red lips with matching fingernails and toenails. She wore a sleeveless, sky-blue top, a white skirt over Coppertone legs, and sandals. If her nose was a little too big, Burr didn't care.

"Are you done undressing me?"

"I'm so sorry. Can I offer you a glass of wine?"

"You may."

Burr dashed off. When he returned, the mystery blonde was at home on the swing, one leg dangling. She was scratching Zeke's left ear. He was in heaven.

Traitor.

He opened the wine and poured them each a glass. He sat next to her in the *de rigueur* Mackinac Island Adirondack chair. She sipped her wine and scratched Zeke's ear. Burr refilled her glass.

I'm not going to be the first one to speak.

He filled her glass again.

Finally, "I'm Jimmy Lyons' wife. Or was."

"I'm so sorry, Mrs. Lyons." He swirled the wine in his glass.

"That doesn't help. Not with a white."

"No, it doesn't." Burr set his glass down.

"What's your dog's name?"

"Zeke," Burr said.

I still don't know her first name.

She scratched Zeke's right ear. The dog turned his head.

"He seems to like the left ear better than the right."

"He does."

Mrs. no-first-name Lyons looked up at him. "Jane. I'm Jane."

"Jane is a lovely name."

"It's a bit plain."

"Respectfully, Jane, there is nothing plain about you."

"Thank you, Mr. Lafayette."

"Burr," Burr said.

Jane Lyons brushed a fugitive hair off her face. "I thought you ought to know that Murdoch Halverson is a cur."

I haven't heard that word since Grace's lawyer used it on me.

"Jimmy used to work for Murdo. Jimmy was a genius with metal manufacturing. Especially screw machines." The widow Lyons brushed the rogue wisp off her face again. "Do you know what a screw machine is?"

"I do."

"Jimmy left to start his own business. We were doing very well until Murdo sued over a patent."

"And?"

"Murdo said it was patent infringement."

"If they were fighting, why were you all together at The Pink Pony?"

"We'd been friends for a long time. Jimmy invited Murdo on the race as a peace offering. Anne and I drove up here to meet them."

The rogue wisp fell back on Jane's face. She ignored it, but it was driving Burr crazy. He reached over to brush it off her face.

"What are you doing?"

Burr stopped himself. "Shooing away a fly. All these horses."

She ignored him. "Murdo waited until everyone left, and then he killed my husband."

"Why did you come all this way to tell me this?"

"You seem like a very smart man, and I don't want Murdoch Halverson to go free."

"What if it wasn't Murdo? Your husband had no enemies?"

"None." She handed Burr her glass and left.

* * *

Burr swung, Zeke at his feet, as before. Two dead soldiers overturned in the ice bucket. He had walked the widow Lyons to her bicycle and offered to escort her to wherever she was going, but she had declined.

Two empty bottles of wine and the sun nowhere near over the yardarm.

"Zeke, here we are on what's supposed to be a good old-fashioned Mackinac Island vacation, and every time I fall asleep on this damn porch, somebody shows up and causes trouble." He dozed off.

* * *

Burr sat in the bar at The Pink Pony, nursing an ice water in front of the infamous Labatt tap. Zeke lay at his feet. It always surprised Burr that he could take Zeke almost anywhere. He thought it was because he never asked permission. It was cocktail hour and The Pink Pony had started filling up, but there was no one sitting at the bar except the two of them. He looked out at the dangling chains.

Maybe things would go better for me if they put another pony up there.

"Mr. Lafayette?"

The auburn-haired beauty with the pointy nose, freckles and ponytail sat down next to him.

"Carole?"

She nodded.

"Would that be with an *e*?"

"How did you know?"

"There's a lot of that going around." She gave him a puzzled look. "May we speak privately?" he said.

"There's no one else at the bar. Except your dog."

"Right."

"Who isn't allowed in here, by the way," she said but made no effort to enforce the rule. She ducked behind the bar, drew each of them a Labatt, then sat next to him.

"My favorite," Burr said.

"I thought you preferred your Labatt with tomato juice and Worcestershire."

"Only on special occasions," he said, hoping she wouldn't ask him if hangovers were special occasions.

"What exactly is your job here?"

"I manage the bar and the bartenders." She drank off the top inch of her beer, which left her with a foam mustache.

"I'd like to ask Karen Vander Voort a few questions."

"She's not here," Carole said.

"I can see that."

"It's her day off."

"Do you like my mustache?" she said.

"I was wondering about the doors."

"The doors?" Carole licked off her mustache.

"Can you open the doors from the inside, after they're locked?" He took another swallow.

"The bartender who closes makes sure the bar and the kitchen are empty. Then they lock the door to the street, the door to the lobby and the back door, the one from the kitchen. They still open from the inside. That's fire code. But no one can get in from the outside."

"Then how did Jimmy Lyons get in here? Or for that matter, the murderer?"

"I have no idea."

"Could he and the murderer have hidden in here?"

"I don't see how." Carole frowned at him. "It's part of the closer's job."

"What about the bathrooms?"

"They're in the lobby."

"Was Karen the closer that night?"

Carole nodded.

"Could she have let them in?"

Carole set her beer down on the bar. "She wouldn't do that."

"One of the witnesses at the preliminary exam said that he saw Murdo come out the kitchen door."

"I don't see how that could have happened." Carole drank from her beer. Another mustache. "Especially if Patrick was doing what you think he was doing." She smiled at him and her mustache dripped into a Fu Manchu. "It was clever of you."

Burr was nothing if not clever. Sometimes too clever by half.

"Maybe she forgot to lock one of the doors."

"They were all locked, all three of them." Carole licked off her Fu Manchu.

* * *

The following afternoon, Burr sat comfortably at the north end of the porch of the Grand Hotel, porch being something of an understatement. Veranda was more like it. A grand, Victorian veranda almost as long as a football field. Twenty-feet wide, underneath a sky-blue beadboard ceiling supported by white columns thirty feet tall. Wicker chairs and cocktail tables all painted in white enamel stretched the length of the veranda, filled with resorters, mostly middle-aged to elderly, sprinkled with a few unruly children. Red-jacketed waiters bussed the tables and plied the idle with alcohol.

Burr sat by himself. Lake Huron, beyond the trees and a hundred feet below the hotel. Then, the Mackinac Bridge stretching across the straits like a dinosaur. The same west wind that lulled him to sleep on the porch at Windward stirred the lake just enough for the sun to sparkle on the wave tops.

Burr dropped his left hand to scratch Zeke … who wasn't there. No dogs at the Grand and the rules strictly enforced. He had called for Murdo, at Aerie, and was told by the maid to meet him at the Grand at three o'clock sharp. And here he was. Next to him, the biggest bottle of San Pellegrino money could buy. And a saucer of lime wedges. After yesterday's run-in with the Kim Crawford, not to mention the Labatt, sparkling water was all he could manage. He drank the sparkling water and waited. And waited. By three-thirty he was losing interest in meeting with Murdo, but he didn't want to get fired, and the ten large was already spoken for. He ordered another San Pellegrino.

At last, the accused arrived. Murdo wore lemon-yellow slacks with midnight-blue whales, a white polo shirt and Weejuns with no socks.

"Hello, Murdo," Burr said, standing. He shook Murdo's hand, not exactly a bone crusher.

Murdo flagged down a waiter. "Dewar's with a twist. You?"

"All set."

Murdo looked at Burr's glass. "Gin?"

"San Pellegrino."

"Of course." Murdo sat in the chair next to Burr, a cocktail table between them.

Murdo said, "How about a friendly game of gin? While we talk?" He asked one of the red-jacketed waiters for a deck of cards.

Does he understand he's been charged with murder?

The scotch arrived along with the cards. "We'll cut for the deal." Murdo slid the deck to Burr, who turned over the Queen of Spades. Murdo swung his hair out of his eyes and turned over the King of Hearts. "Dollar a point. Hundred a game. Fifty for a gin and fifty for an undercut."

"Done," Burr said. Burr discarded the Jack of Diamonds, which Murdo swooped up.

They played.

"Murdo, we have to talk about your defense."

"Of course."

Burr picked up the five of clubs. He was working on a run. "Did you kill Jimmy Lyons?"

"That cuts right to the chase." He picked up Burr's discard and rearranged his hand, then discarded face down. "Gin." Murdo counted Burr's deadwood. "That's fifty-nine in points and fifty for the gin. One hundred and nine in all." Murdo wrote it all down on his cocktail napkin.

"Murdo, did you kill Jimmy Lyons?"

Murdo dealt again. "No. Of course I didn't."

"Who did?"

"I'm sure I don't know. Discard, please."

Burr discarded the King of Spades. Murdo drew.

"Murdo, you were seen arguing with Jimmy at The Pink Pony. Your name tag was on his shirt. Your glasses were found next to his body. Your fingerprints are on the lights that strangled him. You were seen leaving The Pink Pony after hours. And yesterday I found out you were suing him."

"Who told you that?"

Burr ignored him. "And on top of all that, the homicide cop testified that Jimmy was having an affair with Anne."

"She most certainly was not. I was with her the entire evening. She'll testify to that." He flipped his hair off his face again. "For that matter, I will, too."

Burr thought the best way to send Murdo to Jackson State Prison for the rest of his life would be for him to testify on his own behalf. Sympathetic, he wasn't.

"Murdo, it's seldom, if ever, a good idea for the defendant to testify, and who knows if the jury will believe Anne. The prosecutor will try to show that Anne and Jimmy were having an affair and you killed him out of jealousy. And if that doesn't work, he'll say you killed him because of the lawsuit." Burr picked up the King of Diamonds and discarded it.

Murdo picked it up.

Damn it all. He's working on a run in diamonds.

"Anne is my wife."

"My point exactly."

Murdo motioned the waiter for another round. Burr passed.

If I drink any more sparkling water, I'll float out of here.

"Murdo, why were you suing Jimmy?"

"Who told you that?"

"Jane."

"I should have known. I wasn't suing him. Detroit Screw Machine was suing him." *Small point.*

"Do you know what a screw machine is?"

"My grandfather invented the broach."

"Oh, that's right. Jimmy is, was, in his own way, brilliant. We were about the same age, but he worked for me. I taught him all he knew about screw machines. Then he left to start his own shop. While he was working for me, he had come up with a wonderful new idea for mounting the work on the machine. He took the idea to his new company."

"That's a motive."

"Nonsense, the litigation is still pending. You know better than I do that everyone sues everyone. It was nothing personal."

He doesn't miss a beat.

Burr lost four more games. So far, he was down 537 points, which was 537 dollars. Now he didn't have enough for the elevator.

"Murdo, you have to take this seriously. At the very least Karpinen is going to introduce evidence that Anne and Jimmy were having an affair, and whether it's true or not, it's going to make Anne's alibi less believable."

Murdo rearranged his cards.

"Jane told me that you killed Jimmy because he was having an affair with Anne," Burr said, lying.

Murdo looked at him out of the corner of his eyes. "She did, did she?" He drank from the Dewar's with a twist. "I'm sure they weren't. And even if they were, I certainly wouldn't kill him over it."

"She said she was divorcing him," Burr said, lying again.

"I hardly think so," Murdo said.

"Why not?"

"He was worth more to her dead than alive."

"How so?" Burr said.

"Life insurance. If anyone killed Jimmy, I'd say it was Jane." Murdo finished his drink, then looked up at Burr. "Please don't misunderstand me. There is nothing worse than what is happening to me. To us. To Anne and me.

The only reason I wanted to meet here was to keep all this away from her. And the only reason I wanted to play gin was to keep from being even more worried." Murdo picked a card from the deck. "Here's another gin." He spread out his hand, two through four of spades, three sevens, and four aces.

* * *

On the way back from the Grand, Burr stopped at Doud's to pick up dinner. When it was safely in the refrigerator, he and Zeke lit the fire in the cherry red Weber just off the deck in the backyard.

For all of the million-dollar view from the porch, Windward backed up to the forest that covered most of the island with an eight-foot cedar hedge on each side.

Burr looked in the grill. The flames had died down and the charcoal pyramid glowed orange from the bottom up. In another ten minutes it would be time to spread out the coals.

Eve joined him in the backyard. "Now what are you up to?"

"Everyone has to eat. And drink. Speaking of that, stay right here. I'll be right back." Burr opened the screen door and darted into the kitchen. He filled two highball glasses with ice and, feeling completely recovered, poured two shots of Myers's dark rum into each of the glasses, then bitter lemon.

Schweppes is the only bitter lemon worth drinking.

Then another dollop of Myers's. He sliced a lime into four wedges and squeezed two in each glass. Back on the deck, he handed Eve the glass with the rum and bitter lemon. Burr raised his glass. "To Murdo. And to justice."

"I hope they're not mutually exclusive." Eve clinked Burr's glass and studied hers. "This is a very brown drink."

"There's no good reason to waste perfectly good Schweppes."

Eve ignored him. "What if justice means guilty?'

"That would be unfortunate," Burr said.

"How did your meeting go?"

"We played gin."

"How much did you lose?"

"I am skilled at gin."

"How much did you lose?"

"About nine hundred."

"Dollars?"

"Three hours of billable time."

"You haven't gotten that much an hour since Fisher and Allen." She looked at her drink again, then at Burr. "Do you think he did it?"

"Possibly."

She stuck her index finger in her drink and stirred. "I wish you hadn't made this so strong." She sipped again. "You'll never let Murdo testify, but what about Anne?"

"Possibly."

Is she believable?"

"Very, but I'm not sure that I believe her."

"Why not?"

Burr stepped into the woods at the edge of the backyard. He searched and searched. He picked up a four-foot stick, broke off the twigs and about a foot of the skinny end. "Perfect." Back on the grill, he spread the coals with his new grilling stick.

"You simply can't grill without a proper grilling stick," Eve said.

"Exactly," Burr said.

"Are you aware that someone has actually invented grilling tools?"

Burr ignored her. "As you know, I make it a point never to believe what my clients say." Burr poked at the coals again. They glowed a soft orange. "And the higher the stakes, the more they lie." The end of Burr's grilling stick caught fire. "This always happens." He stuck the burning end in the ground.

"Funny how wood always seems to burn."

"Jimmy's widow came to see me yesterday."

"And?"

"And she's convinced Murdo killed her husband."

"And?" Eve stirred her drink with her finger again.

"She said that Jimmy had no enemies. Except Murdo."

"Do you believe her?"

"Of course not, but today I told Murdo that Jane said Anne and Jimmy were having an affair."

"Did she say that?"

"No." He poked at the fire with the fresh end of the grilling stick.

"Do you think Anne and Jimmy were an item?"

"I have no idea," Burr said.

"What did Murdo say?"

"He denied it."

"Do you believe him?"

"Of course not." Burr found the grate which Zeke cleaned off with his tongue.

"That's disgusting."

"I was hoping you didn't see that." Burr arranged the grate in the grill, then disappeared into the kitchen. He returned with a cookie sheet with three oversized fish filets each in their own foil boat. "I think we may actually have to find out who did kill Jimmy."

"How are you going to do that?"

Burr noted that Eve had changed *we* to *you*. Not a good sign. He slid the filet boats onto the grill.

"At least there's something between Zeke's tongue and the fish," Eve said.

"Fresh Lake Superior walleye. These poor devils were swimming this morning, just like the whitefish." Burr drank more of his Myers's and bitter lemon.

"What's that on the fish?"

"Almond slices soaked in Maker's Mark. Walleye is a mild fish and needs a little something. Although I hate to waste perfectly good bourbon on a marinade." He put the top on the grill. "We don't actually have to figure out who did kill Jimmy. We only need to put some doubt in the jury's mind. A reasonable doubt." He opened the vents and smoke poured out. He looked at his watch. "Seventeen minutes. Where's Jacob?"

"Tying flies. You did say you'd take him fishing."

Burr looked at his watch again.

"What's next?" Eve said.

"Grilled asparagus, new potatoes, salad, peach pie. Fresh peaches from St. Joe and a subtle Pinot Noir."

"About your case?"

"I'll know right where to start as soon as I get the list," Burr said.

"The list?"

"I'm going to open the wine. It needs to loosen up a bit." He disappeared into the kitchen.

CHAPTER NINE

It was raining when Burr woke, not a downpour but a steady, patient rain.

"An all-day rain," he said to Zeke lying at the foot of the bed.

After breakfast, Burr put on his foul weather gear and set off for the marina to get the list he needed. Zeke trotted beside the bike, enjoying the rain.

The slips were full. Powerboats, cruising sailboats and a few of the racers that had laid over after the race. Burr turned onto a finger dock and stopped alongside the companionway of *Elysia*, a fifty-foot Chris Craft, vintage 1951. A sedan with a covered cockpit. Shiny, white wooden topsides. Oiled teak decks. Varnished Honduran mahogany cabin sides with six coats of Feldspar refreshed twice a year. Rain beaded up on the varnish and ran off like water off the proverbial duck's back.

"Zeke, there's nothing like bright work well-done." He rapped on the cabin side. "Permission to come aboard?"

No answer. Burr rapped on the cabin side again. "I know the old goat's aboard. He never gets up before noon." Burr admired the gangway, teak planks with waist-high mahogany handrails that matched the rest of *Elysia*. "There's not many gangways around here." Burr walked the gangway to the boat. Zeke tagged along behind. Burr, now aboard, admired the aft deck. White canvas with clear plastic zipped in the entire aft deck, keeping out the rain, rattan deck furniture with navy cushions. "Not exactly slumming."

"Who goes there?" A gravelly voice from below decks.

"Stubby, is that you?"

Shuffling feet, then the door to the main cabin burst open. "Stay where you are." A double-barrel shotgun pointed at Burr's chest.

"For God's sake, Stubby, it's me."

"What the hell are you doing here at this hour?" The safety clicked on.

"What are you doing with that thing?"

"You can't be too careful," Stubby said.

"Mackinac Island is a very dangerous place, with the fudgies, the boaters, and the Boy Scouts."

Stubby scowled at him but leaned the gun against the rail.

Stubby Goodspeed. Five-foot-five, maybe. A barrel for a trunk and the shortest legs Burr had ever seen. Sandy hair, freckles and brown eyes all on a head shaped like a shoebox. He had on the nastiest bathrobe Burr had ever seen, frayed at the cuffs, at the collar, and the hem. His bare, stubby legs stuck out from his bathrobe. Burr hoped he had on more than the bathrobe, navy blue with white piping. At least he matched the furniture.

Stubby spied Zeke. "Dogs are not allowed aboard."

"Come on, Stubby. It's raining."

"He's a Lab. Either he doesn't know the difference or he doesn't care."

"Who fetches your ducks?"

"A Lab in a duck blind is a horse of a different color."

"That would be Zeke," Burr said.

"All right. Just this once." Stubby more or less collapsed into one of the rattan chairs. "What the hell do you want this time of the day?"

"It's 10:30."

"That's what I said. And don't call me Stubby." Stubby hated being called Stubby. Only his friends and enemies called him Stubby. "How about a mimosa?"

"It's only 10:30."

"You said that. I've never known you to turn down a drink." Stubby staggered to the bar, opened the waist-high refrigerator, teak door and all, and mixed the drinks. Burr listened to the rain tap, tap, tapping above him. He felt a drop drip onto his head and slid his chair a foot to the left, comforted that even a boat like *Elysia* had a leak or two. He took in the smells of a wet boat. The teak, canvas, and mildew, and all was right with the world.

"Stubby, I'm here to see you in your official capacity as Commodore of the Bayview Yacht Club."

"The most thankless job in the whole damn country. And I don't get paid."

Not that Stubby needed money. The aging scion of yet another Detroit metal manufacturing family, Stubby was pretty well fixed for blades. He lumbered back from the bar, handed Burr a mimosa and plopped back down in his chair. Stubby took a swallow of the orange juice and champagne. Burr didn't.

He knew Stubby loved flying the commodore's flag next to the Bayview burgee, a triangular pennant in navy and red.

Bayview Yacht Club had sponsored the Port Huron-Mackinac since 1927, one of the biggest, best and most prestigious races anywhere. The members of the Bayview Yacht Club surely thought so.

"If it's about your flag, you can't have it until you pay your dues."

"It wasn't my boat. I was just the skipper."

"I don't give a shit. And I don't care if you finished first. Pay your goddamn dues." Stubby finished half the mimosa. "And you better get that pink pony back. That makes us all look bad." Stubby snickered.

"That's not why I'm here."

"Well, then, what the hell do you want?"

"I'd like to see the crew list of Jimmy Lyons' boat."

"He's dead." Stubby finished his drink.

"That's why I want to see the crew list."

"Why?"

"I represent Murdo Halverson."

"That son of a bitch. I hope he fries."

"You know as well as I do there's no death penalty in Michigan."

"There ought to be. How about another?" Stubby stood up. "You haven't touched yours."

"I'm cutting back."

"You must be hung over."

Stubby, back at the bar, his ample backside once again facing Burr, said, "You should never have left Fisher and Allen. Or Grace. Who was that tart anyway?"

"Suzanne. And she wasn't a tart."

"And you're not a criminal lawyer."

"My elevator is broken." He decided he'd try the mimosa.

"What's that?" Stubby mixed.

"Nothing. Stubby, I need to see the crew list."

"For *Fujimo*?" Stubby said.

"*Fujimo*?"

"Lyons' boat," Stubby said.

"That's kind of a Zen name."

"If you say so," Stubby said.

"I need a few suspects, and *Fujimo's* crew list is as good a place to start as any."

"What in God's name for?"

"Because whoever killed Jimmy had to be on the island that night."

Stubby waddled back to his chair and sat, drink in hand. "Can't do it."

"You're the commodore. You can do anything you want."

"The last thing the Bayview Yacht Club needs is another scandal. There's way too much sleeping around as it is."

"I can subpoena it."

"You wouldn't."

"I would." Burr drank a little more of his mimosa.

"It's just me and Elliot on the boat, and I don't know where a damn thing is."

"Elliot?"

"He's a mouser. And a damn good one."

"Where's your bride?"

"She hates boats. They all do, once you marry them."

Burr nodded.

"Look, if you have to talk to someone, the guy you want to talk to is Buehler. Jim Buehler. He and Lyons had a terrible row. Claimed Lyons fouled him. Big protest hearing, but there were no other boats around. His crew against theirs."

"One-tonners? One white hull? One red?"

"How'd you know?"

"I was behind them. They had a tacking duel at Spectacle Reef. I saw the red boat raise the protest flag."

"For God's sake man, why didn't you come forward?"

Burr thought this was a good time to drink a little more of his mimosa. "I was too far behind to see what happened."

"You were way ahead of the rest of your class." Elliot the mouser appeared, like all cats, from out of nowhere. He jumped up on Stubby's lap. Stubby scratched him behind the ears.

"It's just a sailboat race."

"Not to Buehler. He said Lyons forced him onto the reef and he had to tack away. Said it cost him the race. And he's a hothead. A nouveau riche stockbroker from Troy. He could have done it. Hell, any of you guys could have done it." Elliot jumped down from Stubby's lap. This got Zeke's attention, but he didn't go after the cat, who disappeared below.

"I still need the crew list," Burr said.

Elliot reappeared with a quite dead mouse and dropped it at Stubby's bare feet.

"Sue me."

* * *

Burr and Zeke headed farther out on the main dock. They stopped at *Scaramouche*, the Peterson 34 that Burr had chartered for the race. A fast boat, that's what she was. The transport crew would set off tomorrow, and this would be the last he'd see of her.

Scaramouche could point, especially with her new sails. That's why he'd won his class. That, and the way he had sailed the course. But all that came later. On Saturday morning, July 15th, they had motored out to the starting line, just north of the Blue Water Bridge at the southern end of Lake Huron.

The wind blew about ten from the southeast. They put up the main and rigged the ½ ounce chute. They got a fair start, not a great start, but it was a long race and Burr wanted to stay clear of a foul. He took the first watch, steering by compass and Loran, staggering the eight-man crew. Four hours on, four off with a crew change every two hours.

He sailed the rhumb line up the lake, a straight line to the big black can, the turning mark off Cove Island that marked the entrance to Georgian Bay. *Scaramouche* glided up the lake, quartering before a following sea, nothing more than one-footers. Puffy cumulus clouds dotted the sky. They lost sight of land about six hours out of Port Huron.

They had sandwiches for dinner, roast beef and Swiss on rye. Burr turned the running lights on at nine that night, but they didn't really need them until almost ten. The new moon set at eleven, and then the sky lit up with the summer constellations – Pegasus, Scorpio and Sagittarius. They lost sight of the boats but could see running lights all around them.

The sky turned around the North Star through the night. Fog blew in about three in the morning and they lost sight of the fleet. Burr sent a watchman to the bow with a horn. The sun burned off the fog by nine, and they found themselves in the middle of the fleet. So far, Burr had run an average race, but that was about to change.

* * *

Back on the dock, Burr lingered, standing in the rain, admiring the boats. He felt the same way about boats as he did women. He liked them all. "Zeke, they come in all shapes, sizes, and dispositions." He strolled to the end of the main dock, the end nearest the Chippewa and the Arnold docks.

"What have we here?" A sailboat with a yellow, horseshoe-shaped, man-overboard life vest. Stenciled in a semicircle around the horseshoe, *Fujimo*.

"There she is, Zeke. Big as life. She's fifty feet if she's a foot." White hull, green waterline, nonskid deck, oiled teak trim. Tall, skinny mast with a rake aft. Low-slung cabin. Burr headed down the finger dock. Zeke followed, nonplussed about any boat that wasn't a duck boat. Burr studied the cockpit and the oversized stainless-steel wheel just ahead of the reverse transom. Three winches on each side. Two coffee grinders, the biggest of the winches.

There was no sign of life. Burr paced back and forth on the finger dock. Finally, he climbed aboard. Zeke sat on the dock. Burr stepped down into the cockpit and studied the instruments mounted in the aft of the cabin. Compass, knot meter, depth finder, wind direction, wind speed, apparent wind. He stroked them lovingly.

The hatch cover had been pulled shut, and three teak slats sealed off the companionway. There was a hasp on the hatch cover but no padlock. He slid it back and was greeted by the sweet, smoky smell that he was all too familiar with.

Then there was a flare gun aimed at his face.

"I was just looking around," Burr said.

"Get off," a voice said.

If that thing gets any closer, I can blow my nose in it.

The flare gun waved in Burr's face.

I hope he doesn't get paranoid when he smokes.

"Get off."

"I skippered *Scaramouche*. I saw your stern the whole race and just wanted to take a look."

"*Scaramouche?*" the voice said, flare gun still in Burr's face.

"Peterson 34."

"You can't expect to keep up with a one-tonner. Now get off."

"I don't care if you smoke weed all day and all night. That's what my partner does."

"Does what?"

"Smoke. Every day, and on top of that he's a lawyer." The flare gun hadn't moved. Burr put his right forefinger on the barrel and pushed it away from his nose. "Can I come below?"

"I guess so."

Burr swung his legs over the slats and climbed down into the gloom of the cabin. There weren't many portholes, but then again, *Fujimo* was a racing machine. Burr's eyes adjusted. He finally got a look at the voice behind the gun. This guy was short, too. Taller than Stubby but not by much. Maybe five-seven. Mid-twenties. Dark brown hair, nicely parted, mustache trimmed just above his upper lip. Peeling nose, like all of the racers. Dilated pupils. No surprise there.

He looks like a stoned shortstop.

"Burr Lafayette," he said, sticking his hand out.

The young man shook Burr's hand. "Toad."

"Toad?"

"That's what my friends call me." Toad retrieved a joint from an ashtray at the nav station and struck a match. His tongue flicked in and out of his mouth.

"That explains that."

"What?"

"Nothing."

Toad sucked on the joint, held his breath and passed it to Burr.

Today is a day that encourages substance abuse. It must be the rain.

Burr took a hit and passed it back to Toad, who was sitting on the port quarter berth. He flicked his tongue and took another toke.

Burr sat down at the nav station. The best instruments here, too. A door on the other side of the cabin led to the aft stateroom. Ahead of that, the galley, midships quarter berths, the enclosed head. Ahead of that, the forward cabin.

Spartan but functional.

Toad passed the joint back to Burr. He toked, then remembered Zeke. "Can I bring my dog aboard?"

"Sure," said the now affable Toad.

Burr fetched Zeke from the dock and pulled out the slats in the companionway, but the Lab sat in the rain and looked down at them.

"Labs sure like rain," Toad said.

"They do."

Where do I start?

"*Fujimo* is a great name for a boat. Kind of Zen."

"If you say so. She's fast as hell."

"Are you the boat boy?"

"For the moment."

"I won my class, but I'm also Murdoch Halverson's lawyer."

"What's that got to do with me losing my gig?" He passed the joint to Burr.

"My client has been charged with Mr. Lyons' murder. As long as I'm here, can I ask you a few questions?"

"Like?"

"Like, are you anything else besides the boat boy?"

"Head trimmer."

"That's great."

The trimmer adjusted the headsails to their best possible advantage. Next to the driver, trimming was the most important job on a racing sailboat.

"After Port Huron, I was supposed to take *Fujimo* to Chicago, but I've been stuck here since Jimmy died. But not much longer."

"Why not?"

"Mrs. Lyons is going to can me."

"Why?"

"She's going to sell *Fujimo*."

"Why?" Burr said, as if he didn't know.

"Married women don't like boats."

"Don't I know it."

Grace loved boats. Until we married.

Toad passed him the joint.

I'm going to lose my place if this keeps up.

"I think she needs the money."

"Really?"

"Jimmy pretty much owed everybody. Including me."

"Do you know anyone who might have wanted to murder Jimmy?"

Toad sucked on the joint and thought it over. "Plenty of people." He offered the joint to Burr, who finally passed.

"Like who?"

"Like Jane."

"Jane?"

The ship's bell chimed eight times. "Shit. It's noon. I got to go for my interview."

"Just a second. Would you give me the crew list?"

"I don't think that's a good idea." Toad stubbed out the joint, and put it in his pocket.

"Who do you think might have killed Jimmy?"

"My money is on Jane." He stood up, reached in the hanging locker and pulled out his storm jacket.

Burr thought he might as well try again. "Who was on the crew?"

"No."

"I'm trying to save an innocent man."

"Murdo might be a lot of things, but one thing he's not is innocent."

Burr found a twenty-dollar bill in his pocket and handed it to Toad, who looked at it like he'd never seen one before. He stuffed it in his jeans. "That gets you on board."

"I'm already on board."

"You paid in arrears."

He should be a lawyer when he grows up.

"Questions cost a hundred."

Burr pulled out the rest of his cash and counted it. "I'll buy forty-one dollars' worth." He passed the cash to Toad.

Toad sat down.

"About the crew."

"There were ten of us, including Jimmy."

"Let's start with the ringers." Burr pulled a cocktail napkin and a pencil from his storm gear.

"Why?"

"Because they're the least likely to have a reason to murder Jimmy."

"Eric had the point. I went to State with him. Never gets anything twisted up. Robert and Tom were the grinders. Robert goes to Central. Tom goes to Kalamazoo and plays football. O-line. Big, strong guys, especially Tom. Another guy, Sammy, did the mast. I was head trimmer. Tom backed me up."

Burr coughed.

I could get stoned just sitting here.

He was having a hard time concentrating, but he wrote down the names with the job next to each one.

"That's pretty much it for the ringers." Toad retrieved the joint from his pocket and lit up again.

"What about the others?"

"The other guys, most of them at least, were Jimmy's pals. He and I drove, but so did Murdo and Lionel."

"Lionel?" Burr hoped it wasn't the Lionel he knew. But then how many Lionels could there be in Detroit?

"He had this white hair that would frizz up. Looked like a lion." Toad giggled.

"What did he do?"

"Driver. He was pretty good, but he oversteered."

"His day job."

"He was Jimmy's lawyer."

That's what I was afraid of.

"Who was the navigator?"

"Mostly this guy named Otto. I never met him before, but I think he was in the screw machine business, too." Toad sucked on the joint. "Then there's this guy Dickie. Skinny guy. He really didn't do much. I don't know why he was there."

"Why?"

Toad yawned. "It didn't seem like they got along. All he did was talk to Jimmy about money."

"Anyone else?"

"Benny. He was the cook. That's all he did. Great cook. Lousy sailor. Kind of squishy."

"Squishy?"

"Like this." Toad reached his hand to Burr and shook it. A limp handshake.

"Anybody else?"

"Not that I can think of."

"Who did the pit?"

"The pit?"

"The pit," Burr said again.

"The pit," Toad said again. "Robert. Robert did the pit."

"I thought you said Robert was a grinder."

"He did the pit, too."

It will be a miracle if I can remember any of this.

"Why would anybody kill Jimmy?"

"I already told you." He looked Burr right in the eye. "Money."

"Money?"

"Jimmy lived large but not on his own nickel." Toad snickered again. "I always had a great time with Jimmy. Too bad it's over."

Toad put out the joint, now just a roach, and put it in his pocket. "You used up your forty-one dollars. I got to go to my interview." He started up the companionway. "You got any idea what *Fujimo* stands for?"

"I thought it was just some Zen thing."

Toad's tongue darted in and out. "Zen, my ass." He pulled back the hatch cover, then turned back to Burr. "It means '*Fuck U, Jane. I'm Moving Out.*'"

* * *

Burr, Zeke at his feet, sat in a booth at Jesse's Chuck Wagon. There was a counter with stools, all occupied, on the other side of the diner. Jesse's was on Main Street, two blocks west of the marina. It was known for serving breakfast all day, which was just fine with Burr, who had a powerful appetite and knew why.

Burr sat facing the door. He never sat with his back to any door. The door opened to muttering and general confusion, a dapper man tangled up in a black umbrella stuck in the doorway.

Eve ducked underneath Jacob and his umbrella. She shook the rain off her yellow slicker and sat down across from Burr.

"You smell just like Jacob."

"That's why I'm so hungry."

Jacob gave up on the umbrella and sat down next to Eve, the umbrella upside down on the floor. He had a summer-weight, belted Burberry trench coat over a coral crew neck cotton sweater. He took off his crushed felt fedora. Natty as always, but water dripped from his steel wool hair. Raincoat, hat and umbrella notwithstanding, Jacob had managed to get wet.

"I see we're in another one of your dives."

"It looks to me like you can have anything you want here, as long as it's fried," Eve said.

"You can get breakfast all day. That's what I like about it." Burr took the crew list out of his pocket.

"What's that?" Jacob said.

"It's *Fujimo's* crew list." Burr handed Eve the list.

"Do these people have last names?"

"That's what we need to find out."

"We, meaning me?" Eve studied the list. "Toad?'

"He's the boat boy."

The waitress arrived, a sulky looking young woman with ketchup on her apron. Burr ordered the Chuck Wagon special: eggs over easy, a double order of link sausage, hash browns, rye toast, and tomato juice. And a side of pancakes.

"Do I need ask why you're so hungry," Eve said. She ordered pancakes.

"And you, sir?" the waitress said to Jacob.

"Water."

"Just water?"

"Water will be more than enough."

"Plus, there's Jane," Burr said.

"I thought she was the grieving widow," Eve said.

"Not if she knew what the name of Jimmy's boat meant," Burr said.

"The name?" Jacob said.

"*Fujimo.*" Burr parsed the acronym. Eve snickered. Jacob frowned.

"Why would she kill her husband? All she had to do was divorce him and she'd get half."

Eve knew all about divorce, but Burr didn't think this was the time to bring that up. "If Jimmy was broke, she'd get half of nothing. If she killed him, she'd get the life insurance," Burr said.

"Assuming she was the beneficiary," Jacob said. He took the list from Eve. "Murdo's on this list."

"He was part of the crew," Burr said.

"That doesn't help," Jacob said.

Burr ignored him.

"What about all the other drunks who were on the island that night?" Eve said.

"And there's the guy who protested Jimmy," Burr said.

"Protested?"

"Another boat said she was fouled by *Fujimo*."

"And you'd kill somebody over that?" Jacob said.

"Those are half-million-dollar boats, and the owners have egos to match."

"For all you know, it may have been someone who had nothing to do with the damned sailboat race," Jacob said. He looked out the window. "For all you know, it could have been that street sweeper out there."

CHAPTER TEN

A northwest wind came up during the night and blew out the rain, and the morning dawned crisp and clear. Burr and Zeke sat on the top deck of the *Captain Shepler* bound for Mackinaw City. Burr let Zeke sit against the rail on the upper deck. Zeke, ears flapping in the wind, loved the spray in his face. Burr, who didn't, sat on the aisle.

Burr had avoided leaving the island unless it was absolutely necessary, but it had become painfully clear after meeting with Toad that lawyering from the porch of Windward, however delightful, wasn't going to get the murder charge dismissed.

Once ashore, Burr had the valet retrieve his black Jeep Grand Wagoneer with the fake wood paneling. He opened the passenger door for Zeke, who always insisted on a boost to the passenger seat. Why a dog who broke ice to fetch a duck and bullied through a cattail swale after a pheasant insisted on being helped into a car was beyond Burr.

They headed south on I-75. Burr tried to get the cassette player going in the Jeep, then remembered it was broken, like the rear window wiper he'd broken off before it broke on its own. Then, 250 miles and a tank-and-a-half of gas later, Burr took the Jefferson Avenue exit in downtown Detroit. They passed the Renaissance Center, which housed the offices of Fisher and Allen, and parked just up Griswold in front of the Penobscot Building, a gray Art Deco skyscraper that had been the tallest building in Michigan until the RenCen went up.

He and Zeke rode the Penobscot elevator to the thirty-second floor, then transferred to a second elevator that ran to the top fifteen floors. It shook and rattled all the way to the forty-third floor. Burr remembered why he hated elevators. He didn't agree with Eve's theory that it was a loss-of-control issue.

The damn things aren't safe.

The doors opened to oak paneling and brass lettering that read *Jameson,*

Jones, Worthy, and Goodenough. The law firm took up the whole floor, not that there was much floor space this far up.

"Yes?" said a young woman at the reception desk.

"Burr Lafayette to see Lionel Worthy."

"And your associate?" she said. Total deadpan.

"Co-counsel," Burr said, returning the deadpan.

She phoned into the bowels of the law firm. A few minutes later, Lionel Worthy appeared. Big and strong, thick around the middle. Florid complexion, white hair combed straight back, ending in curls that brushed his collar. Sixty-five-ish.

He smells like an ashtray.

"How nice to see you again, Burr." Lionel Worthy pumped Burr's hand. "And this is?" he said, scratching Zeke's ear.

"Zeke."

"Come on back." He took them to a corner office that looked over the top of the Guardian Building to the Detroit River on one corner and the City-County building on the other. The counselor with the flowing mane sat at his desk in a wine-colored leather office chair.

Burr sat in one of two matching wing chairs facing Worthy. Zeke looked longingly at the other chair, but Burr motioned him to the Oriental rug. Worthy opened a drawer, took out a pack of no-filter Pall Malls and lit up. He blew a cloud of smoke in Burr's direction. Burr coughed. Worthy waved at the smoke, but it still settled over Burr, who coughed again. Worthy smoked half the cigarette, then stubbed it out in an overflowing brass ashtray and lit another one. He sucked on the new one, then said, "What can I do for you?"

He looks like he's sucking lemonade through a straw.

"I represent Murdoch Halverson."

"The Halversons already have lawyers." Worthy blew a lungful of smoke from his nostrils.

He looks like a dragon.

"I'm mixing my metaphors."

"What's that?"

"Nothing," Burr said. "I'm representing Murdoch Halverson on the murder charge."

"Things must be tough since you got booted out of Fisher and Allen."

"I resigned."

Worthy stubbed out his Pall Mall and lit a third.

Burr was damned if he was going to let Lionel Worthy get the better of him. Worthy was a fiery litigator. He was plenty smart, and anything he lacked in brains he made up for in bravado. Burr had beaten him every time they had met in court, and Worthy hadn't forgotten.

"Lionel, were you on *Fujimo*? With Jimmy?" Burr said, hoping against hope there was another Lionel.

"Great name," Lionel said, inhaling.

His hopes dashed, "Your relationship with him must have gone beyond professional."

Worthy exhaled.

"It seems like your client had some money issues," Burr said.

Still no response.

"I hear he owed everybody and his brother. I suppose that includes you."

Worthy's face turned from heart attack red to fire-engine red.

That did it.

"Look here, Lafayette, I represented Jimmy Lyons when he was alive. Now I represent the estate of Jimmy Lyons. His affairs are private."

"Come on, Lionel. Do you want me to order up your deposition?"

"These matters are subject to attorney-client privilege." Worthy waved his hand with the cigarette at Burr. Ashes flew everywhere.

"Your client is dead, and privilege does not extend to strangling with Christmas tree lights."

"Nonsense." Worthy pulled at one of his bushy eyebrows with his nonsmoking hand.

Burr knew the privilege survived death, but he wasn't sure that Lionel did. "I'm just trying to find out who might have wanted Jimmy dead. And it seems like *Fujimo* was full of them."

This should do it.

"Including you."

Worthy turned from fire engine red to cherry red. "Get out. Get out right now. Now that you're nobody, I don't have to sit here and take your arrogant bullshit. Especially in my own office."

"Relax, Lionel. I've got a client. You've got a dead client."

"Just because somebody owes somebody doesn't mean you kill them."

"The crew was at The Pink Pony after the race, including you. And you all had a room at the Chippewa."

"How do you know that?"

"You guys were all drunk. Things happen."

"Just because somebody owes somebody money doesn't mean you kill them," Lionel said again. He turned a shade of red Burr had never seen before.

"If not the crew, then how about Jane?"

"No."

"Does she know what *Fujimo* means?"

"I don't know what she knows, but he was her meal ticket."

"What about the life insurance?"

"Don't you think life insurance is a bit pedestrian?" Worthy said. "From where I sit, this wasn't about money. And my money is on Murdo."

"I thought you said it wasn't about money."

"I think Anne and Jimmy were a little too chummy and Murdo didn't like it." Worthy lit a cigarette off the one he was smoking.

"That's the motive *du jour.*"

Worthy looked at both cigarettes. He crushed them out in the ashtray, stood up walked around his desk. "And then Murdo did this." He reached down for Burr's tie and then wrapped it around his neck like a string of lights.

* * *

Burr snatched the parking ticket off the windshield of the Jeep, stuck it on the windshield of the Lincoln Town Car parked in front of him and drove off.

They made Mackinaw City in time for the last ferry, a small, slowish boat run by the Star Line. The two weary travelers slid into bed just before midnight.

* * *

Burr found Jacob the next morning. "Jacob. I'm told there's a trico hatch coming off the Carp. A big hatch."

"There is?"

"And the brookies are rising for it. They're coming off late morning." This was perfect for Burr, who, other than duck hunting, despised getting up early.

"Really?"

"Really."

Jacob was hooked.

"When can we go?"

"How about tomorrow?"

"Tomorrow? Tomorrow would be great."

There's just one thing."

"One thing?"

"A favor, actually."

"Which is?"

"I need some research done."

"That's what I do."

"Perfect. In Detroit. At the City-County Building."

Jacob didn't say a word. Burr counted to himself. One, two, three, four, five, six, seven … he had never made it past seven. Then …

"What is it this time?"

* * *

Burr tracked down Eve in the hollyhocks, tall, milky green stalks with flowers from top to bottom. Blooms the size of half dollars. The same kaleidoscope pattern on each flower, with different patterns and different colors on each stalk. Eve, on her knees, looked up at him. She had a smudge of dirt on her nose. "Don't even start."

"Start?"

"You are so transparent."

"Me?"

"Tell me what you want me to do and what you have to offer."

She has my number.

"It would be much easier if you could just pay me," she said.

Burr bent down and wiped the smudge off her nose.

* * *

Burr and Jacob, fly rods and waders in hand, along with Zeke, took the ferry to Mackinaw City. They crossed the Mackinac Bridge, which scared Jacob to death, to the U.P., then on to the Carp River. The tricos hatched. The brook trout were ravenous. Jacob was in heaven, and now he owed Burr.

The morning after the fishing adventure, Burr and Jacob waited for the ferry.

"You know how I hate the City-County Building."

"We need to know what, if any, litigation is pending against the late Mr. Lyons. My guess is the patent case is probably in the Eastern District of the Federal District Court. The rest of it is probably in Wayne County Circuit Court, but you're going to have to check Oakland and Macomb, too."

"Damn it."

"I didn't hear a word when you caught those brookies."

"They were beautiful."

"You do have a nice presentation, the way you lay the fly on the river."

"Why, thank you, Burr," Jacob said, always a sucker for piscatorial flattery.

"Give the deckhand this ticket when you land. The valet will bring you that God-awful Corvair."

"It's a Peugeot, and all the windows work."

"And take these." Burr passed Jacob two pills.

"I don't take speed," Jacob said.

"They're Dramamine."

Jacob swallowed both.

* * *

Four days later, the mailman walked up to the porch and handed Burr a fat, eight-by-eleven manila envelope. Zeke, sound asleep at Burr's feet, woke up just enough to growl.

"I can sign for it," Burr said.

"Not unless you're Eve McGinty."

Eve appeared from somewhere in the garden with a different smudge on a different part of her nose. She signed for the package. Burr reached for it, but Eve pulled it out of his reach. She tore off the end of the envelope and slid the contents into her hand.

"May I see them?" Burr said.

"Not until we review our agreement."

"Our agreement?" Burr said, knowing full well what the agreement was.

"These pictures you wanted are in exchange for one eight-by-twenty perennial garden at 1644 Hillcrest Avenue, East Lansing, Michigan, including compost, mulch and the cultivars of my choice."

"Cultivars?"

"Plants," Eve said. "Five hundred now. The balance due on completion."

"If I'd known how easy it was going to be for you to get these pictures, I never would have agreed," Burr said.

"The deal was pictures. We didn't bargain over the degree of difficulty." Eve and her pictures descended the steps to the garden.

"You can't put a garden in until spring."

"*Au contraire*. Fall is perfect."

I don't have five hundred.

Eve came back up the steps. She pulled out a folded check from a pocket of her jeans. "Sign here. You have just enough."

* * *

Burr sat on the deck behind the Chippewa, the harbor in front of him, the Arnold Line dock to his right, and, in between, the door where Murdo supposedly made his escape. A Labatt and the envelope with Eve's pictures in front of him.

Carole sat across from him. She wore a sleeveless emerald top, black slacks and flats. Burr thought she looked terrific.

"I see you're with one of your two constant companions. Where's the other?" she said.

"Two?"

Carole pointed at his beer. "Where's Zeke?"

"He had other plans." Burr drank from his first companion. "I was supposed to meet Karen Vander Voort."

"That's why I'm here."

"Where's Karen?"

"I'm afraid she quit."

That's just ducky.

"Really? When?"

"A week or so ago. Everybody on the island quits. It's just a matter of when."

Carole motioned for the waitress and ordered ice water.

"No Fu Manchu?"

"I'm working." She smiled at him. "All the help is seasonal. They all leave sooner or later."

I might have wasted the money on Eve's pictures.

"Were you here that night?"

"I always work when the racers come in. The tips are great."

"Was there anything out of the ordinary?"

"Other than the drunken sailors? But that's not out of the ordinary."

"Did you know Jimmy Lyons?"

"Not until I found him strangled by the Christmas lights." Carole's water arrived.

"Did you know anyone at his table?"

"I wish I'd had that table. He was throwing money around like there was no tomorrow."

"Did you see anything unusual?"

"Well, there was the Christmas tree which ended up on the bar. And all that underwear. You were there. What do you remember?"

"I'm a little bit fuzzy."

"Except for the pony?"

Who's interviewing who?

"The one with the flat chest and the black hair started it."

"That's Murdo's wife. Did you notice anything at their table? Any arguing or fighting?"

"Not really. There were all kinds of people coming and going."

"If I showed you some pictures, do you think you would recognize anyone?"

"Maybe."

Burr opened up the envelope and spread the pictures on the table. Murdo, Anne, Jimmy and Jane. Jimmy's crew. Buehler, the one who lost the protest.

How could Eve have possibly gotten all these pictures in four days?

Burr pointed at the crew plus Buehler. "Do you remember if any of these guys were there?"

Carole studied the pictures. "Not really. Maybe this one. I remember the cigar." She pointed at the cigar-smoking Buehler. "I think he was yelling at Jimmy, but Jimmy didn't seem to care."

"Anyone else?"

"Him," she said, pointing at Murdo's picture.

So far, this hasn't been worth the bike ride.

"Anyone else?"

"I don't know. The place was packed."

"Were yours on the tree?"

I probably shouldn't have said that.

She didn't seem to care. "I shouldn't have, but a guy at one of my tables bet me a hundred bucks I wouldn't do it."

"Which ones were they?"

She smiled at him. "The little pink ones."

That's not why I'm here. Unfortunately.

"Can you find out if these guys actually checked in?"

"No."

"You could if you wanted to."

She picked up her water but set it back down. "I've known the owner for years. He's doing his best to keep the Pony as far away from this as possible."

Burr's second beer showed up. "How about if you get me the reservation list from *Fujimo* and I'll buy you dinner tonight at the Iroquois?"

"Do you think I'm that cheap?"

"There's nothing cheap about the Iroquois." He took a drink from his beer. "I can get the list if I have to. This will keep the hotel out of it."

Carole scrunched her pointy noise. "Show me a Fu Manchu."

This threw Burr for a loop, largely because he had no idea how to do it. He stared down at his glass. There wasn't nearly enough foam to make a mustache.

Carole reached over and picked up his Labatt. She buried her upper lip in the beer then set the glass back down. "Like this." A perfect Fu Manchu dripped from her upper lip and around the corners of her mouth.

CHAPTER ELEVEN

Burr swung on the swing. A carriage stopped in front of Windward. Jacob climbed out and walked up to Burr, a suitcase in one hand, a fat, brown accordion file in the other. He collapsed in a chair next to Burr.

"How'd you make out?" Burr said.

"Let me catch my breath."

He only walked fifty feet.

"If you must know, I was terribly seasick and the stench from this island makes it worse."

"I'm sorry."

"You'll be getting the bill for my ride up the hill."

Burr nodded.

"Do you have charges with everyone on this island?"

Everyone I can.

Jacob set the file on his lap and creased the crease in his beige slacks between his thumb and forefinger. "Keep that cur away from me," he said, pointing at the always napping Zeke.

Cur. That's the second time this month.

"What'd you find?"

Jacob sat the file upright on his lap. "The late Mr. Lyons had legal issues that went far beyond the litigation with Murdo."

"Really."

Jacob twirled one of his steel-wool curls.

Not a good sign.

"The copying cost me a fortune. Not to mention the gas."

"Corvairs get great mileage."

"Peugeot," Jacob said. "It's a Peugeot."

"You should drive an American car."

"Do you want to know what I found or argue about how poorly made

American cars are?" Jacob re-creased his crease. "It seems that the deceased had lawsuits in almost every jurisdiction and venue in southeast Michigan."

"Such as?"

"A company called Apex Heat Treat has filed a breach of contract suit against New Method Screw Machine in Wayne County Circuit Court."

"And who might they be?"

"The plaintiff's registered agent is Otto Gunther. The defendant is James Lyons' company."

"Is that so?"

"In Macomb County, Dickie Gold is suing New Method Screw Machine on a promissory note."

"Dickie?"

"Then there's Murdo's patent infringement suit in federal district court. In Oakland County, some guy named Benny Fishman is suing Lyons for, of all things, not paying for a suit."

"A suit?"

"A three-piece, with two pairs of pants. Tropical wool. Grey herringbone. Also, five ties, a belt, two handkerchiefs, and a pair of Italian loafers."

"Jimmy had good taste in clothes. Is that all of them?"

"Not quite. Also, a complaint for divorce."

Burr stopped swinging. "Was Jimmy the plaintiff?"

"Yes." Jacob twirled the curl again. "But it was never served."

"How do you know that?"

"I have my ways. He was murdered before it could be served." Jacob looked at Burr but didn't say anything.

Here it comes.

"These matters are unbecoming for an appellate lawyer."

"Who are Jimmy's lawyers?"

"One lawyer," Jacob said, twirling. "Lionel Worthy."

* * *

Burr found Eve among her perennials. Hands on hips, Eve menaced him with her clippers. "I'm sure it's right where you left it." Burr followed her into the library, where she handed him the envelope with the pictures. She started back to the garden.

"Follow me." He led her to Jacob, still recovering on the porch, and spread the pictures on the table next to the porch swing. Then he opened Jacob's file and slid the pleadings under the pictures.

"What are you doing?"

"I've matched the crew of the *Fujimo*, minus the ringers, with their lawsuits."

"What's a ringer?" Jacob said.

Burr ignored him.

"And here's Jimmy's lawyer." He pointed at the lion look alike, Lionel Worthy.

"Lawyers are often friends of their clients," Jacob said.

"True enough, but the Port Huron-Mackinac is the best race in America. Why invite your enemies?" Burr straightened Worthy's picture. "All of these men are suing Jimmy, but they're all on the crew."

The wind stirred, spinning the pictures around and blowing them off the porch. They fluttered into Eve's garden.

* * *

The wind died down Saturday night and Lake Huron turned into a parking lot. Burr switched to the quarter-ounce spinnaker sheets and had one of the crew hold out the lee side of the chute with a whisker pole. They heard bells, horns and whistles all around them all night long, but they couldn't see a thing. The sun burned off the fog by nine Sunday morning. When the fog lifted, there were at least two dozen boats around *Scaramouche*.

By ten there were cat's paws on the lake. Burr took the helm and steered from cat's paw to cat's paw. The wind started to clock and they sailed west of the rhumb line. By two, the wind had clocked all the way to the southwest and they jibed onto port tack. By the time they reached the turning mark at Cove Island, the wind had freshened enough to keep the sails full.

Burr saw *Elysia* idling off the mark and raised her on the VHF. "*Elysia, Elysia, Elysia* … This is *Scaramouche*, sail number US23866, rounding the Cove Island mark at 3:17 p.m."

"Is that you, Burr?"

"It is, Stubby."

"You're making good time."

"I guessed right. So far." Burr cleared his throat. "Sail ahead, US 46732. Sail behind, US 11600. *Scaramouche* out."

* * *

After he picked up the pictures in the garden, Burr changed into his sincere blue suit, his lawyering clothes now in his closet at Windward. He took the ferry to St. Ignace, climbed the steps of the Mackinac County Courthouse, where Murdo had been charged and the very same building that housed the Mackinac County Sheriff's Department, the Mackinac County Prosecuting Attorney's office and the Mackinac County Circuit Court.

One-stop shopping.

He found Detective Emil Conti's office in the basement and sat down across from him, a pockmarked desk between them.

"Detective Conti, I have a right to know what you found."

"Of course, you do, Mr. Lafayette," Conti said, still dressed brown, from sand to cocoa. He made an effort, largely unsuccessful, to straighten his tie, a floral print, also in brown.

The flowers on that tie need watering.

"Detective, may I have the evidence?"

"No."

"Why?"

"I don't have the authority to give you any evidence."

"Let me start over. You testified at the preliminary exam that Murdoch Halverson's fingerprints were on the bulbs on the string of Christmas lights wrapped around Jimmy Lyons' neck. Do I have that right?"

"Yes."

"Good. And were you present when the fingerprints were lifted?"

"Yes."

"Good again."

Conti's big front teeth stuck out like a rat's when he smiled, if rats smiled.

"Were there anyone else's fingerprints on the bulbs?"

"Yes."

"Really? And how do you know?"

"The crime scene people told me."

"Whose fingerprints were they?"

"No idea." Conti fussed with the knot on his tie. Burr didn't think the detective was nervous. Bored maybe, but not nervous.

"Detective Conti, you're not on the witness stand and you're not under oath. If you were, I'd ask the judge to treat you as a hostile witness."

Conti smiled his rat smile.

"At this rate, detective, you'll be ready for your pension before we're done."

"What do you want to know?"

"Tell me about the fingerprints."

"I already told you, the prints were the defendant's."

"Tell me about the others," Burr said.

"Did I say there were others?"

"You did."

"All right. There were other prints, but they were smudged, and the tech couldn't identify them."

"But there were other prints."

"That's what I said."

"Detective, couldn't the other fingerprints belong to someone other than Murdoch Halverson?"

"I doubt it."

"Why would you doubt it?" Burr was getting angry with this twenty-question fiasco.

"The defendant was seen arguing with the deceased. The defendant was seen sneaking out the back of the hotel. We identified the prints as his. There's no reason to go any further."

"Why didn't you testify at the preliminary exam that there were other fingerprints?"

"No one asked."

"No one asked," Burr said.

"I answer what I'm asked. That's it." He looked at his watch. "It's almost lunch time."

"Do you know if the other prints were saved?"

"No."

"No, you don't know, or no, they weren't saved?"

"Yes."

"But for your shoddy investigation, my client might not have been charged," Burr said.

"We'd have charged him anyway."

* * *

Two floors up, Burr popped out of the stairway into the waiting area of the prosecutor's office. The prosecutor's office always sat atop law enforcement, this being the hierarchy of the criminal justice system.

In keeping with the pecking order, the furniture was made from genuine fake wood and the filing cabinets had fewer dents. Burr saw Karpinen looking out his office window at the parking lot. He knocked on Karpinen's open door.

"Not now, Myrna," Karpinen said, his back to the door.

Burr knocked again.

"Myrna, this isn't a good time to talk about what happened last night."

Intrigued, Burr knocked again.

"Myrna, please. I'm sorry. It's just that I find you…" Karpinen turned around. Burr saw the missing front teeth on the upper left side of his mouth. The prosecutor's scalp turned a sunburned shade of red. He limped to his desk, fished his bridge from a glass of water and filled the gap in his teeth.

"How attractive," Burr said.

"What's that?"

Burr walked in and sat on what could only be a Naugahyde chair.

Karpinen shuffled through a pile of papers. "I don't see that you have an appointment."

"That's right."

"Why don't you make an appointment with my secretary and come back at the scheduled time."

"Would that be Myrna?"

Burr watched in horror as Karpinen took out his bridge with his tongue, rolled it around in his mouth, then put it back in.

"What do you want?"

"I want to see all of the evidence you have on file in this case."

"I've given you all the relevant evidence."

"I filed an evidentiary request two weeks ago."

"I don't remember that, but if you did, we most certainly complied. No offsides here."

Burr looked over Karpinen's office. A bookshelf filled with trophies. All hockey. There was the clincher, a hockey stick taped at the business end, leaning against a wall.

Here in the frozen north, what they say is … there are ten months of winter and two months of bad skating. Burr was afraid he was going to be stuck with Karpinen and his clichés *ad nauseum* and *ad infinitum*.

"Mr. Karpinen…"

"Call me Gus."

"Gus, I have just visited with Detective Conti and have reason to believe that I don't have all of the evidence you have."

"You have all you need," Gus said.

"I assume you're familiar with Brady versus Maryland."

Karpinen gave him a blank look.

"*Pertinent* is not the standard. The standard is 'all evidence which may be exculpatory.' That's the standard, and that's what was in the pleading."

"You have all you need."

"That's not for you to say," Burr said, standing. "I think I'll go find Myrna."

"Why would you do that?"

"I think you may be headed to the penalty box."

* * *

Burr climbed higher in the jurisprudential pecking order. Now on the top floor, he found himself in the offices of the circuit court, with real yellow birch paneling timbered by the lumber barons. Burr could almost see his reflection in it. He was preening when a voice said, "Young man, there is a mirror in the men's room." The voice had come from yet another open door, this one to his left. "How did you possibly get in here?"

"The stairs."

"What's that?"

"The stairs," he said again.

"The stairs?"

"The stairs," Burr said for the third time. "I don't care for elevators."

"Oh, the stairs," said the voice. "I don't care for intruders, but you don't look too threatening."

Burr looked down at himself in his sincere blue suit. He supposed he didn't.

"Arvid Lindstrom. Judge of the Mackinac County Circuit Court."

Lindstrom was long and thin. Seventyish. Fit, if fading from long use. Thinning gray hair that looked like it had been pasted to his head. A long nose propped up wire-rim glasses with steely-blue eyes behind them.

"And you are?"

"Burr Lafayette."

"What's that?"

"Burr Lafayette," Burr said again.

"Murdoch Halverson's counsel."

"Yes, sir."

They shook hands. "Come in, young man." Burr couldn't remember the last time he had been called that.

I like the sound of it.

Lindstrom sat down in a mahogany-colored leather chair behind a massive oak desk. Burr had seen smaller cars. Sunlight bathed Lindstrom and his desk. A corner office with paned windows the size of pool tables. Burr thought this was as close to luxury as you could get in the Mackinac County Courthouse.

"Young man, what is it that you want?"

"Your Honor, I don't think the prosecutor has turned over all the evidence he has."

"What's that?"

Burr repeated himself.

If I have to say everything twice, this is going to take until tomorrow.

"What would you have me do about it?"

"I'd like the evidence the prosecutor has, Your Honor. All of it."

"Young man," Lindstrom said again, "Mackinac Island is a big part of our local economy. The biggest part. And it doesn't help business to have a murder over there."

"No, sir, I'm sure it doesn't."

"The tomfoolery with the missing pink pony doesn't trouble me, but Chief Brandstatter isn't too happy about it."

"Sir?"

"You know exactly what I'm talking about." Judge Lindstrom took off his glasses. Without his glasses, he had beady eyes. "That infernal hobby horse. Happens every year." He put his glasses back on. "In any event, I want this murder nonsense worked out between you and Karpinen."

"Worked out?"

Lindstrom motioned Burr around to his right side. "We can make this a lot simpler if you just talk into my right ear." Burr took three steps to Lindstrom's right ear.

"That's better," Lindstrom said. "Worked out. No trial."

"Your Honor, I must have all of the evidence."

"You filed a Brady motion. Karpinen should have given you all he had."

"I don't think he did, Your Honor."

Lindstrom muttered to himself. "What would you have me do?"

"Tell him to give me all the evidence."

"Mercy sake, Mr. Lafayette. I'm the judge, not his conscience."

"What would you have me do?"

"Do what every lawyer who wants something from me does. File a motion. No, don't file a motion. I'll speak to him. No, I won't. I want the two of you to get together and plead this."

"My client didn't kill Jimmy Lyons. I can't plead guilty."

"I don't want this case tried."

"My client didn't kill Jimmy Lyons."

"A likely story." Lindstrom sat there for a moment. "Go find my secretary and ask her to come in here."

"Where might I find her?"

"You found your way in here. You can surely find my secretary."

Burr stood.

"Never mind," Lindstrom said, shouting. "Myrna, would you come here please?" A plump young woman appeared in the doorway, the foil to Lindstrom's Jack Sprat. She had the creamiest, most flawless complexion Burr had ever seen. Her creamy face framed pouty, ruby lips, and a bob framed her creamy face. She sashayed in like a model for a large and tall catalog, the princess of the Mackinac County Courthouse.

"Myrna, go find Gus and tell him to give Mr. Lafayette all of the evidence he has." Lindstrom took off his glasses. "All of it. I'm sure you know where to find him."

Does she ever.

"Yes, Your Honor," she said primly. Myrna turned and walked off, hips swaying like she was on a runway.

Lindstrom winked at Burr.

CHAPTER TWELVE

Burr sat on the patio of the Iroquois and looked out at the water. The Iroquois, a forty-room, four story, white frame hotel with grand towers, rested on the most western point of Main Street, Round Island across the channel. The harbor to the east. The bridge to the west. A spectacular view, even by Mackinac Island standards. He desperately wanted to order a martini, but he thought he should wait.

Ten minutes later, Carole sat across from him. She wore a blue dress with a V-neck tucked at the waist. He stood and kissed her on the cheek.

"You don't even know if I brought the list."

I don't care.

Burr pulled out her chair.

Carole ordered a Pinot Grigio. Burr, still desperate for a martini, thought better of it and ordered a bottle. The wine arrived and Burr proposed a toast. "To summer. May it linger." They touched their glasses. Carole leaned toward him and looked in his eyes. "My dress matches your eyes."

Burr was a fool for flattery, especially from a pretty, younger woman. "No one has ever said that to me before."

Carole sipped her wine. Her lipstick left a pink smudge on her glass, which Burr found provocative. He stared at her glass.

"Is something wrong?"

"How could anything possibly be wrong?"

"You're just sitting there, staring at my wine glass." She picked up her napkin and wiped off the pink smudge. "Is that better?"

"No, it's fine."

"No, it's fine?"

If I don't say something that makes sense, I'm going to ruin everything.

"What about the winter?"

She looked at him like he was crazy.

I'm not crazy. I'm smitten.

"The winter. What do you do in the winter?"

"In the winter, I manage a bar in Key West."

"That sounds like fun."

That's better.

"I wouldn't call it fun, but it pays the bills. And it's warm."

While he tried to think of what to say next, Carole said, "I was an English teacher in Boyne City, but I tired of trying to teach kids who had no interest in the printed word or learning how to read. That, and the cold. One day I got in my car and drove south until I couldn't go any farther."

"That sounds like a great way to live."

"It isn't, but thank you for saying so."

He finished his wine, topped off Carole's glass and poured himself a full one.

If we finish the bottle, maybe I can order a martini.

The waiter showed up to take their orders. Carole asked Burr to order for her. He ordered her the lake perch in a dill sauce. His chef friend had his own herb garden on the west side of the hotel, so Burr knew the dish would be delicious. He ordered veal with morel, a wild mushroom only found in northern climes. His confidence restored, he ordered himself a martini. Carole stuck with the wine.

After dinner, Carole reached into her purse. "If you're not going to ask for it, I'm going to give it to you anyway." She handed a piece of paper to Burr. He reached in the breast pocket of his blazer for the handwritten crew list and set it beside Carole's list.

"If anybody finds out, I'll get fired," Carole said.

"No one will ever know." Burr pretended to look at the lists, but he was watching Carole push her silky white bra strap back under her dress.

"You weren't supposed to see that."

Burr smiled at her. Then he actually studied the reservation list. "There's one more name on the reservation list than on the list Toad gave me."

"Toad?"

Burr counted the names again. Ten on Toad's list. Eleven on Carole's.

"Who's Ronnie Cross?"

"You got this list from the great Toad?"

"You know him?"

"Everyone knows Toad."

"Was he at The Pink Pony that night?"

"I didn't see him."

"Would he be here?"

"Alcohol isn't his drug of choice, but maybe that's why he forgot."

"If he forgot," Burr said.

* * *

Carole gave Burr a good night kiss at the bike rack in front of the hotel. As much as he had wanted the evening to go further, Burr thought fraternizing with someone involved in the murder, however tangentially, probably wasn't the smartest thing to do. On the other hand, all she had done was find Jimmy Lyons' body. What could be the harm in seeing her again.

* * *

At four in the afternoon, Burr and Zeke drove through downtown Harbor Springs, past the Little Traverse Club and into Harbor Point. He parked in the stall next to Aunt Kitty's silver Benz.

Burr straddled the red Huffy and ding-a-linged Norbert as he pedaled past the gate. Zeke trotted alongside. "Good afternoon, Mr. Lafayette," said Norbert, the oldest security guard with the blackest hair and the straightest part Burr had ever seen.

Five minutes later, his aging aunt met him on the porch of Cottage 59.

"I wondered when you'd show up." Zeke leaned against her and she bent over and scratched his left ear. She picked dog hair from her skirt. "When was the last time you brushed him?"

"It's shedding season."

"It's always shedding season." Her back cracked when she straightened back up.

"Shall I?"

She nodded at him and fell into a white Adirondack chair.

Burr crossed the porch. It wrapped three-quarters of the way around the three-story Victorian, circa 1898. Inside, an Oriental rug ran the length of the hall over an oak and maple parquet floor that led to the kitchen. The refrigerator took up the entire wall and needed eight legs to stand up. It had three doors with claw handles, the deluxe version of Windward's refrigerator. The compressor sat on top, humming and grinding.

He opened the freezer and filled two old-fashioned glasses with ice. He poured Bombay into each glass, added a capful of dry vermouth, then one solitary olive in hers, four plus olive juice in his.

Back on the porch, he handed his aunt her martini and sat across a cocktail table from her, a vase with lavender, yellow, pink and orange snapdragons between them.

She took a big swallow. "Too much vermouth."

"I barely waved the cap around the glass," Burr said, playing his part of the ritual.

"Why must you wreck perfectly good gin with vermouth, and you ruined yours with all those olives, not to mention the juice," she said, playing her part.

Burr looked out at the harbor. The Lafayette Cottage, Number 59. All of the cottages on Harbor Point were numbered, no names. The height of reverse snobbery, Burr thought, but he liked it just the same. The last home at the tip of the point, Cottage 59 faced Harbor Springs and Little Traverse Bay on one side, Lake Michigan on the other. An uncommon view among uncommon views. Aerie had nothing on Cottage 59.

He smelled the smells of the place. The water and the wet sand. The cedar hedge and the white pines, eighty-footers that shaded the cottage.

"You have no business taking this case. You're not a criminal lawyer."

"This was your idea."

"Bail. That's all I wanted you to do."

Burr plucked an olive from his drink. As much as he loved the juniper taste of gin, it was the olives and the olive juice that made a martini a martini.

"She cost you your practice, your wife, and almost your life." Aunt Kitty drank again. "How broke are you?"

"Fairly broke."

"You need to give up this appellate practice and get back to what you're good at. Then you won't have to get involved in these criminal fiascos. And you need to find a new wife and get your life in order."

"My life is in order."

"You may be the best commercial litigator in the state, and you're fooling around with an appellate practice that barely pays the bills. Not to mention that pothead of a partner."

"And Eve."

"She's the only thing that keeps you going. Why she does it and how she can afford it is beyond me."

She divorced well.

Burr looked out at the harbor again, the water a pale blue next to the beach, then aqua, turning suddenly to a blue black at the dropoff.

He told Aunt Kitty what he had found out so far, who he had talked to, and what had happened with Conti, Karpinen and Lindstrom.

Aunt Kitty stared at her crystal-clear martini. A maiden lady, she practiced in Detroit, then moved full time to Harbor Point long before there were any year-round residents. She did environmental law, largely pro bono, largely for the Little Traverse Conservancy. She knew all the lawyers and all the judges within a hundred miles of her martini.

"How much more do you need?"

"Another ten thousand."

"I thought you just got ten thousand."

Burr poked around in his glass for an olive but thought better of taking one out. "That paid for the elevator."

"So, your next stop is Detroit and asking for more money?"

Burr reached for an olive.

"Don't you dare." Aunt Kitty set her drink down. "Detroit Screw Machine employs over two hundred people. It more than pays the bills for Martha, Murdo, and Anne." She looked down at her glass but didn't pick it up. "We both know what happened to Colonial Broach. Fortunately, Detroit Screw Machine is thriving."

Where is she going with this?

"For such a smart man, you can be naïve at times. Especially about money. No matter what Murdo may have done and no matter what kind of fool he may be, he's the brains behind Detroit Screw Machine." She picked up her drink. "If you lose this, and Murdo goes to jail, Detroit Screw Machine will be ruined. That's why someone who knows what they're doing needs to take over."

* * *

Burr took M-68 to Indian River, then I-75 south to Detroit. He thought about what Aunt Kitty said, but he was damned if he'd quit now. Plus, he needed the money.

Once in Detroit, Burr took the Lodge downtown, got off at Jefferson and drove past the Renaissance Center, which hadn't renaissanced anything. Half-a-mile later he turned right on Atwater, toward the river. Burr drove through the chain link fence that marked the entrance, past the better part of a hundred cars and pickups, mostly pickups – Chevys, Fords, Dodges – all of them built in the USA, most in Detroit. He parked in a "no parking" spot next to the space marked *Halverson*. He looked up at the Detroit Screw Machine Company, a three-story, rust-colored brick building, vintage 1925, just about the time Detroit took over as the manufacturing capital of the world. The brick had weathered, its surface worn away by the wind, the rain and the snow.

"Zeke, I shan't be long." Just to his right, the Detroit River, half a mile wide. Burr smelled the river smells, the cattails, the gasoline and the sewage. He shaded his eyes and looked around. Detroit Screw Machine wasn't quite an oasis in a desert of abandoned and burned out buildings, but almost. The neighborhood where tool and die, metalworking, and manufacturing once flourished had moved to Warren, Taylor, or Sterling Heights … or was just plain gone. Behind him now, the Renaissance Center was truly an outpost. In between was Arnie's, where he had lunched in his days at Fisher and Allen, a lawyer in a sea of the skilled and unskilled trades. The best olive burger in Detroit, not to mention the fire-brewed Stroh's draft, from the now closed brewery just up Jefferson. Burr thought both he and Detroit had come a long way, and not the way that either of them had expected.

He walked into the lobby – linoleum floor, tan cinder block walls, and six chairs, all of it pleasantly uncomfortable. Designed for the tool salesman, lubricant vendors, and would-be union organizers. A woman of about sixty slid back a glass window in the wall opposite the door. She studied him, arching her eyebrows over the black frames of her glasses. "No solicitors."

"I'm a solicitor only in the British sense of the word," Burr said.

"No salesmen on Tuesdays. Everybody who calls on us knows that."

"I have an appointment with Murdo."

Her eyebrows almost erupted out of her head. "I'm so sorry. It's your coat and tie, although yours is much nicer than most of the salesmen."

"I'm Mr. Halverson's lawyer."

"Right this way."

The door next to the window buzzed and Burr popped through. The eyebrow lady led him through an office area lit by fluorescent lights where about fifteen women typed, filed, and talked on the phone. Out a door and onto the shop floor, a floor that had known decades of boots with steel toes, oil and metal shavings ground into the hardwood, now a gray blond, all traces of the grain gone, but the wood had enough give to make it bearable to stand on for hours at a time.

The screw machines, row upon row of them, hummed, whined and roared. The shop smelled of machine oil, metal shavings, and sweat. The screw machines looked like so many headless monsters, cut off at the waist, with up to eight arms moving in and out from a defenseless piece of metal. Machine tenders in coveralls shuffled between the screw machines, tightening and loosening, taking finished parts off the machines and putting new ones on. The eyebrow lady led Burr down an aisle to a corner office. Windows looked out on the shop floor. Light poured in from windows that faced the river and the parking lot. The office had a desk the size of a Ford Falcon. A drafting table sat next to the window on the river side of the office.

"I thought for sure Mr. Halverson was in here. Why don't you just wait right here." At that moment, a little man with a plaid, open-collared shirt and oil-stained khakis came in.

"I'll take you to him." The little man stuck his hand out. "Floyd Enright." Burr shook his hand. Enright had thin lips, a flat nose, and just about the finest comb over Burr had ever seen. "He's in the prototype room."

Out they went, past the machines, through the tool room and into a shop filled with every metalworking tool known to man: lathes, grinders, drill presses, metal saws. There, working a lathe, was Murdoch Halverson. White shirt and black slacks, tie tucked into his shirt. His hair fell over his safety goggles. Murdo either didn't see Burr or didn't care. The lathe turned. Metal shavings flew. The heat of the day seeped into the shop. The back and armpits of Murdo's shirt were soaked through. Sweat ran down his cheek. He had an uncommon concentration.

He doesn't look a murderer to me. Could it have been an accident? Or a drunken rage? That wouldn't be first-degree murder. Was it jealousy?

Murdo didn't strike him as the jealous type, especially right now, bent over the lathe. Maybe Murdo killed Jimmy because he was afraid Jimmy was taking his business away. But he doesn't look sympathetic. Unless I find something extraordinary or cook up something spectacular, Murdo is in big trouble.Finally, Floyd walked around the lathe to face Murdo so he wouldn't be startled and get caught in the machine. Murdo kept at it, turning and grinding. At last, he turned off the lathe and pulled his goggles to his forehead.

"What now, Floyd?"

"You have a visitor, Mr. Halverson." Enright fussed with his comb over.

"I do?" Murdo turned around. "Why, Burr, how are you?"

"Fine, Murdo. Just fine."

"I'm surprised to see you here."

"We had an appointment this afternoon."

He turned back to the lathe. "I've almost got this jig the way I want it. The way we do it now takes too long to make the fitting. This will speed things up nicely." Murdo rubbed his hands together. "Do you know what a jig is? Of course, you do. Colonial Broach was two blocks over. A shame your father couldn't keep it going."

Burr ignored him. "Can we go to your office and talk about the trial?"

"We can talk here."

Burr looked at Floyd.

"Floyd can stay. Anne and I were together the whole time."

"That may be so."

"It is so." Murdo took off his goggles and his hair spilled over his forehead. He shook his head and flipped his hair out of his eyes.

"What if the jury doesn't believe Anne? Then what?" Burr ran his hands through his hair, front to back. "It would be better, much better, if we could point the finger somewhere else."

"We talked about this at the Grand. I think it was Jane."

"Jimmy worked for you for years. You must know someone who might have wanted to kill him."

"Jimmy and I were best friends. I gave him his start. I did everything for him. Even after he left I helped him. I only sued him because I had to." Murdo took a handkerchief from his pocket, cleaned his glasses and put them back on. "I don't know who his friends were."

"But you and Anne did things with Jimmy and Jane. Didn't you meet any of his other friends?"

"No. Not really."

"You crewed on his boat. By the way, who is Ronnie Cross?"

Murdo's hair fell back into his eyes. He flipped it out of his eyes again.

That's getting annoying.

"There are three floors here. Three floors of screw machines and everything that goes with them. We get all the tough jobs because we know how to make the tools."

Why does that matter?

"Do you know how hard it is to keep a family business going for three generations?"

"I have an inkling," Burr said, who had more than an inkling. "Who is Ronnie Cross?" he said again.

Murdo started to flip his hair again but this time he brushed it off his forehead with his hand. "I have no idea."

"He was part of the crew."

"One of the boys?"

"Maybe a ringer."

"I have no idea what their names were." Murdo looked like he was getting bored with Burr. "You came all this way to ask about one of the boys on the crew?"

"Not exactly."

"How much this time?"

"Ten thousand."

"It's always about money … isn't it, Floyd?" Floyd turned red underneath his comb over. "If it's about money, Burr, go see my mother." Burr gritted his teeth. "Maybe she'll give you some." Murdo turned the lathe back on.

* * *

Burr and Zeke headed northeast on Jefferson, away from downtown. They drove past the shuttered Uniroyal plant, the abandoned Chrysler factory and the burned-out east side of Detroit. Burr had the doors locked and the windows up, just like all the commuters. Zeke scratched at the window. They crossed into Grosse Pointe Park at Alter Road, a six-foot county drain and a chain link fence topped with barbed wire on each side of the pavement. Burr lowered Zeke's window. They were on the tree-lined version of Jefferson in

Grosse Pointe Park, the first of the five Grosse Pointes, home to the wealthy, the would-be wealthy and the formerly wealthy.

Burr turned toward Lake St. Clair. Five blocks later, into Windmill Pointe, one of the Pointe's oldest and finest neighborhoods. At 537 Windmill Pointe Road, he turned into a circle drive and parked in front of an overbearing Tudor with a slate roof.

Martha Halverson answered his knock. "Why, Mr. Lafayette, how nice to see you. Please come in."

The matriarch led him down a beige hall with a hardwood floor and an Oriental runner that Burr thought was probably worth the price of a house in Warren. Past a powder-blue living room, past the requisite paneled library and into the sunroom. Floor to ceiling leaded windows overlooked Lake St. Clair. Beyond that, the Canadian shore and Walpole Marsh, where Burr and Zeke hunted ducks. Martha walked to the windows and cranked them open.

"A little fresh air is always a good thing." She sat him in a plaid, overstuffed chair. She sat kitty-corner to him in an equally dizzyingly plaid chair. "How much this time?"

"Ten thousand," Burr said without flinching.

"That's a bit stiff, isn't it?" Martha didn't flinch either.

"Criminal defense is expensive."

"I agree, but exactly what have you accomplished since I wrote you the first check?"

"Murdo is out on bail."

"You did that the first day."

This isn't going in the right direction.

"Who do you think killed Jimmy Lyons?"

"I have no idea."

"My point exactly. A suspect or two would be helpful," Burr said. "We need a reasonable doubt."

"Isn't Anne enough for that?"

"I hope so, but it would be nice to point the finger at someone."

Martha looked out at the lake, then at Burr. "So, it's ten thousand for a reasonable doubt."

"Yes."

She turned from the window and looked at him. "Mr. Lafayette, the Halversons are not prolific."

"I beg your pardon."

"The Halverson men are not a fertile group."

Burr didn't say anything.

"They don't have heirs. One child a generation. So far, at least. Beginning with Murdo's great-grandfather."

"Mrs. Halverson, I'm not really following you."

She pointed out the window at a slightly smaller but equally overbearing Tudor. "Murdo and Anne live next door. Anne, the former Anne Murphy, comes from a fine family in Winnetka. They live on the sixth hole of the Indian Hill Club. She also happens to come from a large family. Catholic, but nonetheless a fine family. Murdo worships her." She stood and walked over to a French provincial writing table. She opened a drawer and took out her checkbook. Burr thought this promising. "Mr. Lafayette, we all want Detroit Screw Machine to continue in the family. For that to happen, we need an heir, and we're unlikely to have an heir if Murdo is in jail." She dashed off a check and handed it to Burr.

* * *

As was his long-standing habit, Burr left as soon as Martha Halverson handed him the check, long since having discovered that once he had the money, nothing could be gained by further conversation. Indeed, much could be lost, namely the money.

Jefferson turned into Lake Shore. Burr followed it to 763 Sunningdale, a nicely appointed red brick colonial with two sycamores in the front yard, a three-car garage, and a greenhouse in back. His former home, still the home of the beautiful Grace, and also the home on which he still paid the mortgage.

He picked up Zeke-the-boy, and Burr and the two Zekes played fetch on the beach next to the Grosse Pointe Yacht Club. Burr's membership had long since expired, but Maurice, the gate attendant, always let him in.

Lake St. Clair was reasonably clean here but swimming, except in the pool, as well as fetch, violated every rule of the Yacht Club, not to mention Grace's long list. By the time they were done, the two Zekes were equally wet. They finished their day at the Eastland Chuck E Cheese, which fortunately served beer.

Burr took I-75 north to Mackinaw City. He and Zeke boarded the Star Line's last ferry, the spray from its rooster tail disappearing behind them.

CHAPTER THIRTEEN

"Zeke, I wonder if I'm about to open Pandora 's box."

Eve came in. "Unless that's a centerpiece, you need to get that box off the table before we eat."

"This is the Brady box," Burr said, delighted with his cleverness.

"It looks like a banker's box to me. We have hundreds of them."

"This one has all the evidence that Karpinen has."

"What did you find?"

"I haven't opened it yet."

"Open it up. The beef tenderloin will be done soon."

"Don't be in such a rush."

"Come on, Burr." She took the top off.

Burr peered inside the box. It was less than half full.

"Let's find out before the meat goes from rare to well done."

The thought of well-done beef tenderloin shook Burr to the very core. Out came the papers. He rummaged through them. File after file. The crime scene report, the autopsy, interviews. It looked like he already had all of this.

But what about this? Here they are. The fingerprints.

He compared the fingerprints on the Christmas lights to Murdo's. They matched.

"Find anything?"

"Maybe."

"Make the horseradish sauce. I have fresh dill from the herb garden at the Iroquois."

Jacob walked in. "Get to it, Burr. We don't want the meat overdone."

"Just a minute," Burr said. There were four sheets of fingerprints. Burr studied them, print after print. All Murdo's. "Damn it all."

"Damn what all?" Jacob asked.

"Murdo's fingerprints are all over the Christmas lights."

"That's what Karpinen told you," Eve said.

"Please, Eve. Go check the tenderloin," Jacob said.

"Hush. I set the timer."

Burr looked at the prints again. Some of them were blurry. He held up one of the sheets to the light. "Jacob, would you get your magnifying glass? The one you use to tie those size 20 tricos."

"You're no fingerprint expert."

"Please."

Jacob returned with the magnifying glass.

"These are all Murdo's."

The timer went off. "Eve, for God's sake, check the meat," Jacob said.

She didn't move. "What is it, Burr?"

"This can't be all there is," Burr said.

"What?"

"Eve, I beg you. Check the meat."

"Be quiet."

Burr rummaged through the banker's box. Finally, "Here it is."

"Here's what?" Eve said.

Burr pulled out another sheet of fingerprints. "Here it is."

"Here's what?" Eve said.

"Smudges. A sheet of smudges."

"A sheet of smudges?"

"This is what I've been looking for. These are the other fingerprints that were on the lights. It's what Karpinen didn't want me to have." Burr passed the file to Eve. "Keep this in a safe place." He took the file back. "First take out the meat. I'll make the sauce." Burr put the fingerprints back in the box and disappeared into the kitchen.

* * *

Burr chewed on a rare piece of the tenderloin. "I just can't do it."

"I'm your partner."

"It's a family secret." Burr stabbed another piece of zucchini. "This is perfect."

"Thank you," Eve said.

"I know it has horseradish, cream, and dill."

"I'll leave you the recipe in my will."

"What about the smudges?" Eve said.

"They're probably Murdo's, too," Jacob said. "I think you added a dash of tarragon."

"They might be. But they might not."

"You can't base your entire defense on smudges," Eve said.

"Tarragon is not the secret ingredient," Burr said. "A smudge or two may be just the reasonable doubt we need. Eve, I need you to find me an expert on smudges."

It's mayonnaise, but I'll never tell.

* * *

The man with the missing finger pointed the knife at Burr's nose, the tip of the blade so close that Burr's eyes crossed when he looked at it. He didn't think it was a genuine display of affection, stepped back, only to find himself up against a wall.

"That's what I mean." The man took another step toward Burr, who had nowhere else to go. With the knife still perilously close to his nose, and still looking at the world a bit cross-eyed, Burr saw that it was the ring finger on his left hand that was missing.

Why does everyone point weapons at me?

"I'm afraid I don't see what you do mean," Burr said.

The man turned and flung the knife at the wall behind him, where it stuck in the plank. "You can't just jump in here and surprise me. I could have cut myself, what with the knife and all."

It looks like you already have.

"I knocked and you said to come in."

"I got wrapped up in my carving. Don't scare me like that. You're about as bad as my sister. She always spooks me like that."

I wonder if he goes after her with a knife when she spooks him.

"My name is Burr Lafayette. I think my secretary told you I'd be coming."

"That's right." He thrust his hand at Burr, who shook it. "Stanley Mueller. Call me Stan."

Burr had driven south on I-75, this time to Bay City, then up the east side of Saginaw Bay to Fish Point, a wisp of land that stuck out into the bay, barely above lake level. A state refuge and miles of cattail-choked shoreline. Paradise for ducks and geese. Burr was delighted that Eve had sent him to a decoy carver. He'd found the nine-digit Mueller in a garage turned wood shop behind his house. He smelled wood shavings, paint, and mildew. Decoys everywhere in all stages of incompletion. Canvasbacks, bluebills, redheads, mallards, teal.

What a great place.

"This is what I do since I retired."

Burr thought Mueller looked a bit young to be retired. Medium height, trim. His head was shaped like a cement block. He had short black hair without a touch of gray and a nose that couldn't belong to a teetotaler. But it was the glasses that got Burr's attention. Thick lenses in big, black frames that gave Mueller frog eyes.

"Did it for the state police for almost thirty years, but I still work prints. Freelance, dontcha know. Mostly for criminal lawyers. I don't much like that part."

"My client is not a criminal."

"They never are. Let me see what you got."

Burr handed the file to Mueller, who opened a door at the back of the garage and motioned for Burr to follow into his office. Sunlight filled the room. Mueller sat down at a metal desk and turned on a powerful lamp that drowned out the sunlight. He studied the fingerprints, glasses on, glasses off, then with a magnifying glass. After about fifteen minutes, he closed the file, opened one of the drawers, and pulled out a bottle of Jim Beam and two glasses. He poured two fingers in each and handed one to Burr.

That explains his nose.

Mueller drank the two fingers of whiskey and poured himself another.

"The prints lifted from the lights definitely match Murdoch Halverson's," Mueller said. "What kind of name is Murdoch anyway?"

"It's a family name. I'm interested in the other fingerprints."

"The other fingerprints?"

"Yes."

"You mean the smudges?"

"Can you identify them?"

The retired fingerprint expert shook his head. He drank the second two fingers. He bent over the smudges again, magnifying glass in hand. After about five minutes, he stood up and went out a door at the back of the office.

Burr followed him outside to what looked like a very successful vegetable garden – beans, peas, tomatoes, zucchini, and the tallest sweet corn Burr had ever seen, mixed with a few even taller plants.

"I might be able to make out some of those smudges. Might. No guarantees, mind you."

"That would be helpful." Burr sipped his whiskey.

"Problem is, I don't have a law-enforcement database anymore, so even if I could make them out, I've got nothing to compare them to."

Burr kicked at the dirt. "I may be able to get you fingerprints to compare."

"That's what I'd need." Stanley reached into his shirt pocket and pulled out a hand-rolled cigarette. "It will be expensive."

Everything I do is expensive.

Stanley lit up. The sweet smoke drifted over to Burr.

I'm surrounded by potheads.

"Medicinal. For my glaucoma." He pointed at the tall, shaggy plants growing in the corn. "This is my pharmacy."

* * *

"All rise," Henry Crow said.

So the judges share the same bailiff.

Judge Lindstrom made his entrance.

"Be seated," Henry Crow said.

Burr sat in the gallery with a collection of mostly men, mostly middle-aged, all in ties, a group he assumed was composed entirely of lawyers. He looked around Lindstrom's courtroom, a cut above Judge Maki's, a circuit judge a decided rank and pay grade higher than a district judge. Lindstrom's courtroom had hardwood floors, a fresh coat of vanilla paint on the walls and, miracle of miracles, a window. A window just above a portrait of Father Marquette. A big window framing a sugar maple in the prime of life.

"Welcome to motion day," Judge Lindstrom said. He slipped on reading glasses. "Where shall we begin?" he asked himself. The judge flipped through his files. Casually, Burr thought, especially considering what might be at stake for the various and sundry litigants.

Motion day was a day for lawyers, not witnesses, not clients, not juries.

A day when lawyers fought with other lawyers over legal issues, usually procedural niff naws such as evidence, witnesses, consents, stipulations. Matters civil and criminal. Here and there, a constitutional issue, *habeas corpus*, due process and illegal search and seizure.

The lawyers in the gallery waited, patiently and impatiently, until their turn. Burr had found neither rhyme nor reason to the order that judges followed on motion day. In a more prosperous time, judges actually liked Burr and called him first.

This, however, was not a prosperous time. Burr waited and waited. Through the evidence motion in a grand larceny case, through the unlawful search and seizure motion in a drug bust, through the stipulation in a timber accident, through the settlement agreement in a property line dispute. And so on. *Ad nauseum. Ad infinitum.* It was bad enough that he had to sit with his back to the door. It would be worse yet if Karpinen sat behind him, but so far, he hadn't seen the prosecutor, which was a bit dicey for him. Karpinen would likely be defaulted if he wasn't here when Burr's motion was called.

Burr drummed his fingers, tapped his pencil, left for the restroom during a long-winded motion about a railroad right-of-way, dozed during a motion for alimony that dragged on and on, more so because Lindstrom was deaf as a stone in his left ear.

Then Karpinen showed up. He sat down near the front of the courtroom and nodded at the judge. Lindstrom summarily disposed of the motion at hand, something about a recalcitrant witness. It didn't look like either lawyer was happy with the ruling.

"People versus Halverson," said the clerk, a dowdy woman of indeterminate age. Karpinen limped to the prosecutor's table, Burr to the defense table. Burr sat and shuffled his papers.

"Mr. Lafayette," Judge Lindstrom said.

"Yes, Your Honor," Burr said.

"Did you have something you wanted to say?"

"Thank you, Your Honor," Burr said, standing. He pulled down the cuffs of his white shirt, which didn't need pulling down, and straightened his royal blue tie with the white checks that didn't need straightening.

"When you're done preening, come over here and say it to my good ear."

"Gus, you stand next to Mr. Lafayette."

Karpinen limped up to Burr.

"How's the hip today?" the judge said.

"It's my knee."

"Right." The judge looked at Burr. "Did you have something you wanted to say, Mr. Lafayette?"

"Your Honor, an examination of the fingerprints provided by the prosecutor has revealed that there may indeed be fingerprints of additional persons on the murder weapon. That is, the Christmas tree lights. The defense asks that subpoenas be issued to those persons listed on the motion in order that we may determine who these additional fingerprints belong to."

"Your Honor, the other fingerprints aren't identifiable. They're smudges."

Lindstrom turned his good ear to Karpinen. "Smudges?"

"That's right, smudges."

The judge turned his good ear to Burr.

"Your Honor, our expert believes he might be able to determine who they belong to."

"That's impossible, Your Honor. If it could have been done, we would have done it."

"You didn't try," Burr said.

"Stop it, both of you." Lindstrom studied the motion. Then he counted on his fingers. "I count seven. You want me to compel seven people to submit to fingerprinting based on what the prosecutor terms smudges?"

"Actually, there are eight, Your Honor."

"While you're at it, why don't you ask me to order everyone who was in The Pink Pony that night to be fingerprinted?"

"I don't think that will be necessary, Your Honor."

"I'm sure you are aware that fingerprinting, especially fingerprinting when there is very little basis for supposing any of these persons are, or might be, suspects, is an intrusion almost without precedent."

"Your Honor, this is crucial to the defense."

"He's offside," Karpinen said.

Lindstrom ignored Karpinen.

"Counsel, at this point, the poor souls on this list are not suspects. They are barely persons of interest. I will not have their Fourth Amendment rights trampled on. If at some point, any of these people become persons of interest, I may reconsider." Lindstrom stared at Burr, then Karpinen. "And one more thing. It is now approaching Labor Day. Finish your preparation, then

we'll have our trial. And by God, it had better be over before deer season."
Lindstrom smacked his gavel on its base. "Motion denied."

CHAPTER FOURTEEN

"This is lunacy and you know it."

"Jacob, it's not lunacy. It's a calculated risk."

"It's reckless."

Burr sliced off a piece of the strip steak. He dipped it in the sauce and chewed it slowly. *It's good, but it's not as good as mine.*

"We have all to gain and nothing to lose."

"I am an attorney, a researcher, and a writer of appellant briefs. I know nothing of fingerprints."

Burr washed the aged Black Angus down with a swallow of a fairly pedestrian Meritage, the California wannabe of Bordeaux. "No one will suspect a thing."

"Your wretched fingerprint expert should do it. If he could stay sober and straight long enough."

"He has good-looking plants. You might want to get to know him."

"I know what you're thinking. You're thinking that you can buy me this steak and I'll do your bidding." Jacob took another bite "It won't work, not this time." Jacob took a bite of his Caesar salad. "The dressing is spectacular."

"It's the anchovies." Burr had brought Jacob to the Machus Red Fox on Telegraph in Bloomfield Township. A one-story squarish building with mud brown timbers and ivory stucco. It was so dark inside that Burr wished he'd brought a flashlight. He'd held the candle-in-the-glass centerpiece up against the menu, and even then, had to ask the waiter for help. But the Red Fox did lend itself to assignations. Assignations of all kinds, romantic and otherwise.

"It's much more cost effective if you do it," Burr said.

"You mean cheaper." Jacob turned his attention back to his steak.

Burr took a plastic box the size of a cigarette pack from his navy-blue blazer and handed it to Jacob.

"What is this?"

"Try it out on me."

"Try what."

"Take my fingerprints."

"In here? It's much too dark."

"If you can do it here, you can do it anywhere."

Jacob studied the package. He poked his salad. "This is a silly place to experiment."

Burr sipped his wine, much smoother now.

I guess it just takes a little longer to open up.

He smiled at Jacob. "Silly isn't a word I would use for the Machus Red Fox. Especially at this table."

"Why not?"

"This was the last place Jimmy Hoffa was seen alive."

Jacob stopped chewing.

"For all I know, Jimmy Hoffa is part of the anchovy paste in the dressing."

* * *

They spent the night at the Townsend in downtown Birmingham, far and away the best hotel in metro Detroit. It occurred to Burr that the money he saved substituting Jacob for Mueller, he'd just spent on the Townsend.

I love a good hotel.

Just before eleven the next morning, Burr and Jacob walked into the shop of R. Benjamin Fishman, Importer, Clothier and Haberdasher. He'd been the cook on *Fujimo*. Burr thought it highly unlikely that the cook was the killer, so this would be a virtually risk-free place to experiment.

Only two doors down from the Townsend, Fishman's was a small shop with a plate glass window that drowned a well-dressed mannequin in sunlight. Burr looked at a label on a sport coat. Pricey indeed.

"May I help you?"

"Burr Lafayette." He extended a hand. R. Benjamin Fishman shook it, a bit weakly, Burr thought.

Fishman was half a head shorter than Burr. He had longish, dishwater blond hair. Thinning on top and combed straight back from a tan forehead. Pointed features softened a bit by overeating. Not chubby, but headed that way. He was dressed to the nines.

"How may I help you?"

"Mr. Fishman, I represent Murdoch Halverson, who has been accused of murdering Jimmy Lyons."

Fishman took a step back. "What could that possibly have to do with me?"

Burr didn't say a word. He'd learned long ago that hardly anyone can stand silence for more than a few minutes. While he waited for Fishman to say something, Burr looked over the shop. Suits, sport coats, slacks, shirts, ties, belts. All top drawer. He'd heard of Fishman, but he'd always shopped at Brooks Brothers, on the hill in Grosse Pointe. Once in a while at the Claymore Shop, just down the street here in Birmingham.

Maybe I should shop here. When I have the money.

Fishman shifted his weight from one foot to the other. He straightened his tie, swept his hair back, then with the fingernail of his left pinkie, he scratched at an invisible spot on his trousers.

What's going on with that fingernail?

Fishman had trimmed the rest of his nails, but not the pinkie's. It was at least an inch long. "An old tailor's trick," Fishman said. "You do look like you know how to dress. Very nice tropical wool, if a bit worn. If you'll excuse me, I'm quite busy."

Burr couldn't quite see what R. Benjamin Fishman was busy with, but he was convinced Fishman would never agree to be fingerprinted.

Fishman started off toward the back of the shop. He stopped and looked at Jacob. "The fellow over there is natty." Jacob, who had been admiring an almost-black bolt of worsted wool, looked up. Fishman walked over to him. "I can have a suit made of that material for you," he said. "I see you like your slacks pleated and cuffed. As do I." Fishman lifted his right pant leg. "I admire a natty dresser."

Jacob offered his hand to Fishman, who shook it. "Jacob Wertheim." Jacob straightened his glasses.

"Benny," R. Benjamin said.

"Do you recommend a vest?"

"I favor vests, but on less than tall men, men like us, they can make us look a bit elfish."

Jacob nodded, knowingly. "Two pairs of pants?"

"Certainly."

"Why don't you write it up?" Jacob said.

That's going to cost fifteen hundred bucks if it costs a nickel.

Since Jacob only spent money on fishing and clothes, he could afford it. Burr, on the other hand, had an ex-wife, an ex-mortgage, child support and a not so bustling office building.

Benny walked over to the stand-up desk where the cash register stood. He reached underneath and returned with a pad of paper, pen and chalk. He took the cloth tape measure draped around his neck and wrapped it around Jacob's neck. "Fifteen-and-a-half," he said, writing it on his yellow pad.

"Benny," Burr said, "did Jimmy Lyons owe you money?"

Benny didn't look up. "Jimmy Lyons owed everyone money."

I've heard that before.

"May I ask how much?"

"Almost ten thousand." The clothier wrapped the tape around Jacob's chest. "Forty."

"That's a lot of money," Burr said.

"It is to me." Benny measured Jacob's waist. "Thirty-four. You're a trim fellow." Benny looked over at Burr. "But not enough to kill over."

"Of course not," Burr said.

Benny got down on one knee and measured Jacob's inseam.

"Besides, I finally got paid."

"You did?" Burr nearly jumped out of his tropical wool slacks. As did Jacob.

"Hold still, Mr. Wertheim, or I'll grab you where you don't want to be grabbed."

"Who paid you?" Burr said.

"Lionel Worthy."

This time Burr did jump out of his skin.

Benny stood up, tape measure back around his neck. "All done. I'll just write this up." Back at the counter, he tallied his numbers with an adding machine and ripped off the tape in triumph. "One-thousand, nine-hundred, and ninety-six dollars. I'll give it to you for nineteen-hundred even."

Jacob wasn't fazed. He picked through the ties. There were hundreds of them.

"Pick out any three. On me."

"Why, thank you. That's most generous." Jacob brought three ties to the counter.

"Why do you think Worthy paid you?" Burr said.

"He's the executor of Jimmy's estate. And it was a legitimate debt."

"Where do you think he got the money?" Burr said.

"I assume it was from the life insurance," Benny said.

Jacob opened his mouth to say something, but Burr put his finger over his lips.

"How about a belt to go with this?" Benny said. "No not a belt. Braces would be good. You'd look good in braces."

"I think braces would be most excellent," Jacob said.

"Benny, do you know Ronnie Cross?"

"He was part of the crew. Big, strapping lad." Turning to Jacob, "There will be a five-hundred-dollar deposit."

"Of course," Jacob got out his checkbook. When he leaned over to write the check, his glasses slipped off his nose, clattered on the counter and fell at Benny's feet.

Benny picked them up. "Let me clean them for you."

"That's all right." Jacob grabbed the glasses from Benny and dropped them into the front pocket of his jacket. He wrote the check and the two would-be detectives left as quickly as they could.

* * *

Back in Burr's room, Jacob sat at the French Provincial writing table, poring over the smudge on his glasses, the fingerprinting kit just off to his right.

"Jacob, you're about to ruin this."

"Nonsense. I almost have it."

Burr peered over Jacob's shoulder.

"You're ruining the light."

"The light has nothing to do with it. You can't see a damn thing without your glasses."

"Nonsense," Jacob said again.

"Then why do you have glasses?"

"Myopia. They're for distance only." Jacob fiddled with a white powder, then sprinkled it on his lens.

"They look like bifocals to me."

Jacob dropped his glasses. "Damn."

"You've ruined it."

Jacob picked up his glasses. "Who the devil is Ronnie Cross?"

"Part of the crew."

"What difference does it make?"

"Probably none. It's just that he was on the reservation list at the Chippewa but not on Toad's list."

"He probably just forgot. After all, he was smoking."

"I'll remember you said that."

Jacob sprinkled more powder on his glasses.

"It was brilliant of you to drop your glasses and get a print from Benny, but you're about to give it all back."

Jacob fussed with his glasses, then the kit, then the glasses. "*Voila.* This should suit your expert just fine." He handed Burr a perfect likeness of the whirls, whorls and twirls of Benny's thumb and forefinger.

* * *

Otto Gunther, president and owner of Apex Heat Treat, stood six-five if he stood an inch, and he weighed at least two-seventy-five. Burr was sure he could play defensive end for the Lions, who could use one. They sat in the men's grill at the Detroit Athletic Club, on Madison just up the street from Jefferson. Burr quite liked the dark, almost black, paneling, the heavy oak furniture and the uniformed waiters in the men's grill. He'd used the Fisher and Allen membership to get in, the news of his departure fortunately hadn't reached the DAC's membership department. Jacob lurked by himself at a table in the corner.

The plan was to buy Gunther lunch and get his fingerprints from the menu, but after the slouching, white-coated waiter took their orders, he took their menus with him.

Now what am I going to do?

"Jimmy was a friend," Gunther said in a German accent. "But he cheated me."

Burr nodded, although he couldn't quite make the connection between friend and cheating.

"He did many things for me. He got me new customers. He was so likable, but I should have known better."

This would have been so much easier if the waiter hadn't taken our menus.

"But then he didn't pay me."

"Pay you?"

"Heat treat. Do you know what heat treat is?"

Burr nodded again.

"It was fine at first. But then he started paying me late. At the end, not at all."

"Why did you sail with Jimmy if he was cheating you?"

"He said it would give us a chance to work out a payment plan. How could I refuse?"

"And did you?"

"We did."

The waiter brought their lunch. Gunther had ordered the ribeye for two. A chicken Caesar for Burr.

Gunther ate and ate, no more talking.

Maybe I can get them from his silverware.

Finally, Gunther pushed his plate away. He'd demolished the better part of two pounds of steak.

As if on cue, the waiter cleared their plates, including the silverware.

Damn it all.

The waiter came back. "Would you care for dessert?"

"I'm full," Gunther said.

"We'd like to see the dessert menu," Burr said.

"I can tell you," the waiter said.

"We'd like to see menus," Burr said.

"I'm full," Gunther said again.

The waiter gave Burr the look that all waiters at men's clubs had perfected, but he came back with two dessert menus. Gunther didn't take his.

Nuts.

Burr studied his menu then dropped it next to Gunther. The waiter bent over. Burr pushed him out of the way. "Otto, would you please hand me my menu."

Gunther grunted but reached down and handed Burr the menu. Burr studied the menu again, careful to hold it by the edges. "Would you give us a few minutes."

The waiter gave him another look then left.

Burr put his menu down, ever so carefully. "Did Jimmy ever pay you?"

"No. Foolish, I know. Especially for a German. But I liked him."

"Do you think you'll get paid?"

Gunther looked at Burr. "I'd be surprised if I ever got paid. I suppose it depends on that wife of his and his miserable lawyer."

"Where were you the night Jimmy was killed?"

The not so gentle giant stood. "My wife was with me from the time we reached the island until the time we left. She can back me up."

"Wives are good for that."

"I beg your pardon."

Burr shook his head.

"If you'll excuse me, I will be going." Gunther left.

Jacob came over to Burr's table. Burr handed Jacob the menu who spirited it away. The slouching waiter showed up.

"Just a check," Burr said.

* * *

Burr retrieved his Jeep and a peeved Zeke from valet parking and drove them back up Jefferson to the Grosse Pointe Yacht Club. Zeke had spent the better part of the last two days in the Jeep. All was forgiven after Burr took him swimming again.

If people got over things as quickly as dogs, the world would be a much nicer place.

They headed back down Jefferson to Detroit. Just inside the city limits, Burr turned left onto Conner. He drove past a rundown collection of small metal shops and frame houses, some abandoned, some not. They ended up at one of Detroit's remaining, although private, bright spots. The Bayview Yacht Club, founded in 1915 and sponsor of the Port Huron-Mackinac, sat on a spit of land at the south end of Lake St. Clair near the mouth of the Detroit River. A one-story brick building, docks scattered in every available space. Burr marveled at the millions of dollars of boats separated from economic ruin by no more than a chain link fence and an unarmed security guard.

He stopped at the gate. "*Scaramouche*," he said to the guard. He thought he'd just about run out of clubby meeting places, but he also thought his name was probably still on the list. A drink at Bayview had been the only bait that lured the elusive Dickie Gold to a meeting.

The gate, a single piece of wood painted yellow that a moped could break through, lifted and Burr was in. He parked in what little shade he could find and cracked the windows for Zeke. His shirt stuck to his back in the clamminess of the late August afternoon. Inside the yacht club, he stopped to admire the trophies and pennants of Bayview's storied history. Unfortunately, the place reminded him a bit of his former self, more money than sense. Half a million for a fifty-foot racing machine good for nothing after two or three years.

"A testament to the money to be made in the making of metal parts."

"I beg your pardon?" This from yet another uniformed waiter, this one a portly black man with grizzled hair and a career smile.

"Thinking out loud."

The waiter smiled knowingly. He had years of experience dealing with people who had more money than brains. "May I help you?"

"Two over there, please." Burr pointed to the window overlooking the docks. He could see no earthly reason to sit outside in the heat. In keeping with his long-standing policy, Burr sat facing the door. The bar was empty except for one sloshed patron of indeterminate age struggling to stay afloat on a barstool.

The bar was just as Burr remembered it, varnished paneling, bright work that would make any yachtsman proud. A bar so bright he could see his reflection. Tables scattered about. Burr nursed a Perrier and lime on the rocks, refreshing but boring, until his guest marched in. He was no more than five-seven and thin to the point of skinny.

"You must be Lafayette. Unless he's the drunk on the bar stool."

"I am."

"Dickie Gold," he said, sitting down. He had shiny black hair, neatly cut and neatly parted. Owlish glasses over black eyes. A too big nose over too small teeth. Standard issue blue blazer over a white Lacoste. Burr was sure he was sockless. He liked Dickie Gold immediately, no matter what he may have done.

The veteran waiter arrived. "Gentleman?" he said.

"Gin gimlet up," Dickie Gold said.

"Make that two," Burr said. "With Bombay." He lusted after a dirty martini. They knew how to make them here at Bayview, but he thought it best to do his best to keep his wits about him.

"Sapphire?"

"With Rose's," although he had serious reservations about the wisdom of mixing lime juice with gin.

"Of course," the waiter said.

"So good of you to invite me. I did want to see you." Dickie smiled a smile of small white teeth, except for a gold tooth flashing from the back of his mouth. "Bit of a hike from Southfield."

"It is, but it's nice to be on the water."

Why does he want to see me? I'm the one who wants to see him.

The drinks arrived. A clinking of glasses. "To justice," Dickie said.

"To justice," Burr said, even more bewildered. Burr drank his gimlet.

The lime juice just about ruins the gin.

"Let's get this murder business over with. I want my money." Dickie smacked his lips.

"I beg your pardon."

"Go and settle this. I'm sure the prosecutor will take some sort of plea."

"Plea?"

Dickie took another swallow. "Yes, plea. I'm not going to get paid from the estate until this thing is done, and I want my money."

"My client didn't kill Jimmy."

"Of course he did. If I have to, I'll testify that I saw him do it."

"I beg your pardon," Burr said again.

"This is very simple. I'm a moneylender and I want my money."

"How do you know the estate has any money to pay you? Jimmy owed everybody."

"I always get paid first."

"How do I know that you didn't strangle him with the Christmas lights?"

"If he was dead, how would I get paid?"

"Life insurance."

"Life insurance?" This piqued Gold's interest. "Who's the beneficiary?"

"Jane, I think."

Gold slumped. "The debt was not joint and several."

I don't like him after all, and I'm sure he's wearing socks.

"Let's get this over with. You're in my way of getting paid. If it's not that stuffed shirt Murdoch Halverson, figure it out and move on." Gold finished his gimlet.

"Did you kill him?"

"I could have. The miserable son-of-a-bitch was the worst loan I ever made." His tooth flashed. "Strangling isn't my style. It's more of an Italian thing. If violence was necessary, I'd hire someone."

Burr picked up his drink, then set it down.

I can't drink gin with lime juice.

Gold studied his empty glass.

I hope to God he doesn't want another.

Gold unfolded his napkin. "My attorney told me not to meet with you." Carefully, very carefully, he wiped off the glass.

Burr smiled weakly at the moneylender.

"I'm going to make it easy for you." He pressed his thumb and forefinger of each hand on the glass.

CHAPTER FIFTEEN

The next morning Burr leaned against the white split-rail fence, the red barn just behind him. This was probably the only barn left in all of the Grosse Pointes and one of the few barns he'd ever seen that didn't need a fresh coat of paint. The barn, the fence, and the corrals housed the horses of the Grosse Pointe Hunt Club. It stood smack in the middle of Grosse Pointe Farms, left there when the rows of corn had been plowed under for rows of houses. The original Pointers had run fox here not so long ago. A few of them still had horses, but the club had morphed into tennis and a restaurant with a menu that promoted acid reflux.

The Hunt Club had slipped his mind until he stopped by the widow Jane's house and the maid had told him she was riding. The clubbiness of Grosse Pointe annoyed him, but then again, he'd been a dues-paying member of the yacht club at one time.

Jane rode by, her ponytail bouncing as she trotted the chestnut gelding.

He was afraid his silly fingerprint plan wasn't going to work. For that matter, he had no idea if any of his would-be suspects would actually have fingerprints on the lights or what it would mean if they did. But he still wanted the widow Lyons' fingerprints and the fingerprints of that pompous ass, Lionel Worthy, who was many things but stupid wasn't one of them.

To the business at hand. Jane dismounted and led her horse back to the stables right past Burr, standing on the other side of the fence.

"Jane," he said.

The blonde in the jodhpurs and riding helmet, carrying gloves and a riding crop, kept walking, leading her 1,200-pound charge to the barn.

"Jane," he said again. "May I speak with you?"

She looked right through him.

"It's Burr. Burr Lafayette."

She looked at him but kept walking. "I know who you are, and I don't have anything to say to you."

"Do you want to know who killed your husband?"

"Not particularly."

Burr admired the curves her riding habit couldn't hide. And her face. No makeup except her ruby red lips. "Who is Ronnie Cross?"

Jane stopped, turned around and looked at him, then started walking again. "No idea."

"He was part of Jimmy's crew."

"If you say so." She didn't look like a bereaved widow to him, and she certainly didn't look broke.

Burr hopped the fence and scooted up beside her.

"You're trespassing."

"I was trespassing before. I'm just closer now."

"Lionel told me not to talk to you."

"I thought he was your husband's lawyer."

"He's the family lawyer and I'm what's left of the family."

"If Mr. Worthy represents New Method Screw Machines, your husband's estate, and you, all at the same time, there may well be a conflict."

"I don't care about the fine points, Mr. Lafayette. I'm a widow."

"From what I hear, your husband was broke. He owed everybody in town."

"This conversation is over."

She was about twenty feet from the stable, and Burr thought the conversation, such as it was, was about to be over anyway.

How the devil am I going to get her fingerprints?

He had a not too happy Jacob standing by with Zeke in the Jeep, but he couldn't see any way he could get her helmet, and Jacob would never go near a horse. Maybe he could sneak in and try the saddle.

"About the life insurance."

"The what?"

"I'm told you came into some money. Life insurance, I think."

"How dare you," she said, turning red over her tan.

"You don't seem like you're in mourning."

Jane dropped the reins and slapped him.

Burr's cheek stung but he didn't flinch. "In fact, you seem to be living rather well. Now that you're a widow." This absolutely enraged her. She raised the crop and swung it at him. He grabbed it by the end before she could strike him. "The lady doth protest too much, methinks." Her gelding had had enough of the drama and started for the barn on his own.

She tried to jerk the end of the crop out of Burr's hand, but he hung on. "Let go."

"I think Sea Biscuit is hungry." She looked at her horse, then Burr. The two of them had a tug of war with the riding crop. After about seven or eight tugs, Jane let go of the crop and ran after her horse.

Back at the Jeep, Burr handed the crop to Jacob, now an expert, who said that fingerprints would be difficult to lift from the handle of the riding crop, but he was sure he could do it.

* * *

Burr drove back downtown and rode the rickety transfer elevator to the top of the Penobscot Building.

This one will be interesting.

The receptionist led Burr to Worthy's office. The flowing-maned counselor sat behind his desk in a cloud of smoke. Burr sat down across from him.

"Glad you're here, Lafayette. Saves me the trouble."

Burr nodded, as if he knew what Worthy meant, which he didn't.

"Stay away from my client," Worthy said, sucking on his cigarette.

"I thought your client was dead."

"I have a new client."

"And who might that be?"

"You know who it is."

Burr waved the smoke away from his face.

"It's Jane, and I don't want you anywhere near her."

"The beautiful widow Lyons is a suspect." Burr's eyes started to water.

"That's ridiculous. She's grieving."

"She's so distraught she went riding at the Hunt Club this morning."

"We all grieve differently. Be a good boy and leave her alone."

Be a good boy.

"Lionel, about the life insurance."

"Life insurance?"

"Whatever Jimmy's money troubles were, Jane seems to be pretty well fixed for blades. And you seem to have enough money to pay Jimmy's importer, clothier and haberdasher."

"I have no idea what you're talking about." Worthy dropped his cigarette in the ashtray and lit another. The cigarette in the ashtray kept on burning.

I may have to call the fire department.

"So, Lionel, who was the beneficiary on the policy? If it's New Method or Lyons, the creditors will have something to say about it. Which means that the executor, who I assume is you, could have some liability. On the other hand, if Jane is the beneficiary, then she got the money." Burr coughed. "If she knew Jimmy was going to file for divorce, she had all the more reason to kill him. As broke he was, he was worth more to her dead than alive." He coughed again. "Which makes her a suspect." He waved the cigarette smoke out of his face. "The way I see it, you could have three clients. New Method Screw Machine, the estate of James Lyons, or Jane Lyons. Which one is it?"

"This is none of your business."

"And possibly a fourth. Just who is Ronnie Cross?"

"Who?"

Burr couldn't tell if Worthy was surprised or just pretending to be. "You know who. Ronnie Cross. He was part of the crew." Burr was convinced that Worthy was lying, but for the life of him, he had no idea why.

Worthy dropped the second lit cigarette into the ashtray. He picked up the pack of Pall Malls, stuck his fingers in it, then looked inside it. He crumpled the pack and dropped it in the ashtray.

We're going to have a fire.

Worthy opened his desk drawers, one by one, and rummaged through them. "Damn it." He pushed a buzzer. The receptionist opened the door and handed Worthy another pack of cigarettes. "There are to be cigarettes in my desk at all times."

"Yes, Mr. Worthy." She opened a desk drawer and took out another ashtray. She headed toward the door with the smoking ashtray, waving at the smoke on her way out. "You're going to start a fire."

Worthy opened the new pack and lit up again. "Did Jimmy keep you paid up so you could fend off all the creditors? And of all the creditors, why did you pay Benny Fishman? Or did you kill Jimmy because he didn't pay you?" Burr threw his hands up in the air. "The possibilities are endless."

"None of this is any of your concern," Worthy said, puffing.

Burr was a bit surprised the lion hadn't roared at him yet. He coughed.
This has to stop.

He walked to the window behind Worthy and opened it. Fresh air rushed in. He took a deep breath.

"What in God's name are you doing?"

Burr ignored the smoking chimney and sat down. "You were both at The Pink Pony that night. Unless you tell me different, Jane has a motive and so do you."

"Counselor, discovery is limited in criminal cases. You must know that." He tapped his cigarette in the ashtray. Most of the ash ended up on his desk. "So, whatever you want to find out, you'll have to find out at trial. I understand you couldn't get a subpoena for fingerprints. Jane can't be forced to incriminate herself, and I have attorney-client privilege." Worthy pulled a handkerchief from his pocket and wiped down his desk. He buzzed again. The receptionist reappeared. "See to it that Mr. Lafayette is not left alone in my office, and that he doesn't touch anything." Worthy stood up, put on his jacket. On his way out, he reached into his side pocket and put on a pair of black goatskin gloves.

* * *

Burr counted to ten and then left. As soon as he reached the sidewalk, he flagged down Jacob who had been hovering nearby in the Jeep. Jacob slid over next to Zeke who had been riding shotgun. Burr hopped in the driver's seat.

"Back seat," Burr said. Zeke wasn't happy about losing shotgun, but he jumped into the backseat. "He went into that ramp," Jacob said, pointing. "But he hasn't come out yet." A few minutes later, Worthy roared out of the ramp in a black, late model BMW sedan.

"Why doesn't anyone drive an American car," Burr said, not asking.

"Because they're lemons," Jacob said, picking an invisible blond dog hair off his summer-weight khaki suit.

Burr followed the BMW up Jefferson toward Grosse Pointe. Worthy turned left on Moross. They followed Worthy into the Country Club of Detroit. "Here we go again."

The Little Club is about the only place I haven't been.

Worthy parked and went inside. "At least he isn't using valet parking, and he's not wearing gloves." Burr cruised up next to the BMW. Jacob lifted the fingerprints from the door and off they went.

* * *

Burr drove Jacob to his car and the two of them split up, Jacob taking all the prints to Stanley Mueller at Fish Point.

Burr took I-75 north to Big Beaver Road in Troy. He headed west. Just before Somerset Mall, he turned left into a parking lot that surrounded two identical, side by side, twenty-story office buildings. Black steel with tinted windows. He parked in the shade of the north building and cracked the Jeep windows. "Zeke, I won't be long."

Burr rode the elevator to the top floor.

At least it isn't rickety.

The elevator opened to a sleek, silver nameplate that read *Roney and Company.* The receptionist showed him to the owner of the red boat, James M. Buehler. The stockbroker stood at a stand-up workstation facing the window. He had on a headset and his office reeked of cigar smoke.

Here we go again.

Buehler shouted into his headset. Then he threw it on the table and turned to Burr. A nouveau stockbroker if Burr had ever seen one. Fortyish. Tan. Short, not quite stocky. A fifty-dollar haircut and black, bushy eyebrows that the barber had missed. A jaw that looked like it was looking for a fight and a nose that had found one. He sported a midnight-blue suit that made Jacob's look like it was from Goodwill.

Buehler sat down at a desk that matched the workstation.

A fat cigar stuck out of Buehler's teeth, right in the middle of his mouth, and it bounced up and down when he spoke. "You here about the race?"

"In a manner of speaking." Burr coughed, the cigar smoke already getting to him. He looked over Buehler's shoulder at the windows.

At least Worthy's window opened.

"It's about time. That son of a bitch Lyons fouled me. He tried to push *Sea Wolf* on the reef."

"*Fujimo* was on starboard tack," Burr said.

"He still can't force me on an obstacle."

"How close were you?"

Buehler ignored him. "But for that damn Lyons, I'd have won. I didn't spend five hundred grand to finish second."

"I'm sure you didn't."

"And the ringers. I paid them, too." He bit off the end of his cigar and spit it in the wastebasket. He stuck what was left in the corner of his mouth and chewed on it. "So, it's about time you idiots at Bayview made it right."

"Actually, Mr. Buehler, I'm here about the murder of Jimmy Lyons."

Buehler stopped chewing his cigar. He took it out of his mouth and looked at it. He crushed it in the ashtray and threw it into the wastebasket. Buehler pulled his cuffs down. Pearl cufflinks.

They're not mother-of-pearl, either.

Buehler stood. "I have to go. And so do you." He hurried out the door. His assistant came in and ushered Burr out.

* * *

Burr hardened up at the turning mark, hoisted the light one and dropped the chute in the shadow of the main. He kept *Scaramouche* on port tack and took her up as far he could. If the wind held from the southwest, he thought he could make the island on this tack, but he thought the wind would keep clocking.

He waited until the pole had been secured to the deck, the chute had been repacked in the turtle and the sheets had been coiled and stowed. Then he tacked over onto starboard. It was a risk, but if the wind kept clocking, he wanted to sail toward the shift.

They sailed through Sunday night. By dawn on Monday, the wind had gone all the way to the west and kicked up to fifteen. They were at the edge for the light one, but they moved the cars aft on the track and flattened the sail.

At 7:30 he flopped over to port tack. An hour later, *Scaramouche* was east of Spectacle Reef, just behind the big boats. He'd guessed right again.

Ahead of *Scaramouche* and just north of the reef, two one-tonners were in a tacking duel. He thought there was a lot of race left to be doing that. One white hull. One red. Burr couldn't make out the names.

Off the shore of the northern Lower Peninsula and well into Lake Huron, Spectacle Reef rose from the bottom of the lake. From two-hundred feet to six feet. Just below the water, boulders everywhere.

If they get too close to the reef, they'll rip a hole in their hulls.

The one-tonners tacked on each other. Again and again, the white boat pushing the red boat closer and closer to the reef. Tack after tack. Burr turned the helm over to one of his crew and watched through binoculars. The white boat pressed and pressed. Then, all at once, the red boat dipped the stern of the white boat and sailed off to the north on a reach. Once she had cleared the bad air of the white boat, she hardened up and hoisted her red protest flag.

Scaramouche, with no one around her, tacked onto port and cleared the reef. Burr didn't know how close the one-tonners had gotten to Spectacle Reef, but he knew they had been close. He stayed on port tack until the wind dropped again. The wind backed a little more. Burr tacked back and forth on the rhumb line and crossed the finish line between the committee boat and the red can off Mission Point. Just after eight on Monday night.

"*Elysia, Elysia, Elysia*. This is *Scaramouche*, sail number US 23866, crossing at 8:11 p.m. No sail ahead. No sail behind."

Stubby came on. "You won your class." *Elysia* fired the finishing gun.

Burr found a berth at the state docks. As soon as they tied up, Burr and his crew headed to The Pink Pony.

* * *

Burr left Buehler's office without the stockbroker's fingerprints.

Now what am I going to do?

He took I-75 north, then on to East Lansing via I-69. As soon as the city inspector approved the repairs to the elevator, it was back to his island paradise to wait for the story of the fingerprints. He hoped he liked the ending.

Buying the Masonic Temple, circa 1927, had seemed like a good idea at the time. It wasn't big, even by East Lansing standards. Six stories and narrow, very narrow. A burnt-red brick building. He'd taken the top floor for himself. Half for his office, the other half, his living quarters. The renovations, especially the elevator, had nearly broken him.

Burr sat in Michelangelo's and twirled the angel hair around his fork. As much as he loved pasta, he could never eat enough to cover the rent that Scooter, the restaurateur, owed him. Zeke sucked in a No. 12 angel hair noodle and smacked his lips. Burr swirled the Chianti that Scooter stocked just for him.

Scooter, pasty complexion and all, appeared at Burr's table. "How is it, Mr. Lafayette?"

"Fine, Scooter. It's fine."

"I'm sorry, Mr. Lafayette. Dogs aren't allowed."

They started their ritual. "He's a seeing eye dog, Scooter."

"He may be, but you're not blind."

"I'm also not six months behind in the rent. That's nine grand."

Scooter left.

He's not much of a tenant, but I'm probably not much of a landlord.

After lunch, Burr and Zeke started up the stairs to the roof. He was slightly winded by the time he reached the third floor, but he was damned if he would take the elevator, fixed or not. By the time he reached the top floor, he was out of breath.

Burr wandered through his office and his apartment. He quite liked them both, but he quite disliked being cash flow negative. Having caught his breath, he and Zeke climbed the last flight of stairs and stepped out on the flat, gravel-covered, tarred roof. Michigan State University a block south, the city of East Lansing to the north, east, and west. He gave a quick look at the elevator room that topped the building and was the source of his troubles. It was hot on the roof, and he hoped this wouldn't take too long.

He heard the machinery in the elevator room clanking. "Zeke, old pal, it sounds like it's working. A few minutes later, the door to the roof opened and out popped the city building inspector, followed by one of East Lansing's finest, sidearm in holster, unlike the flashlight-armed Chief Brandstatter.

Why in the world do we need a cop to certify this God-forsaken elevator?

"Good afternoon, Mr. Otis," Burr said.

"Don't press your luck, Lafayette," the inspector said, a gangly man with glasses that dug into the bridge of his nose. With all the ups and downs he'd had with the damned elevator, Burr thought pressing his luck was just the thing to do. The inspector walked over to the elevator room and unlocked the door. He disappeared inside. The policeman, a Hardy to the inspector's Laurel, glared at Burr, hands on his hips. Burr decided not to wonder why he was here. More clanking from inside the room. At last, the inspector came out. Burr was sweating from the heat on the roof.

The inspector took off his glasses. "Mr. Lafayette, I'm afraid I have no choice but to certify this elevator. Extraordinary."

"Thank you. Now I really must be off."

The cop stepped forward. "Not just yet, Mr. Lafayette." He took off his hat, his creamy skin remarkably similar to Oliver Hardy's.

"Officer Friendly. I have an appointment."

"Step over here, Mr. Lafayette." The cop walked around to the east side of the elevator room, out of sight. Burr followed him around the corner.

"What are these?" said the officer, not so friendly.

"I'm sure I don't know," Burr said, who did.

There before him in five-gallon ceramic pots, a half-dozen cannabis plants. About seven feet tall, healthy looking and well-tended.

"I'm sure you know that these are marijuana plants," the cop said. "And while possession of less than an ounce of marijuana is a misdemeanor in East Lansing, growing this much dope is a felony."

"I am aware of that," Burr said, not liking at all where this was headed.

"Are these your plants?"

"No."

"Do you know whose they are?"

Burr wiped the sweat off his brow. "No, I don't," he said, but did.

"Since you're the owner of this building, I have no choice but to arrest you."

"That's ridiculous."

"It is, isn't it?" Officer Friendly took the handcuffs from his belt.

CHAPTER SIXTEEN

Burr woke up with a terrible kink in his back. He sat up, swung his legs off the bunk and stood up, or tried to. He fell back on the bunk. He tried to stand up again and fell back again. *Maybe standing up isn't a such a good idea.*

Burr had done all he could to convince Officer Friendly that the hand-cuffs weren't necessary. Actually, he had begged. Officer Friendly, whose given name was Majeski, said he always cuffed felons. It didn't matter to Majeski that Burr wasn't a felon until he was convicted or that Burr said they weren't his plants, and calling him Officer Friendly probably hadn't helped. The cop led him through the lobby of his building, where Burr left Zeke in Scooter's care. The cop drove him the two blocks to the jail on Abbott Road, in the basement of the City of East Lansing offices, one floor below 54-B District Court, where Burr was charged with possession of marijuana in excess of one ounce. The judge, a pudgy man in his fifties, set bail at one-hundred-thousand dollars. Ten-thousand would have freed Burr, but the judge – wisely, Burr thought – wouldn't take a personal check.

So, here he was in the drunk tank, sober as a judge, with a kink in his back and waiting to be rescued.

Eve arrived at noon. The jailer unlocked his cell.

"Sleep well?" she said.

"Like a baby." Burr managed to stand this time, but he was bent over at the waist and the neck.

"You look like a pretzel," Eve said.

"What took you so long?"

"It's three and a half hours after you get off the island."

"What about yesterday?"

"I had to deadhead the zinnias yesterday."

"Of course."

"About the bail," she said.

Burr shuffled past her. "What about the bail?"

"A cashier's check. From my personal account. How are you going to pay me back?"

Burr handed her the check he had just gotten from Martha Halverson and headed to the stairs.

"This is just peachy. We're right back where we started."

Burr tried the stairs. His right leg seemed to work just fine, but he couldn't quite get his left leg going. Finally, he lifted it with both hands.

Eve passed him on the way up. At the top of the stairs, she turned back to him. "Just how are you going to pay me back?"

Eve waited for him at the top of the stairs.

"I enjoy a regular paycheck. At least I used to." She stormed out.

Burr limped after her. He retrieved Zeke from Scooter. His dog, unlike Burr, was no worse for wear, the pasta diet apparently agreeing with him. Burr ripped up the parking ticket on the Jeep and drove off.

By late afternoon, Burr had reached the sanctuary of Windward's porch swing. Jacob sat next to him.

"I'll be shocked if Mueller can make any sense out of any of those fingerprints," Jacob said. "And if he does, Karpinen will roast him. He's blind as a bat."

Burr scowled at Jacob, who smiled back at him.

"Back a little stiff?" Jacob said.

"Just a bit."

"Sleep in the wrong position?"

"I spent last night in the East Lansing jail. In the drunk tank. On a steel bunk. Which is why my back is like a two-by-four. I've been charged with felony possession of a controlled substance. It took the ten thousand-dollar advance to post bail."

Jacob mumbled something.

"There were six of the healthiest marijuana plants I have ever seen growing on my roof. Behind the elevator room. You need to write me a check."

Jacob took off his glasses and looked at Burr. "How tall were they?"

"At least seven feet."

Jacob beamed.

"We have no money and there will be hell to pay if Karpinen finds out about the drug charge."

"It will never stand."

"How did those plants get so big? With you here on Mackinac Island."

"Scooter watered them."

"Why in God's name did you put those plants behind the elevator room?"

"That's where the best sun is."

* * *

Burr pedaled down British Landing Road to the lake, past the fort, the cemetery, the airport, the golf course, which had been the battlefield. Ten minutes later, Carole opened the door. She wore a sleeveless peach dress with little yellow flowers. It was nicely above her knees, nicely below her neck, and it showed off all her curves. Her dress went with her hair, and her white sandals showed off her tan. She kissed him on the cheek and invited him in.

It was a small, two-story white frame house, kitchen and living room with an island in between and a half bath on the first floor. Two bedrooms upstairs. She left him in front of a window that filled most of one wall and returned with a drink in each hand.

"Bombay. Very dry, very dirty."

"How did you know?"

"I was at the Pony that night, too." She took him to a glass door at the far-right side of the room. "If I stand on my tiptoes and look way over there, I can see the lake through the trees. The view's better when the leaves are gone, but by then it's too cold out here."

"It's beautiful."

"It's not exactly beautiful, but it's mine." She opened the door and they went out to the deck. "How about if you light the grill while I go make the salads."

Two martinis later, they'd finished the chicken and the salads. Carole put the dishes in the sink. "Come with me." She took him outside, a blanket in one arm. She handed him a bottle of wine and two glasses.

They took a path through the woods, across the road and through a break in the cedars to the beach. They walked across the rocks to a patch of sand. Carole spread out the blanket. Burr opened the wine and poured them each a glass.

Kim Crawford. How did she know?

Lake Huron in front of them. Cedars behind.

Carole sat down next to him. She pulled her dress down. "I'm not really dressed for this."

"What a view," Burr said.

They finished the bottle. Carole scrunched up next to Burr. He kissed her on the lips. She kissed him back. He put his hand on her knee, then slid his hand under the hem of her dress. He stroked the inside of her thigh. Carole sighed. Burr reached further up her leg and felt her silky panties. Carole's breathing sped up. Burr brushed his fingers across her panties.

Then she pushed him away.

Now what.

Carole reached under her dress and wiggled out of her panties.

* * *

"Another twenty-five yards and we're free and clear," Stanley Mueller said.

Another twenty-five yards and they'll haul me out of here in a pine box. Which is all I can afford.

"You all right?"

"Fine," Burr said.

"We're hard aground. Put your shoulder into it."

Burr pushed the boat again.

"We're moving"

A foot. Maybe.

Sweat ran down Burr's forehead and down his back. He was cooking in his waders.

Mueller had called and said he'd matched some of the prints. Burr had asked him to bring the prints to the island, but Mueller said he didn't drive much anymore. Burr asked Mueller to mail the prints, but he wouldn't hear of it.

So here they were, a quarter mile out in Saginaw Bay. Hard aground in ankle deep water courtesy of a southeast wind and the heaviest duck boat Burr ever had the misfortune to push. The boat was magnificent, even if it weighed as much as an elephant. An eighteen-footer with a V-hull and a blind brushed with fresh cut cedar. A work of art. Plus, hand-carved Canada goose decoys. Cedar with lead keels. Hand painted in black and white.

The only reason I'm here is so he has someone to hunt with.

Another shove and the boat floated. Zeke showed up from somewhere with a stick in his mouth and jumped in the boat. Mueller pulled the starter cord and they were off. Ten more minutes and Mueller cut the engine. Burr dropped anchor in two feet of water. It dug into the sand and the bow swung into what little wind there was. Burr set the goose decoys upwind from the boat, and Mueller passed him mallards and teal.

These belong in a museum, not in Saginaw Bay.

Burr climbed in and sat on the bench. Zeke looked out the dog door. Burr lit the first cigarette of the season. The smoke burned his throat.

"That'll kill you," Mueller said.

My guess is something else will kill me first.

Five minutes later there were ducks everywhere but not a goose in sight. "Stanley, about the fingerprints."

"Quiet. You'll spook the geese."

"There's not a goose within a mile of us."

"Right there." Mueller nodded to the south. "He's coming in."

"That's a crow."

"It's not shooting hours anyway."

"About the fingerprints."

"There's time for that later," Mueller said.

"What did you find?"

Mueller dug through his bag and found his calls. He untangled the lanyards and strung them around his neck.

"Whoever lifted those prints did a piss poor job. Piss poor. As long as you've got 'em, pass me a cigarette." Burr handed Mueller a cigarette and flipped open his lighter, a gold Zippo from better days.

Mueller puffed on the cigarette like it was a pipe. "It was a piss poor job of lifting prints. Some of those smudges aren't Murphy's."

"Murdo's."

"What kind of name is that anyway?"

"It's short for Murdoch."

Mueller puffed on the cigarette again. "I wish I had one of my glaucoma cigarettes."

"You mean a joint?"

"Joints are for dopers. Mine are medicinal." He flicked the cigarette over the side. "There were other prints on them lights."

Maybe this wasn't a waste of time. "Did you match them to any of the ones we gave you?"

"Hard to know for sure, but I'd say so."

"Who matched?"

"I don't remember."

* * *

A week later, Burr made his last trip south before the trial. School was about to start, and Burr had promised Zeke-the-boy he'd sign him up for football. Grace was dead set against it, but if Zeke-the-boy's pain threshold was anything like his own, his sole heir's football career wouldn't last long.

They took in a Tigers game on Saturday. Gibson homered. Trammel and Whittaker turned three double plays, Petry pitched a complete game, and the Tigers beat the Yankees 5-1. Burr made sure Zeke ate too much unhealthy food. He and the two Zekes had their own sleepover at the Edge Motel. Breakfast at the Big Boy at Vernier and Mack, where the chief attraction was hot chocolate with whipped cream thick enough to make a snowball.

CHAPTER SEVENTEEN

Burr tap, tap, tapped his brand-new Number Two yellow pencil. He looked up and to his left at the window. There was a little green left on the sugar maple, but most of the leaves had turned orange and yellow. It was still September, but fall always had a head start in St. Ignace.

Murdo sat to his left in what his client had said was his shabbiest suit, not shabby by Burr's new standards, but it would have to do. Jacob sat next to Murdo. Behind them Eve, Anne next to her, demure in a stodgy brown dress that did nothing for her. She'd also followed directions. Martha, who did and wore what she damn well pleased, sat next to Anne.

I hope I don't need her for anything.

Aunt Kitty sat next to the matriarch.

Burr looked across the aisle at the prosecutor with the gimpy knee, smiling to himself.

We haven't even started yet.

Past Karpinen, the jury box. It was empty for now, and that's why they were here today.

Burr thought Karpinen might well have reason to smile. For all the sleuthing he and Jacob had done, all they had were a few smudges and a nearsighted fingerprint expert. He had a few suspects, but Murdo probably had more reason to murder Jimmy than any of the others. At least no one had seen him do it.

Here he was on the opening day of the trial, and the best he could do for a defense was reasonable doubt. He had nothing else to show for all he'd done.

"All rise," Henry Crow said.

They all stood. Chairs scraped the floor. Clothing rustled. Assorted noises from the gallery, packed to the gills, the murder still front-page news, especially since *The St. Ignace News* was a weekly.

The Honorable Judge Arvid Lindstrom entered from the back of the courtroom, flowing to the podium in his black robes. He smiled at the court reporter, a young blonde with a small nose and big ears, who sat just below him and to his right. Lindstrom sat.

"Be seated," Henry Crow said.

Lindstrom cracked his gavel. "We are here for the trial of Murdoch O. Halverson, who is accused of murdering James Lyons during the early morning hours of July 18th at The Pink Pony on Mackinac Island. Gentlemen, we'll begin with jury selection. Bailiff, call the first person from the jury pool."

"Eugenie Gunthorpe," the bailiff said. From somewhere in the back of the courtroom, a massive woman in her fifties struggled to her feet and started down the aisle.

Lindstrom looked down at a file on his desk, "Just a minute. Stay right there, Ms. Gunthorpe."

"It's Missus," said the missus.

Lindstrom ignored her, but Burr thought the judge probably hadn't heard her.

"Mr. Lafayette, Mr. Karpinen, please approach the bench." Burr walked and Karpinen limped up to the judge. He picked up the file in front of him and looked down at Burr. "Is it true that you've been charged with felony possession of marijuana?"

"No, Your Honor."

"Don't lie to me counsel." Lindstrom put the file down and tapped it with his glasses. "According to this, which Mr. Karpinen was good enough to provide me, you have been charged with growing marijuana on the roof of your building in East Lansing."

Damn it all. "I will not have a lawyer accused of a felony in my courtroom."

"Your Honor, I haven't been charged with a crime."

"Have you been arraigned?"

"Yes, Your Honor, but . . ."

"No buts. Get out." Lindstrom pointed his gavel at the door in the rear of the courtroom. "I will not have accused felons practicing in my courtroom."

Burr looked out the window. A fiery orange maple leaf fell from the tree. He looked back to Lindstrom. "Your Honor, there's nothing in the court rules that permits a sitting judge to do this."

Lindstrom gave him a deadly look. "Mr. Lafayette, I am an unimportant man in an unimportant place. A circuit judge in a backwoods county. But," he said, brightening, "within these four walls, I am God." Lindstrom paused. "God," he said again. "And if I say get out and don't come back until you have dealt with your felonious behavior, then that is what you shall do."

"Your Honor," Burr said. "I object."

"Good for you. Make sure you write that down, Billie," he said to the court reporter, who rather seemed to be enjoying the drama. "This godforsaken trial will surely be over by the time your appeal is heard. Now, get out."

"Your Honor," Burr said, "you've prejudiced the prospective jurors against me."

"Since this is the last time anyone in this courtroom is ever going to see you, I can't see how that matters." Lindstrom smiled at the thought of never seeing Burr again. "Besides, no one up here likes Detroiters anyway."

"East Lansing," Burr said.

"What's that?"

"Your Honor, I request a delay so that my client may obtain new counsel." *Maybe that'll give me enough time to straighten out Jacob's plants.*

"Who's that sitting next to the defendant?" Lindstrom pointed at Jacob.

"Jacob Wertheim, Your Honor. My co-counsel."

I shouldn't have said co-counsel.

"Wertheim can do it." Lindstrom turned to the bailiff. "Henry, escort Mr. Lafayette out of my courtroom. You may use force if necessary." Henry Crow walked up to Burr and wrapped his pitcher's mitt of a hand around Burr's forearm.

Burr shook off Crow's hand. "Just what I need. Another judge with a paint-by-numbers law degree."

"I heard that." Lindstrom turned red. "I most certainly do have your number."

"Yes, you do, Your Honor. You most certainly do." He walked up the aisle, trying to maintain what little dignity he had left.

* * *

The best that Burr could do was a ten-minute recess, and now he and Jacob stood outside the courtroom underneath the sugar maple. "Pick us a good jury."

"Who would that be?"

"All men, if you can. We need a jury of men who sympathize with rich people, who drink too much, and whose wives take off their panties and decorate stolen Christmas trees."

I don't know if I could pick a jury like that.

"That's your gift, not mine," Jacob said.

"Then well-to-do men. That will do."

"Are there any within two hundred miles of here?"

"If you can't get prosperous men, then just get men." Sweat beaded on Jacob's forehead.

If only Eve had a law license.

"Jacob, you can do it," Burr said, although he doubted it. "I'll be back as soon as I can."

"What if I have to make the opening argument?"

"Feign illness."

"I won't have to feign." He bent over and threw up on Burr's shoes.

* * *

Burr took the ferry back to the island, rescued Zeke from the not too watchful eyes of Willard, then took the ferry to Mackinaw City and his Jeep. Three hours, a tank and a half of gas and two quarts of oil later, Burr sat across from Robert W. Stocker II, the East Lansing city attorney. Zeke and the Jeep waited curbside.

Stocker's skin hung in folds from his lower jaw, the remains of a once-fat face. Apparently, his hair had gone with the fat and what was left of it was combed straight back. He swayed side to side when he spoke, and the reading glasses that hung from a silver chain around his neck swung back and forth.

Like the pink pony.

"Mr. Stocker, we both know that six potted marijuana plants on my roof do not make me a drug trafficker."

Stocker smiled at him.

"This is a charge that won't stick. And you know it."

Stocker kept smiling.

"It's going to be dismissed at the preliminary exam."

The smile turned into a grin.

"Is there something in particular you want from me?" Burr said, not smiling.

"We are seeking justice, Mr. Lafayette."

"That's terrific, because the just thing to do is to drop this."

"It's out of our hands."

If he uses the royal 'we' one more time, I'm going to strangle him. At least then I'll be charged with a real crime.

"Mr. Stocker, I am a resident of East Lansing. I own a commercial real estate development. I'm a taxpayer." He pointed at Stocker. "I am a law-abiding citizen, and I would like to be treated as such."

"Mr. Lafayette, there actually is something you could do." Stocker reached for a brown accordion file on the corner of his desk and set it down in front of him.

"I'm all ears."

"You could pay your parking tickets."

"Of course. And if I pay them, you'll see to it that the charges are dismissed?"

"I will."

Stocker put on his reading glasses and rummaged through the file. He gave up and dumped it on the desk.

There must be two hundred tickets there.

Stocker shook his head, and the loose skin below his chin swung back and forth like the wattles on a turkey. "There must be two hundred tickets here."

They can't all be mine.

"These are all yours." Stocker shuffled through the tickets. "Here it is." Stocker picked up one lonely piece of paper. "Two-thousand, eight-hundred, eighty-two dollars and thirteen cents."

"I'm surprised I didn't get towed."

"I am, too. Mr. Lafayette. You're a scofflaw. A scofflaw." He wagged his finger at Burr. "Pay what you owe and we can all move on."

"I'm not paying all that.

"Oh, but you are."

"There's no place to park in East Lansing," Burr said.

Stocker took off his reading glasses. "I'd say you found plenty of places to park."

"I'm not going to pay that much."

"Mr. Lafayette, take a look out the window." The driver of an H&H

Mobil tow truck had just hoisted the front of his Jeep. Zeke, inside, didn't look pleased. Burr got out his checkbook.

* * *

Two-thousand, eight-hundred, eighty-two dollars and thirteen cents, and one rubber check later, plus the gas and the oil his Jeep burns, Burr snuck into Lindstrom's courtroom.

I hope my credit is still good with Eve.

He took a pew near the back of the courtroom. He didn't think Lindstrom had seen him come in, and he was certain the judge hadn't heard him. Burr looked at the jury. Eight women and four men. He'd hoped for more men, but at least they looked reasonably prosperous.

"Ladies and gentlemen, we have a tragic situation. A man has been murdered. Strangled." Karpinen paused to let this sink in.

A nice touch.

The jury squirmed in their collective chairs.

"Strangled with a string of Christmas lights." Another pause. More squirming. Burr felt the jury's queasiness spread through the courtroom.

Karpinen's doing well.

"In The Pink Pony, of all places," Karpinen said. "In The Pink Pony. Strangled by the defendant, Murdoch Halverson." The jury gasped. Murdo looked away, the opposite of what Burr had told him to do. He'd told Murdo to look at the jury. Look at them and give them your most convincing *I am innocent look.* Don't glare at them. Don't smile at them. Just give them a sincere look.

Object. Jacob, object. Do something.

It was all Burr could do to keep from jumping to his feet and shouting. Not that he had any reason to object, but Karpinen was on a roll and Burr wanted to stop him. Jacob would never do it. He was far too shy, and he followed the rules, at least in court.

Karpinen turned back to the jury. "The accused murdered Jimmy Lyons. He was called Jimmy, not James. Everyone liked him. He had many, many friends. He had a business with fifty employees, fifty good-paying jobs. Jimmy was a brilliant tool and die man."

Burr shook his head. In any other state you'd have to explain what tool and die meant, but not in Michigan.

"What will happen to them? "

If anyone could understand the importance of a job, it was surely here, Burr thought. "And what about his widow, Jane Lyons?"

Karpinen took a step to the side, partially facing the gallery. He frowned when he shifted his weight to his bad leg. Karpinen nodded but didn't point to the widow Lyons. She had done as she was told, wearing a black suit, her hair in a bun and no makeup. The once-upon-a-time beautiful Jane Lyons looked down at her lap, hands clasped.

She's been well coached.

Karpinen turned back to the jury. "What will become of her?" Another pause.

Burr could barely stand the drama. He had to get back in, but Lindstrom would never allow him to interrupt Karpinen's opening statement. That would be too much, even for Burr.

Karpinen stood there, sorrowfully. He looked down at his feet, then a cold stare at Murdo. He turned to Jane and let out a deep sigh. Then back to the jury. The silence roared through the courtroom. Karpinen had center stage and showed no sign of doing anything but standing there.

If Karpinen keeps this up, the jury's going to convict Murdo on the spot.

Burr sneezed so loud that it echoed through the courtroom. The blast from his lungs parted the hair of the matron in front of him.

Lindstrom, also hypnotized by Karpinen's theatrics, broke free from the prosecutor's spell. Karpinen hopped on his good leg. The eyes of the courtroom searched for the sneezer. Burr shrunk in his seat, then looked around for the spell breaker.

Karpinen started again, the trance broken. "Ladies and gentlemen, I am aware that my saying things does not make them so. Just because I say that Lake State has a great power play does not mean they do." Karpinen smiled at the jury. They smiled back at him. Lake State did, indeed, have a great power play. "And just because I say that Murdoch Halverson murdered Jimmy Lyons doesn't mean that he did. What I must do is prove that Murdoch Halverson murdered Jimmy Lyons." Karpinen looked at Murdo, then back at the jury. "And this I will do. When I'm done, the red light will flash and there will be no doubt that the puck is in the net."

"Please, I love hockey, but please make him stop," Burr said under his breath. The woman whose hair he had parted shushed him.

"I will prove that Murdoch Halverson killed Jimmy Lyons with malice aforethought. That is the legal definition of first-degree murder, but all that it means is that Murdoch Halverson had a plan to kill Jimmy, and he did kill him.

"I'm going to show you how he did it, how I know he did it, and who saw him do it."

Jacob, you've got to object. No one saw Murdo kill Jimmy. You can't let Karpinen put that idea in their head. It's not true, and we'll have a devil of a time getting it out of their heads.

"And," Karpinen said, "I'll tell you why Murdoch Halverson killed Jimmy. In fact, I'll tell you right now."

Karpinen limped toward Murdo. Jacob cringed. "What you may hear is that Jimmy had some financial problems. That he owed the defendant money. I have no idea if that's true. Maybe it is, maybe it isn't. It doesn't matter." Karpinen looked back at the jury. "Rich people like the defendant don't kill because someone owes them money. That's what lawyers are for." He smiled at the jury again. "That's what guys like him are for." Karpinen pointed at Jacob, who cringed. "Let me tell you why the defendant murdered Jimmy. Let me tell you why."

I know what's coming next.

"It wasn't for money," Karpinen said. "It wasn't for the money. Not at all." The prosecutor walked to the jury box. He leaned on the railing and spoke softly, as if to old friends who needed to hear something privately. Something that would not be welcome news. "None of us are perfect," he said. "Not me, not you. Certainly not Jimmy. Jimmy wasn't perfect. He made mistakes. We all do. But Jimmy's mistake cost him his life." Karpinen took a step back from the jury. "He certainly didn't deserve to die for it."

Karpinen took another step back from the jury box. "This is why the defendant, Murdoch Halverson, murdered Jimmy: It was because of her." Karpinen wheeled around and pointed at Anne.

"That woman, the defendant's wife, seduced Jimmy. She seduced Jimmy, and her husband, the defendant Murdoch Halverson, was jealous. He was so jealous that he murdered Jimmy. He bided his time. He waited until just the right time, a time when he thought no one would ever find out." Karpinen turned back to the jury. He stepped back to the jury box and leaned over the rail. "And when the time was right, the defendant Murdoch Halverson strangled Jimmy with a string of Christmas tree lights. Why? Because Anne Halverson seduced Jimmy Lyons." He pointed at Anne again. "Murdoch Halverson waited until just the right time. Then he killed Jimmy Lyons because he was jealous." He pointed at Murdo.

Burr shrank against the pew. He almost slid to the floor.

Karpinen limped back to his chair. Jacob struggled to his feet. He started mumbling to his shoes. Burr couldn't hear a word he said. Neither could the jury, and neither could Lindstrom.

"Speak up," Lindstrom said. "Speak up."

"I am," Jacob said, just above a whisper.

"It's your turn," Lindstrom said.

"Your Honor," Jacob said.

Burr jumped to his feet and raced up the aisle. "Burr Lafayette, Your Honor. Counsel for the defendant."

"I know full well who you are, and you are not to practice in my court-room. Out." Lindstrom pointed toward the door with his gavel.

Burr reached inside his jacket and took out the dismissal and a receipt for two-thousand, eight-hundred, eighty-two dollars and thirteen cents. "Your Honor, the false charges have been dismissed with prejudice."

"I don't believe it," Lindstrom said.

Burr handed the papers to the court reporter, who passed them up to Lindstrom. He studied the dismissal. "That's a lot of parking tickets." He folded the dismissal and passed it back to the court reporter, who passed it back to Burr.

"Get out of my courtroom," Lindstrom said.

"Your Honor, I've done everything you asked. I have every right to defend my client."

"Mr. Lafayette, you are, at best, a scofflaw, and I won't have a scofflaw practicing in my court."

"Respectfully, Your Honor, your actions are *ultra vires*," Burr said, gritting his teeth.

"What?"

"Highly illegal."

"I know what it means. Now, get out."

Burr hated himself for what he was about to do, but sometimes begging was the only way. "Your Honor, if it please the court, I apologize for my previous behavior and humbly ask the court to allow me to defend my client."

Lindstrom chewed on his lower lip. "Approach the bench, Mr. Lafayette." Burr took another step.

If I get much closer, I'll be sitting in his lap.

Lindstrom motioned for him to come even closer. Burr took a baby step, the toes of his shoes touching the podium. Lindstrom leaned down to Burr. "As I'm sure you know, the pink pony is still missing. Under the circumstances, I would advise you to behave yourself. Now that the jury knows you're a miscreant, welcome back."

Lindstrom leaned back in his chair. "While it grieves the court, you are hereby reinstated. You may proceed with your opening statement."

CHAPTER EIGHTEEN

Burr turned on his heel and walked straight to the jury.

I'm already in the hole.

"Ladies and gentlemen, my name is Burr Lafayette. I am Murdoch Halverson's lawyer." Burr smiled at the jury, not a hearty smile, but a smile that said *you can believe me.* He pulled down his cuffs, straightened his tie, then looked down at his shoes. They still needed polishing, especially after the episode with Jacob.

Burr thought it a bad idea to mention a single word about what just happened with Lindstrom. He had found it best to follow the lead of The Deuce – Henry Ford II – whose motto was, *Never complain. Never explain.* As angry as he was at the confederacy of idiots who had gotten him into this mess, this was, after all, not about him.

Burr looked up at the jury. "Ladies and gentlemen," he said again, "it's one thing to accuse someone of murder. It's quite another to prove it. The easiest thing in the world to do is make a false accusation. But there must be proof. Proof that someone murdered James Lyons," he said, careful not to mention Murdo's name in the same sentence as Jimmy's. "In fact, it's not clear that Mr. Lyons was murdered. Did you know that?"

The jury didn't know, but they wanted to. Was this even the same case? They leaned toward him as if they were one.

"That's right. It's possible that Mr. Lyons was so drunk that he strangled himself." Burr paused. "Did you know that?"

They didn't, but they wanted to know about that, too.

Karpinen stood. "I object, Your Honor. There's not a shred of evidence that this was anything but a murder."

"Sustained," Lindstrom said.

Sustained?

Burr turned to Lindstrom. "Your Honor, this is an opening argument. We're not submitting proofs yet."

"Your comments are inflammatory," Lindstrom said.

"Your Honor, the prosecutor was allowed to make accusations without any basis in fact."

"I will prove that the defendant killed Jimmy Lyons because his wife was having an affair," Karpinen said.

"And I will prove that Mr. Lyons was so drunk he strangled himself."

"Stop it, both of you," Lindstrom said. "Mr. Lafayette you may proceed, but watch what you say. You're one step away from another parking ticket."

Karpinen had stopped Burr's momentum, just like Burr had done with his sneeze.

"Ladies and gentlemen, Mr. Lyons was very drunk that night. A blood test showed that. That will be part of the testimony. But enough of that for now."

Burr stepped toward the jury. "That isn't the half of it. There's more. Much more. Saying something doesn't make it so." Burr pointed at Karpinen. "He still has to prove it. So far, all he's done is wave his arms." The jury looked at Karpinen. Burr wanted them to see Karpinen as the evil one. "This man has to prove that Mr. Halverson killed Mr. Lyons. And you know what? There isn't a single person who saw Mr. Halverson so much as touch Mr. Lyons. So, it's going to be very difficult to prove that Mr. Halverson murdered Mr. Lyons. Very difficult indeed."

Burr took two more steps toward the jury. "I'm going to show you that there are others who could have killed Mr. Lyons and who had a reason to do so." He took two more steps, now right to the railing.

"And one more thing. Convicting someone of murder is a tall order. A very tall order." Burr put his hands on the railing. "Do you know why?" They didn't, but wanted to know about this, too. "You cannot convict anyone of a crime unless you believe beyond a reasonable doubt that a crime was committed. Beyond a reasonable doubt." Burr stepped back. "That's a tall order. It's not just that a crime might have been committed or that you think a crime was committed. You cannot convict even if you simply believe a crime was committed. You must believe beyond a reasonable doubt." Burr leaned in toward the jury. "You must be convinced beyond a reasonable doubt." He pointed at Karpinen. "And he can't do that. He can't. There are holes in his case. Holes everywhere. There are more holes in this case than in a slice of Swiss cheese."

"That's quite enough, Mr. Lafayette," Lindstrom said. "Do you have anything further?"

"Yes, Your Honor."

"We will reconvene in the morning."

He must not have heard me.

Burr started to object, but Lindstrom slammed his gavel. "We are adjourned."

* * *

The next morning, Karpinen called his first witness. "Miss Hennessey, you were the first one to find Jimmy Lyons, is that right?"

"Objection," Burr said. "She doesn't know if she was the first one to find the deceased."

"Please, Mr. Lafayette, isn't it a bit early in the day to split hairs?" the judge said.

"Your Honor, the witness can only testify to what she knows."

"Reluctantly, I agree with you," Lindstrom said.

Karpinen limped around in a circle. "Miss Hennessey, did you find the body of Jimmy Lyons?"

"Yes," she said.

"Miss Hennessey, would you please tell us what happened on the morning of July 18th?"

"It was a Tuesday, and I open the bar on Tuesdays."

"Would that be The Pink Pony? In the Chippewa Hotel?"

"Yes. Tuesday isn't usually very busy, but the race had just finished so I knew the bar would be crowded for lunch. I got there about ten and unlocked the door to the bar, the one from the lobby."

"What time do you open the bar?" Karpinen limped to the right of Lindstrom so the jury could have a clear view of Carole.

"At eleven."

"What did you do after you unlocked the door?"

"It took a minute or so for my eyes to adjust to the dark. Then I saw the Christmas tree on the bar."

The prosecutor kept going. "What did you do then?"

"That little Christmas tree," she said. "It had…"

Karpinen cut her off. "Not the tree, what did you do next? Did you walk over to the bar?"

Burr popped up. "Objection, Your Honor. The prosecutor is interrupting the witness and then leading her."

"Overruled," Lindstrom said, softly.

"Your Honor, the prosecutor is telling his own tale."

"I ruled on your objection," Lindstrom said, not so softly this time. "Sit down and be quiet, Mr. Lafayette." Lindstrom tapped his gavel.

"Your Honor," Burr said, still standing.

"Sit down and be quiet." Lindstrom banged his gavel.

Burr sat, satisfied that he had accomplished what he set out to do, which was to undermine Karpinen's credibility.

"Now then, Miss Hennessey," Karpinen said, "what did you find when you reached the bar?"

"You mean on the tree?"

"No, not on the tree."

Good work, Carole.

She sat up straight and squeezed her knees together. "There was a man sitting in a chair behind the bar."

"And?" Karpinen just couldn't get her going.

"And he was dead."

"And?"

"And what?"

"Did he have Christmas tree lights wrapped around his neck?"

"Objection," Burr said, still sitting.

"Overruled."

"What was the question?" Carole said.

Karpinen glared at Carole.

I did a pretty good job of coaching her.

"Please tell us in detail what the body looked like. The lights. The face. Everything."

She squeezed her knees tighter. "Well, the man had blond hair. He was slouched over in the chair and his hair hung over his forehead. His eyes kind of bugged out and the tip of his tongue stuck out of the corner of his mouth."

"Thank you, Miss Hennessey. Was there anything wrapped around his neck?" She started to say something. Karpinen held up his hand and shushed her. He limped a step closer to her. "Miss Hennessey, please tell us in detail."

"There was a string of Christmas lights around his neck."

"Like a necklace?"

"No, they were tight. Very tight. They were wrapped around his neck, then once around the Labatt tap, and then plugged in. Tight. Like they had strangled him."

"Objection," Burr said. "The witness doesn't know the cause of death."

"I'll give you that one," Lindstrom said. "Sustained."

"Miss Hennessey. Can you tell us what was on the dead man's shirt?"

"There was a name tag. The paper kind, with the sticky back."

"And what did it say?"

"It said *Murdo*."

The jury gasped.

"Murdo," Karpinen said. "Murdo. The name tag said Murdo."

Burr whispered to Jacob. "He got all the mileage he could out of that."

"Thank you, Miss Hennessey." Karpinen limped back to the prosecutor's table. He picked up a folder and walked back to the witness. He took an eight-by-ten photograph from the folder and showed it to the witness. "Is this a picture of the dead man?"

Burr stood. "Objection, Your Honor. If the prosecution wants to use physical evidence, it must be introduced."

"You're a bit fussy, Mr. Lafayette," Lindstrom said.

"Your Honor, I didn't write the rules of evidence."

"Mr. Lafayette, at this rate, deer season will be over before we're finished with this witness." Lindstrom looked at Karpinen.

"Your Honor, the state would like to introduce this photograph as People's Exhibit One."

"Mr. Lafayette?"

"No objection, Your Honor."

"Miss Hennessey, is this a photograph of the dead man?"

"Yes."

Karpinen walked to the jury box and handed the photograph to the foreman, Mrs. Gunthorpe, the first woman Lindstrom called from the jury pool. It was the photograph of the strangled Jimmy Lyons, eyes bulging and tongue hanging out. She shuddered.

"Please pass it around," Karpinen said.

She cringed, then passed Jimmy to the juror next to her.

Burr was afraid this would happen, but there was nothing he could do about it.

When all of the jurors had finished cringing, Karpinen handed the photograph to the clerk, then, "Ladies and gentlemen, Miss Hennessey has identified the dead man as the deceased Jimmy Lyons. And as you just heard, she has testified that she found him sitting on a chair with a name tag on his shirt that read *Murdo*, the accused." Karpinen pointed at Murdo, then back to the jury. "There you have it. Jimmy was murdered, strangled, by a string of lights. Christmas lights wrapped around Mr. Lyons' neck."

Burr stood. "Objection, Your Honor. It hasn't been shown that Mr. Lyons was strangled. Let alone murdered."

"Mr. Lafayette, will you please stop this nitpicking?"

"Respectfully, Your Honor, the defense jumps to conclusions without any basis in fact."

"I suppose you think Jimmy Lyons drowned," Karpinen said.

"I think you and your case are only upright because you've got training wheels on your bicycle."

"That's enough," Lindstrom said. "Mr. Karpinen?"

"No further questions, Your Honor." Karpinen limped back to his seat.

Burr walked up to Carole. He liked the way she'd pinned her hair back. Alluring in a modest way.

"Mr. Lafayette," Judge Lindstrom said, "are you going to question Miss Hennessey or just ogle her?"

Burr wanted to give Lindstrom a withering look, thought better of it, then tried to address Carole without ogling. "Miss Hennessey, you said you entered The Pink Pony from the lobby of the hotel. Is that right?"

"Yes."

"Was the door locked?"

"Yes."

"After you entered, did you check the door to the street?"

"Yes."

"Was that door locked?"

"Yes, and there's a door from the kitchen that opens out the back. That was locked, too."

"Thank you, Miss Hennessey. I was just getting to that."

Carole nodded at him.

"And why did you check to make sure all the doors were locked?"

"For security. To make sure that the closer, the bartender from the night before, locked up."

"I see." Burr looked at the jury.

They were curious. Just where was he taking them?

"So, you found Mr. Lyons inside The Pink Pony. Locked inside. Is that right?"

"Yes."

"How can that be?" Burr put his hands in his pockets. "Miss Hennessey, do you need a key to lock the doors?"

"You need a key to lock all the doors."

"Do the doors lock behind you when you leave?"

"Yes, but when you're outside, you need a key to open them."

"Thank you. And who has the key?"

She wiggled in her chair. "The keys are kept behind the front desk of the hotel. In a drawer."

"Who has access to the keys?"

"The desk clerk. You need to get the key from the desk clerk."

"Is there another set?"

"The manager has a set."

That was all he needed. "Thank you, Miss Hennessey." Burr turned to the jury. "Ladies and gentlemen, the prosecutor would have you believe that Mr. Halverson killed Mr. Lyons, but he forgot to mention that Miss Hennessey, the first person to find Mr. Lyons, has testified that all the doors were locked." Burr stopped. He looked down at his shoes. Then back at the jury. "So how exactly would Mr. Halverson get in the bar and out again? Without a key?"

"Objection," Karpinen said. "There are many ways it could have happened."

"It's not your turn," Burr said.

"Mr. Lafayette, while this may come as a surprise to you, I am in charge here," Lindstrom said. Then to Karpinen, "Overruled."

"Thank you, Your Honor," Burr said. "Miss Hennessey, was there very much drinking going on in The Pink Pony that night?"

"Yes."

"Were the patrons unruly?"

"Yes," she said.

"In your opinion, was The Pink Pony pretty wild that night?" Burr said.

"Objection," Karpinen said.

"Sustained," Lindstrom said. "Mr. Lafayette, you already plowed that ground."

"Your Honor, what happens at The Pink Pony when the Mackinac racers reach the island is not a secret."

"I'm told that you have firsthand knowledge," Lindstrom said.

Burr walked back to the defense table. "Nothing further, Your Honor."

Karpinen called Winifred Burgdorfer, the aged medical examiner. "Dr. Burgdorfer, would you please tell us the cause of death?"

"Strangulation." Her voice boomed. Whatever infirmities old age had visited upon the good doctor, a weak voice wasn't one of them.

"Are you saying that Jimmy Lyons was strangled?"

"Of course that's what I'm saying."

"And what was the instrument of death?" Karpinen said.

"He was strangled by a string of Christmas tree lights."

"And how do you know that?"

"I examined the body," she said.

"Your witness," Karpinen said.

Burr tapped his pencil. He'd have to be careful with Dr. Burgdorfer. He needed to make his point, but he didn't want to antagonize the jury. Half of them were probably her patients.

"Counselor," Lindstrom said, "do you have any questions for Dr. Burgdorfer or are you just going to entertain us with your pencil tapping?"

Burr walked up to the witness. "Dr. Burgdorfer…" he said, then stopped short.

She looked at him. He looked back. She twisted in her chair. Finally, "What is it that you want?" she said.

"Are you the medical examiner – the coroner – for Mackinac County?"

"Yes."

"Are you a doctor?" he said as kindly as he could.

"Of course, I'm a doctor," she said, irritated.

"Are you a medical doctor?" he said, even more kindly.

"No," she said, this time defiantly.

"I thought you said you were a doctor."

"I am a doctor."

"But you're not a medical doctor?"

"No."

Karpinen struggled to his feet. "I object, Your Honor. Counsel is badgering the witness. Dr. Burgdorfer's credentials are impeccable."

"Sustained," Lindstrom said.

"Your Honor, the qualifications of an expert witness are always subject to scrutiny."

Lindstrom thought this over. Finally, "Continue, Mr. Lafayette, but please remember that Dr. Burgdorfer is a longtime and well-respected member of our community."

"Yes, Your Honor," Burr said. "Dr. Burgdorfer, exactly what kind of doctor are you?"

"I am an osteopath," she boomed.

"An osteopath," Burr said. "I see. And that is a kind of doctor?"

"Yes." She growled at him.

"Like a chiropractor?"

"No." Burr watched the color rise to her makeup-free face.

"But both chiropractors and osteopaths crack backs."

"In Michigan, an osteopath can do anything a medical doctor can do."

Burr ignored her. He'd taken this as far as he could, and all he'd wanted to do was put a little doubt in the jurors' minds about the good doctor's capability. "Dr. Burgdorfer, did you examine Mr. Lyons at The Pink Pony?"

"No."

"Where, may I ask, did you examine him?"

"At the morgue."

"So, you didn't actually see Mr. Lyons where he died."

"No."

"I see."

Maybe the jury will think all this this was amateur hour.

"Miss Burgdorfer ..."

"Doctor," she said.

"Of course," Burr said, "did you check the alcohol content of Mr. Lyons' blood?"

"Yes."

"And what was the alcohol content in Mr. Lyons' blood?"

".21."

".21," Burr said. "That's high, isn't it?"

"That's not for me to say."

"Miss..." Burr stopped, "...Doctor Burgdorfer, what is the blood alcohol content in Michigan for drunk driving?"

".08," she said, without hesitation.

".08," Burr said. "Mr. Lyons' blood alcohol content was .21. That is high. In fact, it's almost three times as high as the definition of legally drunk," Burr said, not asking. "Would you say Mr. Lyons was drunk at the time of his death?"

"Yes."

"Was he dead drunk?"

"Objection."

"Sustained."

"Dr. Burgdorfer, is it possible that Mr. Lyons could have been alone in The Pink Pony, wrapped the lights around his own neck, passed out, and strangled himself?"

"No."

"Why not?"

"Because he would have woken up."

"Not if he was that drunk," Burr said to the jury.

"Objection," Karpinen said. "Counsel has no idea what happened."

"Sustained."

Burr turned to the jury. "Ladies and gentlemen, Mr. Lyons was drunk. Very drunk. He was found dead inside The Pink Pony. Locked in. From the inside. I submit to you that Mr. Lyons did this to himself. That Mr. Lyons killed himself."

Karpinen started to stand. Burr waved him down. "All done, Mr. Karpinen."

Lindstrom adjourned them for lunch.

The Halversons left together. Aunt Kitty stopped Burr on the courthouse steps. "Just what do you think you're doing?"

"Doing?"

"Getting yourself thrown out like that. You've just about lost before you started."

"Aunt Kitty…"

"Don't Aunt Kitty me. Martha is mad as hops. I'm sure she's going to call the family lawyers."

I doubt that one of them was growing pot on top of their building.

"And then what will you do?"

* * *

After lunch, the bailiff called them back to order. Martha's lawyers hadn't shown up yet, but St. Ignace was at least a five-hour drive from Detroit.

Karpinen called Emil Conti. The rodent-like detective took the witness stand and faced the courtroom.

Karpinen got through the perfunctory questions quickly. "Detective Conti, were you in charge of the examination at the crime scene?"

"Objection," Burr said, popping to his feet. "It has not yet been determined that a crime was committed."

"You just can't help yourself, can you?" Lindstrom wagged his finger at Burr. "I've had just about enough of your niff naws."

"Your Honor…"

Lindstrom cut him off. "That's it. One more of those teeny-weeny points of order and I'm going to throw you out. And if I do, your bashful friend will take over." Karpinen wagged at him again. "Do I make myself clear?"

"Yes, Your Honor." Burr sat.

Karpinen limped back and forth in front of Conti, establishing the conduct and procedures of the sheriff's department. Absolutely top drawer, at least according to Detective Conti. Karpinen asked Conti to identify Murdo's tortoise-shell glasses, which the prosecutor introduced into evidence. On cue, Murdo made a show of putting on his new wire-rimmed glasses.

But then Karpinen got to the meat in the sandwich. "Detective Conti, did you examine the Christmas lights used to strangle Jimmy Lyons for fingerprints?"

Burr started to stand, then sat.

Lindstrom's right. I just can't help myself.

"I did," Conti said.

Karpinen limped to his table and picked up another file. Back at the witness stand, he opened the file and handed a square of paper to Conti. "Detective, would you please identify this?"

Conti scrunched his rat nose over the paper. "These are the fingerprints found on the Christmas tree lights."

"Thank you." Then to the clerk, "Please enter this as People's Exhibit Two. Then to Burr, "Counselor?" Burr waved him off.

"Please identify this," Karpinen said, handing Conti another paper, also to be introduced into evidence.

"Those are the defendant's fingerprints."

"And how do you know this?"

"I watched him being fingerprinted."

"Where was that?"

"At the jail."

"At the jail," Karpinen said.

Burr knew Karpinen would do everything he could to link Murdo to *murder, defendant, crime scene,* and *jail.*

Karpinen introduced Murdo's prints into evidence. "Detective Conti, what can you tell us about these two sets of fingerprints?" Burr knew a good lawyer wouldn't ask an open-ended question unless he knew the answer. Burr didn't like Karpinen much, but he thought the prosecutor was a pretty good lawyer.

Conti sat up straight, thrust out his shoulders, such as they were, and stuck out his chin, which was missing in action. He cleared his throat.

Drum roll.

"The fingerprints on the Christmas lights match those of the defendant."

"Are you saying that the defendant Murdoch Halverson's fingerprints are on the murder weapon?"

"Yes. I am."

The jury shuddered.

"No further questions."

Burr walked up to the detective. "Mr. Conti, were you the first law enforcement official to arrive at The Pink Pony?"

"No," Conti said, quietly.

"I see," Burr said, taking a step back. "Did someone from the Mackinac County Sheriff's Department arrive before you?"

"No," Conti said, slightly louder.

"Really? But your department conducted the investigation. Is that right?"

"Yes," he said, a little louder.

"Mr. Conti, what law enforcement officer was the first to arrive at The Pink Pony?"

"Arthur Brandstatter, the Mackinac Island Chief of Police."

"Is that the fudgie cop?"

The jury snickered.

"Objection," Karpinen said.

"Stop it, Mr. Lafayette," Lindstrom said.

Burr continued. "Who called you?"

"Chief Brandstatter."

"I see. Mr. Conti, when you arrived, was there yellow tape on the doors?"

"No."

"Was there yellow tape anywhere?"

"No," Conti said. Burr had backed up halfway to his table. "I'm sorry I can't quite hear you."

"No, there was no tape anywhere."

"Where was Mr. Brandstatter?"

"He was in the lobby."

"What was he doing?"

Conti looked at his shoes, then at Burr. "He was drinking a cup of coffee."

"I see," Burr said. "Mr. Conti…"

"It's Detective. Detective Conti."

"Of course, it is." Burr had finally gotten under the rodent's skin. "Is it possible that someone or perhaps multiple people could have been in The Pink Pony before you arrived?"

"No."

"Mr. Conti … " Burr said, "… excuse me, Detective Conti, was there anyone standing guard at any of the three doors when you arrived?"

"No."

"So, it's possible that the evidence could have been corrupted?"

"No."

Burr put his hands in his pockets. "Come on, detective. The head cop on Mackinac Island is drinking coffee when you get there. There are no guards. There's no police tape, but you say that there's no possibility that anyone may have gotten inside the bar?" Burr took a step toward Conti. "Come on, detective. This is inexcusable police work and you know it."

"Objection, Your Honor," Karpinen barked at the judge. "The witness already answered the question."

Burr turned to Karpinen. "I'm surprised you waited so long." He turned to the jury. "Ladies and gentlemen, I think it's clear that any evidence found in The Pink Pony may well have been corrupted by the shoddy police work done by Mr. Brandstatter."

"What's that?" Lindstrom said, also barking.

Burr turned back to Karpinen. "Nothing, Your Honor."

"Look at me when you're speaking to me," Lindstrom said.

"Yes, Your Honor." Burr looked at Conti and moved in for the kill. "Detective Conti, were there any other fingerprints on the Christmas lights?"

"What?" This startled Conti.

"I said, were there any other fingerprints on the Christmas tree lights?"

"No," Conti said, not too sure of himself.

"Really?" Burr looked at the jury, then back at Conti. "Detective, could you identify every fingerprint on the lights?"

"No."

"Why is that?"

"Well," he said, "some were smudged."

"Smudged?" Burr arched his eyebrows. "So, there were some finger-prints that you could not identify. Is that right?"

"Yes."

Burr had him now and Conti knew it. "So, it's possible, Detective Conti, that there may have been fingerprints of other people on the lights?"

"They were the defendant's fingerprints, but they were smudged."

"If they were smudged, how do you know they were Mr. Halverson's?" Burr stepped right up to Conti. "You don't, do you?"

"Objection," Karpinen said. "Calls for speculation."

I was hoping he'd say that.

"Your Honor, this isn't speculation. I asked a simple question that requires a yes or no answer. Either he knows or he doesn't."

Karpinen glared at Burr. Burr, who was doing a lot of smiling, smiled at Karpinen.

"Answer the question," Lindstrom said.

"No."

"No, what?"

"No, I don't know."

"No, you don't know what?"

"No, I don't know who the smudges belonged to."

Burr turned to the jury. They nodded at him.

* * *

Predictably, Karpinen dredged up Patrick Gurvin, the Casanova on the beach who said he saw Murdo sneak out the back door of The Pink Pony after it had closed. Burr thought the prosecutor got the boy's testimony about as skillfully as he could, considering what Gurvin had been up to. Burr, artfully, but as directly as he could, did his best to discredit the red-faced lad, even though Lindstrom stopped him well before Burr reached the *coitus interruptus* part of the story. From the tittering of the twelve, Burr was sure that the jury had more than a pretty good idea of what had taken place on the sands of Mackinac Island that night.

Burr thought that Karpinen had been smart not to call Brandstatter, even though the prosecutor had the chief on his witness list. Burr would take care of that when he presented his defense. Carole, despite Burr's coaching, had been a much better witness for Karpinen than Brandstatter would ever have been.

What Burr couldn't understand was why Karpinen hadn't called Karen Vander Voort, the bartender who had the most damning testimony at the preliminary exam. Not only had she poured the shots for Jimmy at the bar, she'd also poured the drinks for Jimmy's table. Worse, she'd been close enough to their table to witness all their shenanigans, including Murdo rearranging the lights around Jimmy's neck. Not to mention the lingerie debacle. Worse yet, she'd testified that she was sober as a judge, which surely put her in a class by herself. But she did say she was the last one out and had locked all the doors. Maybe that was why Karpinen didn't call her.

Thank God for that.

But his prayers weren't answered for long.

"The state calls Detective Emil Conti."

"Did you forget something, Mr. Karpinen?" Lindstrom sneered at his sometime colleague.

"Your Honor," Karpinen said, "Detective Conti is necessary to establish some additional testimony."

"Why didn't you think of that before?"

"Your Honor, if you permit me to examine Mr. Conti, it will become very clear, very quickly."

"Very well, but get on with it," Lindstrom said. He pointed at Burr. "Don't say a word. Your objection is noted and overruled."

Conti took the stand again. He smiled at Karpinen as though they were the best of friends, which, Burr thought, they probably were. "Detective Conti, I'm sure you're aware that you are still under oath." Conti nodded. "Detective Conti, you interviewed Karen Vander Voort about what she saw on the night that Jimmy was killed. Is that right?"

"Yes."

"Please tell us what she told you."

Burr jumped to his feet like a jack in the box. "Objection, Your Honor. This is hearsay."

Lindstrom pursed his lips.

The old goat might finally agree with me.

"Mr. Karpinen?" the judge said.

"Your Honor, we can't seem to locate Ms. Vander Voort. That's why we need to question Detective Conti."

"Your Honor, that's the whole point of the hearsay rule. If the prosecutor wants to question Miss Vander Voort, he needs to find her."

"I know what hearsay is, Mr. Lafayette." Lindstrom looked at Karpinen.

"Miss Vander Voort has somehow disappeared," Karpinen said.

Burr, still on his feet, said, "It's a fundamental constitutional principle that the accused have the opportunity to confront their accusers. Your Honor, secondhand testimony is very likely to be inaccurate."

"Your Honor," Karpinen said, "Miss Vander Voort testified at the preliminary exam. We have her transcript."

"Why don't you start with that," Lindstrom said.

Karpinen picked up a folder from his table.

Damn it all.

Karpinen introduced the transcript into evidence as People's Exhibit

Three, then he turned to a paper-clipped page. "Detective Conti, please read from here."

"Your Honor," Burr said. "Having a policeman read from the transcript gives the testimony more credence than it should have. The clerk should read the testimony."

"Stop with your namby-pamby objections, Mr. Lafayette," Lindstrom said. "Detective Conti, please read whatever it is that it seems to be so important to everyone."

"Yes, Your Honor."

Conti read aloud. "The four of them, the two couples, sat at a table next to the bar. At first, they were all having a good time. Then the wife, Mrs. Lyons, got mad and left." Conti stopped, then looked up at Karpinen, who nodded to him.

They practiced this.

Conti continued. "Do you know what she was mad at? Then Miss Vander Voort said, 'I think she was mad at Mrs. Halverson.' 'Why was that?' you asked, 'Because she was flirting with Mr. Lyons.'"

"Your Honor," Burr said, "this is ludicrous. We can't possibly tell who is saying what to whom about anything."

"Mercy, mercy, mercy," Lindstrom said. "Mr. Karpinen, you read your questions. Detective Conti, you be Miss Vander Voort."

"This is like a tryout for the St. Ignace civic players," Burr said.

"I didn't hear that Mr. Lafayette," Lindstrom said. "Continue, Mr. Karpinen."

The detective and the prosecutor went back and forth. The point of all this silliness was that if Karen Vander Voort was right about what she saw, there was little doubt that more than enough alcohol had been served, that Jimmy and Anne had something for each other, and that Murdo was jealous.

Burr popped up again. "Your Honor, we have no idea if Mr. Halverson was jealous. That's the opinion of a missing witness."

"You're quite right, Mr. Lafayette," Judge Lindstrom said.

"That is precisely my point. And since she's not here, I can't question her," Burr said.

"You could have questioned her at the preliminary exam," Lindstrom said.

"Your Honor, that's not what happens at a preliminary exam."

Lindstrom shooed Burr away with his hands. "Are you quite done, Mr. Karpinen?"

"Not yet, Your Honor." Karpinen turned to another paper-clipped page. "Detective Conti, please read from here." Karpinen pointed to the middle of the page.

"Then Mr. Lyons came back with a little Christmas tree, a short one. It was nailed to two little slats so it would stand up. He set it on the bar. Every-one thought it was funny.'"

"'What happened then?'" Karpinen read.

"'Well, Mr. Lyons had some Christmas lights, the big old-fashioned kind. C-9's, I think.'"

Burr shook his head.

Conti read on. "'By the time Mr. Lyons was done, the tree had lights wrapped around it. I plugged them in for Jimmy.'"

"'Then what happened?'" Karpinen said.

"'Women started decorating it with their underwear.'"

"'Really, and who started this?'"

Conti read from the transcript. "'Mrs. Halverson,'" he said.

"'Could you elaborate?'"

"'Well, Mrs. Halverson reached up under her top and took off her bra. Then she put it on the tree. Like an ornament.'"

"'What happened next?'"

"'Then some of the other women did it. Pretty soon, I saw Mrs. Halver-son come back to the tree. She reached up under her skirt and took off her panties. She put them on the tree, too.'"

Conti looked at Judge Lindstrom. "Now Mr. Lafayette says something." Should I read his part?"

Burr flew out of his chair. "Objection, Your Honor."

"Would you like to read your own part?" Lindstrom said. Burr could barely contain himself.

"Thank you, detective," the judge said, "I think we'll skip that. You may continue."

Conti started again. "Before Mr. Lyons put the lights on the tree, Mr. Halverson wrapped them around Mr. Lyons' neck."

"Objection, Your Honor!" Burr shouted at the judge. "That is not in the transcript."

"Mr. Karpinen?"

"Your Honor, this is what Miss Vander Voort told Detective Conti."

"You mean it's not in the transcript."

"Not exactly."

"Exactly in or exactly out?"

"Miss Vander Voort told this to Detective Conti when he interviewed her."

"So, it's not in the transcript?"

"No," Karpinen said.

Burr stood again. "Your Honor, I move that this entire testimony be stricken from the record. There's no way to know what really happened. For all we know, Miss Vander Voort might have been mistaken as to what really happened. Not only is the prosecutor trying to mislead the jury, this is hearsay at its worst."

"Strike that testimony from the record," Lindstrom said.

"What testimony is that, Your Honor?"

"I've seen that movie, Gus. Strike it all." Lindstrom slammed his gavel. "We are adjourned for the day."

But the damage had been done.

CHAPTER NINETEEN

The next morning, Burr sat at the defense table and looked out at the maple tree. The wind was blowing and leaves were falling off the tree. Karpinen was questioning Lionel Worthy, Jimmy Lyons' lion-maned attorney. His white shirt set off the ruddiness in his face, and his nostrils flared when he spoke.

"Mr. Worthy," Karpinen said, "was Mr. Halverson suing Mr. Lyons?"

"Yes, he was."

"Objection," Burr said. "Mr. Halverson was not suing Mr. Lyons."

"Mr. Worthy," Karpinen said, "was Mr. Halverson's company suing Mr. Lyons' company."

"Yes."

"So, there was a lawsuit between the two companies."

"That's right."

"Thank you," Karpinen said. "Mr. Worthy, did you ever see Mr. Halverson get angry at Mr. Lyons?"

"I did."

"Did he make any threatening remarks?"

"He did."

"Such as?"

"We were standing outside a conference room during a break at a deposition. Mr. Halverson told Mr. Lyons that if he, Mr. Lyons, so much as looked at Mrs. Halverson again, he would kill him."

"So, the threat had nothing to do with money," Karpinen said. "Mr. Halverson was jealous."

"That's right."

"Thank you, Mr. Worthy. I have no further questions."

Burr tapped his pencil. He walked up to Worthy, who still smelled like an ashtray. He took a step back. "Mr. Worthy, how much was Mr. Halverson's company suing Mr. Lyons' company for?"

"I don't remember."

"You're the company's lawyer, but you don't remember."

"Yes."

Worthy had been around the block more than once.

Burr started over. "Yes, you were the lawyer for Mr. Lyons' company, New Method Screw Machine?"

"Yes."

"And, yes, you don't remember how much New Method was being sued for?"

"Yes."

"Let me refresh your memory, Mr. Worthy." Burr introduced into evidence the complaint that Detroit Screw Machine Company had filed against New Method Screw Machine.

"Mr. Worthy, please read this number." Burr handed him the complaint. "It's right there." Burr pointed. "What's that number?"

"I don't know."

"Why not?"

"I don't have my reading glasses."

"You are ever so cute, Mr. Worthy," Burr said.

"Objection, Your Honor."

"Do not abuse the witness, Mr. Lafayette."

Burr walked back to the defense table and snatched Jacob's rimless glasses off his nose. "Try these." Burr handed him the glasses. Worthy dropped them on the floor.

"Your Honor, if this continues, I'm going to ask the court to declare Mr. Worthy a hostile witness."

"For the love of Mike," Lindstrom said, "read it yourself."

I made my point.

Burr turned to the jury. "It says here that Mr. Lyons was being sued for three-million dollars." He paused to let the three-million sink in. He turned back to Worthy. "Does that sound about right, Mr. Worthy? Three-million dollars? That's a lot of money, isn't it?"

"I don't remember."

"Mr. Worthy, the question was, is three-million dollars a lot of money?"

"I don't know."

"I'd say that's a lot of money." Burr turned back to the jury. "Wouldn't you?"

"Objection, Your Honor," Karpinen said. "Counsel is preaching to the jury."

"My question was for Mr. Worthy, who doesn't seem to know anything or remember anything."

"Behave yourself," Lindstrom said.

"Yes, Your Honor," Burr said. "Mr. Worthy, would you say it's reasonable that if someone owed you that much money you might be angry about it?" Worthy started to speak but Burr held up his hand. "I withdraw the question."

"Mr. Worthy, were you on Mr. Lyons' boat during this year's Port Huron-Mackinac race?"

"Yes."

"Yes, you raced with Mr. Lyons this year on his boat?"

"Yes."

"And did Mr. Halverson also race with Mr. Lyons this year during the Port Huron-Mackinac?"

Silence.

"Mr. Worthy?"

"Yes."

"Yes, Mr. Halverson raced on Mr. Lyons' boat. That doesn't seem like they were enemies, does it?"

"I don't know."

"Of course you don't, Mr. Worthy. No further questions, Your Honor."

* * *

Burr took another look at Karpinen's witness list. For the life of him, he didn't know why Robert Huffman was on the list. For that matter, he had no idea who Robert Huffman was.

The bailiff swore in the witness.

It turned out that Huffman worked at the front desk at the Townsend Hotel in Birmingham, Burr's favorite hotel. A fortyish man, a bit plump in his black suit and a bit funereal for a desk clerk, but it did give him an air of believability. That and his square jaw and high forehead.

"Mr. Huffman, do you recognize this woman?" Karpinen said, pointing at Anne.

"I do. Indeed, I do," Huffman said, smiling.

Unctuous, Burr thought, cloying and unctuous, just like every good desk clerk.

"For the record," Karpinen said, "Mr. Huffman is pointing at Mrs. Halverson. Mr. Huffman, did you ever see Mr. Halverson at the Townsend?"

"Yes, I did."

"And did you ever see Mr. Lyons at the Townsend?"

"Yes."

"Mr. Huffman, were you at the front desk when Mr. Lyons checked in? That is, you checked him in?"

"That's right." He smiled a conspiratorial smile.

"How many times would you say you checked him in?"

The desk clerk bit his lip, thought a moment. "Six or eight, I'd say."

"Six or eight," Karpinen said. "Do you remember the last time?"

"A couple of months ago. In June, I think." He smiled again, telling all his secrets.

"Did you ever see Mrs. Halverson with Mr. Lyons?"

"Yes."

"Please tell us about it."

"I'd see them in the bar. The bar across from the front desk."

"Did you ever see them go up the elevator together?"

"Once or twice." He smiled like he he'd just told a secret no one else knew.

"Were they together? Like a couple."

"I'd say so."

"I have no further questions."

Burr looked over at Murdo, who was staring at his hands on the table in front of him. The fingers of each hand locked in the other. Burr looked at Anne. She looked away.

This is a disaster.

Burr stood and slowly made his way to the smiling desk clerk

"Mr. Huffman, did you ever check Mrs. Halverson in?"

"No, not that I remember."

"Did Mr. Lyons and Mrs. Halverson ever check in together?"

"Not that I remember," said the desk clerk, still smiling.

"Did you ever see them leave together?"

"I don't know."

"Did you, or didn't you?"

"No, I guess not." The smile faded just a tad.

"Did you ever see them holding hands?"

"No."

"Kissing?"

"No."

"I see." Burr stepped closer to Huffman. Burr loved the Townsend and knew it like his former house. He'd carried on there once or twice himself. Luckily, Huffman hadn't been on duty at the time. Burr smiled at the desk clerk, whose own smile brightened, but not for long.   "Mr. Huffman, the elevator that you saw Mr. Lyons and Mrs. Halverson get in, goes up to guest rooms, is that right?"

"Yes, it does."

"Doesn't that very same elevator go down to the parking garage underneath the hotel."

"Yes."

"Isn't it possible that Mr. Lyons and Mrs. Halverson weren't going upstairs at all? Isn't it possible that they were leaving?"

"I suppose," the desk clerk said, his smile fading.

"You suppose," Burr said. "You suppose? How would you know? How could you know?"

The now frowning desk clerk started to answer, but Burr held up his hand. "I have no further questions." Burr sat. Murdo looked like he'd just seen a ghost. "What do you know about this?" Burr said, under his breath.

"Nothing."

Burr didn't believe Murdo. He didn't think Huffman had hurt him much, but it was about to get worse.

Karpinen called Greta Bienenstock, the bookkeeper at the Townsend.

What now?

Mrs. Bienenstock was a widow and had been for thirty years, just about as long as she'd been bookkeeper at the Townsend. The widow Bienenstock wasn't a day over fifty and she looked as though widowhood agreed with her. If she was an inch over five feet tall, it was only because she wore four-inch, not-too-sensible heels. She had a round face with red round lips and black shoulder length hair with silver barrettes that kept it out of her dark blue eyes. She wore a tailored linen suit and didn't look a bit like a bookkeeper.

"Mrs. Bienenstock, does the Townsend have charge accounts?"

"A few."

"Did Mrs. Halverson have a charge account at the Townsend?"

In spite of her silver barrettes, Mrs. Bienenstock swept her black hair out of her eyes. "Yes."

Karpinen nodded at her and walked to his table, smiling at the jury as he went. He picked up still another folder and made the round trip to Mrs. Bienenstock. He opened the folder and held up still another piece of paper in triumph. He turned to Lindstrom. "Your Honor, the people would like to introduce the billing record of Anne Halverson at the Townsend Hotel as People's Exhibit Four." Lindstrom looked at Burr.

Burr stood slowly. "Your Honor, I cannot for the life of me understand why a charge account at a hotel in Birmingham, nearly three hundred miles away, has any possible relevance to the gross injustice of charging my client with murder."

"Your point?" Lindstrom said.

"I object," Burr said, still standing.

"Overruled," Lindstrom said. "Proceed, Mr. Karpinen, but be advised that there is a modicum of sense in Mr. Lafayette's objection."

"Yes, Your Honor." The prosecutor handed his witness a piece of paper from the file. "Mrs. Bienenstock, did you make the entries on this billing record?"

"Yes."

"Would you please tell us about Mrs. Halverson's billing record."

"This is a client account record. It shows the charges to the client and the payments."

"Thank you, Mrs. Bienenstock. Would you please tell us what this billing record says?"

"This is the client account, the billing record, for Anne M. Halverson, 539 Windmill Pointe Drive, Grosse Pointe Park, Michigan. It shows the room, dinner and bar charges. And the payments."

"About how many charges are there?" Karpinen said.

Mrs. Bienenstock made a point of poking the charge account with her finger as she counted. Finally, she said, "About twenty."

"Over what period?"

She studied the record again. "For about the past eighteen months."

"Were all the charges paid?"

"Yes."

"So, Mrs. Halverson had a charge account at the Townsend. For room, dinner and bar. And yet she lived in Grosse Pointe which is only half an hour away. Is that right?"

"Yes."

"No further questions."

Burr stood.

Why do I always get the tough cases?

Burr walked up the bookkeeper.

Because I need the money.

"May I look at this?" Burr said. Mrs. Bienenstock looked at Lindstrom, who nodded. She passed the account record to Burr. He pretended to study it, then, "Mrs. Bienenstock, where is your office at the Townsend?"

"My office?"

"Yes, where do you work?"

"I have an office on the first floor."

"Can you see the lobby from your office?"

"No."

"Can you see the guests check in or out?"

"No."

"I see," Burr said. "Did you ever see Mrs. Halverson at the Townsend?"

"No, not really."

"Have you ever seen Mrs. Halverson before today?"

"No."

"So, you sent the bills out and you recorded the payments, but for all you know Santa and his elves might have been staying at the hotel."

Karpinen popped up. "Objection, Your Honor."

He's pretty spry for a busted-up hockey player.

"Please, Mr. Lafayette. Show some manners," Lindstrom said.

"Your Honor, my point is that this billing record doesn't show anything. There's no way to know who paid these charges much less who stayed in the room."

"Your Honor," Karpinen said. "These are charges and payments in Anne Halverson's name and the bill was sent to her home. What else are we to assume?"

"We are to assume that this evidence should not be admitted," Burr said. "It's not even evidence."

"Quiet." Lindstrom said. "The evidence stands as admitted. You watch your manners." Lindstrom wagged his finger at him.

Burr turned away from Lindstrom. "You know about as much about the rules of evidence as Karpinen."

"What's that?" Lindstrom said.

"I said, no further questions, Your Honor."

"That's what I thought you said," Lindstrom said.

Burr stalked to the defense table and sat.

Karpinen called Sheila Jablonski, a maid at the Townsend who lived in Hamtramck. The witness, a pimply-faced lass who looked barely old enough to drive, wiggled in her chair.

"Miss Jablonski, please tell us what you saw on May 19th of this year."

"I saw the 'tree of them in the hotel that day."

"Who were the three of them?"

"The missus, that one," she said, pointing at Anne. "She run right past me. Down the hall there. Lickety-split."

I haven't heard that in twenty years.

"Who did you see and where?" Karpinen said.

"I seen her," she said, pointing at Anne again.

"Please record that the witness has identified Anne Halverson," Karpinen said. "What else did you see?"

"I seen him." She pointed to Murdo. "And the dead guy."

Karpinen produced the photograph of Jimmy Lyons. He handed her the photograph. "You mean, Mr. Lyons?"

"That's him all-right."

Karpinen looked at the court reporter. "For the record, Miss Jablonski has identified Mr. Halverson and Jimmy Lyons as the two men she saw in the hall." Back to the witness. "Where exactly in the hall were they?"

"They was outside room 602."

"And what were they doing?"

"They was arguing."

"Could you tell what they were arguing about?"

"No, but that one, Mr. Halverson I guess his name is, he sure was mad."

"Thank you, Miss Jablonski. And did you enter room 602?"

"Sure did. I had to clean the whole floor. All the rooms."

"What did you see in the room?"

"Back up a minute. Like I said, they all hightailed it out of there. Then I goes in the room. And the room's hardly been used except the covers is all rumpled."

"Thank you, Miss Jablonski."

Burr stood. "Your Honor, this testimony barely rises to the level of a soap opera and certainly isn't worthy of admission."

"Overruled."

"So, Miss Jablonski," Karpinen said, "just to make sure I have it right, you saw Mrs. Halverson rush past you in the hall. You saw Mr. Halverson and Mr. Lyons arguing outside room 602. And you saw the bed clothes rumpled inside Room 602." Karpinen paused to let all this sink in. "Do I have that right?"

"Bed clothes?" the maid said. "You mean the covers?"

"Yes, Miss Jablonski. The covers."

"That's about it."

Karpinen turned to the jury. "Ladies and gentlemen, it's painfully clear that Anne Halverson and Jimmy Lyons were having an affair at the Townsend Hotel in Birmingham and that Anne Halverson's husband, the accused…" Karpinen pointed at Murdo… "caught them." He turned back to Judge Lindstrom. "I have no further questions." The prosecutor dragged himself back to his chair.

At least he's getting tired.

Burr, not exactly fresh as a daisy, had a point to make, but it was risky, especially since he was about to ask a question to which he didn't know the answer, but with the way things were going, he thought it was worth a try.

"Miss Jablonski, did you see either Mrs. Halverson, Mr. Halverson, or Mr. Lyons inside Room 602?"

"Nope."

"Did you check them in?"

"No, I'm a maid."

"Thank you, Miss Jablonski." He looked at Lindstrom. "I have no further questions."

"Redirect, Your Honor," Karpinen said.

Lindstrom sagged in his chair. "All right, but this better be quick."

Karpinen stood, then leaned on his table. "Miss Jablonski, I forgot to ask you an important question." He stood up as straight as he could. "When you saw Mr. Halverson in the hallway, was he holding anything?"

"He sure was." The maid glowed.

"And what was it?" Karpinen said.

Burr wasn't sure what was coming but he was pretty sure he wasn't going to like it.

"A key," she said, absolutely glowing.

"What kind of key?"

"A room key," she said.

"Could you see a room number on it?"

"You know what number it was. We went over it. It was the key to 602." She pointed at Murdo. "He was holding in his hand and shaking it at the dead guy who wasn't dead yet."

"For the record, Your Honor, let it be known that Miss Jablonski pointed at the defendant Murdoch Halverson." Karpinen sat down.

"Anything else for you, Mr. Lafayette?" Lindstrom said.

Burr ignored the judge and tapped his pencil. He stopped tapping, looked at his pencil, then broke it in two. "Murdo," he said under his breath, "what else haven't you told me? Better yet, why didn't you tell me about Anne and Jimmy?"

"It's not what it looks like," Murdo said.

"I used to live in Grosse Pointe," Burr said, "and I have some idea what goes on there. But we're not in Grosse Pointe, and if you think you get to live by different rules than those twelve people sitting over there against the wall, you may well spend the rest of your life in an eight-by-ten cell thinking it over." Murdo looked away. Eve handed Burr another pencil.

"Did you hear me, Mr. Lafayette?" Judge Lindstrom said.

Burr looked up at the judge. "No questions, Your Honor."

* * *

Karpinen called his last witness, James M. Buehler, the rich, belligerent stockbroker from Troy whose fingerprints Burr couldn't get.

"Mr. Buehler," Karpinen said, "were you in the lobby of the Chippewa Hotel the night of July 17th?"

"I was."

"What time were you there?"

"Just before the bar closed."

"And why were you there?"

"I wanted to have a word with Mr. Lyons."

"What about?"

"He fouled me at the end of the race, and it cost me the pennant. I was going to have it out with him."

"Please tell us what happened," Karpinen said.

"I couldn't get anywhere close to Lyons in the bar. It was too damn crowded."

"Watch your language, Mr. Buehler," Lindstrom said.

Buehler continued. "When they kicked us all out of the bar, I thought I'd catch up with him in the lobby. I saw Lyons and Halverson, right outside the door to the bar. I lit a cigar, and when I looked up, they were gone."

"Where do you think Mr. Halverson and Mr. Lyons went?"

"They had to have gone back into the bar. It was too crowded for anybody to move very far, very fast."

"Objection, Your Honor," Burr said. "Speculation."

"Mr. Karpinen, you've gone a bit too far," Lindstrom said.

Karpinen nodded at the judge. "Mr. Buehler, was the lobby crowded?"

"It was packed."

"And you saw Mr. Halverson and Jimmy Lyons standing in the lobby next to the door to The Pink Pony."

"Yes." Buehler looked like he was losing his patience.

"And then they weren't there," Karpinen said.

"That's what I said."

"Did you see them anywhere else in the lobby?"

"No."

Karpinen turned to the jury. "Ladies and gentlemen, Mr. Buehler may have been the last one to see Jimmy Lyons alive. Except, of course, for the defendant. I submit to you that they went back into the bar after it closed, and then the defendant murdered Mr. Lyons."

Burr jumped up. "Your Honor, this is outrageous. It's pure speculation."

Karpinen looked at the judge. "It's a possibility, Your Honor."

"I'll allow it."

Burr sat down, furious.

"Thank you, Mr. Buehler. I have no further questions." He walked back to his table and sat.

Burr had had just about enough of Karpinen and his witnesses. He approached the witness stand. "Mr. Buehler, you said you raced in the Port Huron-Mackinac?"

"Yes."

"Did you sleep much during the race?"

"I got enough."

"Would you say you got eight hours of sleep a night?"

"No."

"Six?"

"Probably not."

"Four?"

"I got enough sleep," Buehler said.

Burr thought Buehler looked like he was the one who usually asked the questions.

"Were you drinking beer in the bar?" Burr said.

"I don't drink beer."

"What were you drinking?"

"Salty dogs." Buehler smiled at him.

"And that is?"

"Grapefruit juice, vodka, with a dash of salt."

"How many would you say you had?"

"I'm sure I don't remember."

"But you remember seeing Mr. Halverson and Mr. Lyons outside the door to the bar?"

"That's right."

"But then you bent your head down to light a cigar and when you had it lit and looked back up, they were gone."

"That's right."

"How long does it take to light a cigar?"

"I don't know. Not very long." He glared at Burr.

"You have to unwrap it, bite the end off, put it in your mouth, strike a match, and puff until the cigar is lit." Burr mimed a demonstration, taking as long as he possibly could. "Do I have that right?"

"I use a cigar cutter and a lighter."

"Of course, you do," Burr said.

"Objection, Your Honor," Karpinen said. "Counsel has no idea how Mr. Buehler actually would light a cigar."

"Perhaps you'd demonstrate, Mr. Buehler," Burr said. He offered his new pencil to the annoyed witness.

"That's quite enough, Mr. Lafayette," Lindstrom said.

"Mr. Buehler, it appears that lighting a cigar is a complicated and time-consuming process. Isn't it possible that by the time you were done lighting your cigar, Mr. Halverson had simply walked out of the lobby and into the street?" Burr turned away from Buehler. "I have no further questions, Your Honor."

"Not possible. It was too crowded," Buehler said.

Damn it all.

"That wasn't a question," Burr said, his back to Buehler.

"It sure sounded like one," Buehler said.

Burr turned back to the belligerent witness. "Mr. Buehler, where did you sleep the night Jimmy Lyons was killed?"

"What?"

"I said where did you sleep the night Jimmy Lyons was killed?"

"That's none of your business," Buehler said.

Burr looked up at Judge Lindstrom. "Answer the question, Mr. Buehler," the judge said.

"That's my business," Buehler said.

"Mr. Buehler, you will answer the question or I will have the bailiff put you in jail until you do answer," Judge Lindstrom said.

"I slept on my boat," Buehler said.

"Was anyone else on the boat?" Burr said.

"No," Buehler said.

"I have nothing further." Burr walked back to the defense table.

"Mr. Karpinen?" Lindstrom said.

"The prosecution rests, Your Honor," Karpinen said.

"Will wonders never cease," Lindstrom said. He made a show of looking at his watch. "It being almost five o'clock, we will recess for the day." He tapped his gavel and walked out without a further word.

CHAPTER TWENTY

Burr looked up at the window in Lindstrom's courtroom. A steady rain tap, tap, tapped on the window, like the tap of his pencil. The maple outside was almost bare. He stood and walked to the jury. "Ladies and gentlemen, I'm going to finish as I began. The prosecutor must prove beyond a reasonable doubt that Mr. Halverson killed Mr. Lyons." He stepped closer to them. "Beyond a reasonable doubt," he said again, leaning on the rail of the jury box. He looked at them one at a time, then spoke softly. "And reasonable doubt doesn't mean you think he might have done it. Or that he could have done it. It doesn't even mean that you think he probably killed Mr. Lyons. It means that you are almost positive that he killed Mr. Lyons. Almost positive."

"Objection, Your Honor. That's not the meaning of reasonable doubt," Karpinen said."

"Sustained," Lindstrom said. "Can't you leave it at reasonable doubt, Mr. Lafayette?"

I didn't think he could hear me.

"Ladies and gentlemen, whatever words are used, reasonable doubt is a high standard. We don't have to know who did kill Mr. Lyons, if in fact he was killed. For all we know, he may have been so drunk he strangled himself. As I said, we don't have to know who did kill Mr. Lyons in order to acquit Mr. Halverson. To convict Mr. Halverson, you must believe beyond a reasonable doubt that Mr. Halverson did, in fact, kill Mr. Lyons." Burr turned away from the jury. He wanted to give this a moment to sink in. He looked up at the window again and saw the rain running down the windowpane.

He turned back to the jury. "Ladies and gentlemen, as I've said, the evidence doesn't support a conviction. Because the prosecutor doesn't have much in the way of evidence. No one saw my client murder Mr. Lyons. And the evidence he does have is flimsy, at best. The prosecutor has conveniently neglected to provide evidence. Evidence that shows someone else, actually many others, could have killed Mr. Lyons. And the evidence he does have may not be good evidence. It may have been corrupted by shoddy police work." Burr paused again, almost ready for the grand finale. He looked at his shoes, which still needed polishing.

"Ladies and gentlemen, perhaps I should have started and ended with what I am about to tell you. Mrs. Halverson will testify who she was with that evening. And do you know who she was with?" Burr stopped again. He stuck his hands in his pockets. He counted to ten, then pointed at Anne. "She was with her husband the entire evening. So, Mr. Halverson couldn't possibly have murdered Mr. Lyons."

Karpinen's jaw dropped. Burr had heard it from Anne *ad nauseum*, but this was the first the prosecutor had heard it. Which was exactly why Burr hadn't brought it up at the preliminary exam. "Mr. and Mrs. Halverson were with each other the entire evening. And that is why you must find Mr. Halverson not guilty." He looked at them again, one by one. Each one in the eye.

* * *

Burr called Chief Art Brandstatter. He'd considered cutting right to the chase, starting and finishing with Anne, but he'd thought better of it. He thought it was probably better to poke as many holes in Karpinen's case as he could.

"Chief Brandstatter, are you the chief law enforcement officer on Mackinac Island?"

"That's right." Brandstatter smiled at him.

"Chief Brandstatter, what were you doing at The Pink Pony on the morning of July 18th, the morning James Lyons died?"

"I was investigating the murder of Jimmy Lyons."

"Of course you were. But before that? What were you doing before that?"

"That's what I was doing."

"Weren't you on the sidewalk outside The Pink Pony trying to figure out what happened to the pink pony itself, the little pink hobby horse that hangs outside the bar? The one that costs all of about twenty-five dollars?"

"It costs a lot more than that."

"Weren't you looking for a little pink pony outside The Pink Pony while Jimmy Lyons was dead inside The Pink Pony? On the other side of the door?"

Chief Brandstatter's smile turned upside down. "How was I supposed to know he was in there?"

"Chief Brandstatter, how did you finally find out that Mr. Lyons was dead inside The Pink Pony?"

"Someone from the hotel told me."

"I see. And what did you do?"

"I went inside."

"And what did you do when you got there?"

"I investigated."

"For the record, chief, how many murders have you investigated?"

"One."

"Really, please tell us about it."

"This one."

"So chief, in your entire career in law enforcement, this is your first murder. Is that right?"

"I've done plenty of investigating."

"But this is your first and only murder. Is that right?"

"I suppose so."

"Your first and only murder." Burr looked at the jury, then back at Brandstatter. "Did you put up any police tape?"

Brandstatter squirmed in his chair. "No."

"I see. Did you talk to anyone?"

"I sure did." The chief had a new smile.

"Inside the bar?"

"Yes."

"Where Mr. Lyons was?"

"Yes."

"When did you contact the Mackinac County Sheriff's Department?"

"When I was done."

"And when would that be?"

"After an hour or so. Maybe two."

"Chief, were there any other people in the bar while you were investigating Mr. Lyon's death?"

"A few."

"A few," Burr said. "So, Chief Brandstatter, let me make sure I understand you. Jimmy Lyons was dead, no more than twenty feet away from you, while you were investigating the disappearance of a little pink plastic pony. And when you finally figured out Mr. Lyons was dead, you didn't secure the crime scene. And on top of that, any one of a number of people were in and out of the bar. Any one of whom could have killed Mr. Lyons and destroyed evidence. Is that about it?"

"It wasn't that way at all. And you know it," Brandstatter said, but he looked a little beat up.

As if on cue, "Objection, Your Honor," Karpinen said. "This is irrelevant."

Burr couldn't have scripted it any better. He turned to the jury. "This is the most relevant part of this entire trial. The prosecutor has taken great pains to show that the sheriff's department did a professional, expert and thorough job. But he conveniently omitted the fact that the first law enforcement officer at the scene botched the investigation before it ever started. The crime scene and the evidence were corrupted before Detective Conti and his crew, however able they may have been, even got there. The entire investigation is tainted."

Lindstrom chewed on his cheek. "As much as I don't like Mr. Lafayette's approach, I'm going to allow this." To Burr, "Anything else?"

"One more question, Your Honor." Burr turned to the woebegone cop. "Chief Brandstatter, have you found the missing pink pony?"

"No, but...."

Burr held up his hand and shushed him.

* * *

Burr didn't think Karpinen's cross-examination of the once again jolly chief had hurt him so far. Karpinen had established that Brandstatter had been in law enforcement for the past thirty-five years, but Burr thought the jury was smart enough to understand the difference between experience and expertise. At least he hoped they were.

Then Karpinen got to the part that Burr knew he would get to. It was a calculated risk that Burr hoped wouldn't backfire.

Karpinen looked at Burr, then at Brandstatter. "Chief, do you have any suspects in the theft of the pink pony?"

"I object, Your Honor," Burr said, jumping up. "Irrelevant."

"If the investigation into the theft is relevant, then so is the suspect," Karpinen said.

"I'm not sure I follow that, but you may continue." Lindstrom paused. "Briefly."

"Thank you, Your Honor," Karpinen said. "Chief, who are the suspects in the theft of the pink pony?"

Brandstatter cleared his throat. He grinned at Burr, then with as much gravity as a fat, jolly policeman on a tourist island could muster, "There is only one suspect in the theft of the pink pony." He cleared his throat. "The only suspect is him," he said, pointing at Burr. "Him," he said again. "Burr Lafayette." The courtroom exploded into a rhapsody of *oohs, ahs* and *titters*. Burr thought Karpinen would get to this, but he thought it was worth the risk. He did his best to silence the giggling jury with a steely glare.

Karpinen wasn't done. "Chief Brandstatter, you were investigating the theft of the pink pony. And at the time you were not aware that a murder had been committed?"

"I most certainly was not."

"For all you know, Mr. Lafayette may have been stealing the pink pony at the very time Mr. Halverson was murdering Jimmy Lyons." The courtroom exploded again.

Burr leapt to his feet.

"Sit down, Mr. Lafayette. You started this," Lindstrom said. He smashed his gavel on its pedestal. "That is quite enough, Mr. Karpinen. Ladies and gentlemen, you will disregard Mr. Karpinen's last statement."

"No further questions, Your Honor," Karpinen said.

Chief Brandstatter stopped at the defense table on his way to the gallery. "Don't be so smug about the pony. I found a witness."

Burr stuck his wrists out so Brandstatter could cuff him. "What are you waiting for?"

"As soon as I get his affidavit, I'm going to lock you up."

"Have at it, Sherlock."

* * *

Burr called Stanley Mueller, his fingerprint expert. If Murdo and Anne had mastered dressing down, Murdo in a tweedy sport coat the color of dead leaves and a too wide, striped tie, and Anne in a should-have-been-belted green and black tartan, fresh from the Junior League thrift shop, Burr wished that Stanley Mueller had taken it up a notch, from tacky to shabby.

Burr's fingerprint expert wore a burgundy sport coat, or was it maroon, and dishwater blue pants. Slacks would give too much credit to what looked like pressed denim. A wrinkled white shirt completed the patriotic trio. His red, white, and blue plaid tie matched the rest of him. The knot in his tie was the size of a fist and hadn't heard the fashion news about tie clips. Then there were the glasses, thicker than Burr remembered, thick enough to be coasters. Burr hoped that they gave him a scholarly appearance. He'd asked Mueller to keep his left hand, the one with the missing finger, on his lap.

Burr led Mueller through his many qualifications, then reached the meat of the fingerprint sandwich.

"Mr. Mueller," Burr said, "Detective Conti has testified that the only fingerprints on the Christmas lights were those of Mr. Halverson." Burr straightened his tie and resisted the temptation to tighten Mueller's knot and line it up with his neck. "Do you agree with Detective Conti?"

"No," Mueller said. "No, I don't."

"Did you examine the fingerprints found on the Christmas tree lights?"

"I did."

"And what did you find?"

"In addition to Mr. Halverson's fingerprints, I found at least three other sets of fingerprints on the lights."

"Really?" Burr said, as if he didn't know. "Could you identify them?"

"Two of them matched fingerprints I had in my possession."

"Mr. Mueller, from your examination can you tell us who these finger-prints belong to?"

The lame prosecutor leapt to his feet. "I object. This is outrageous."

"Mr. Mueller, where did you get these fingerprints?" Lindstrom said.

"From Mr. Lafayette," Mueller said.

Karpinen looked over at Burr.

If looks could kill, Karpinen would be the one on trial.

"Your Honor, you expressly refused to grant Mr. Lafayette a court order to obtain fingerprints. And he has done the very thing you prohibited. The fingerprints that Mr. Lafayette obtained must not be admitted into evidence."

"Slow down, Gus," Lindstrom said. "Mr. Lafayette, did these people give you permission to take their fingerprints?"

Burr turned to Lindstrom. "Your Honor, it's well established that finger-prints obtained in a public place are admissible."

"I asked you if they consented," Lindstrom said.

"Your Honor, the rule of law is that being in a public place is implied consent."

"Balderdash," Karpinen said.

"Balderdash?" Burr said.

"This constitutes an illegal search and is prohibited by the Fourth Amendment. You expressly forbid this, Your Honor."

"Lordy, Lordy, Lordy," Lindstrom said. "Gus, I had no idea you were so concerned about my authority." Lindstrom chewed on his cheek. Then he studied his fingertips. Finally, he said, "Mr. Lafayette, did these people give you their express consent to have their fingerprints taken?"

"Your Honor," Burr said.

"A simple yes or no will suffice."

"Your Honor..."

"Yes or no."

Except for Anne, Burr's defense turned on Mueller and the fingerprints. He couldn't afford to lose on this. "It's well established that…"

"I take that as a no," Lindstrom said. "Mr. Lafayette, you may question Mr. Mueller about the fingerprints obtained by the sheriff's department and about any fingerprints you obtained with the express consent of the person fingerprinted. If you cross the line by so much as your big toe, I will remove you from these proceedings until they're ice fishing on the straits." Lind-strom studied his fingertips again. "Do I make myself clear?"

"Yes, Your Honor."

My goose is cooked.

"Proceed, Mr. Lafayette," Lindstrom said. "If you're done with the witness, I'll give the prosecutor his turn."

Burr was tempted to get Jane's and Worthy's names tied to the finger-prints, but he thought that if he did that, Lindstrom probably would throw him out. If he was careful, he might be able to salvage something.

"Mr. Mueller, you testified that there were three sets of fingerprints on the Christmas lights that belonged to people other than Mr. Halverson. Is that right?"

"Yes."

Burr looked at the jury to make sure they were following along.

"So, Mr. Mueller, in spite of what Detective Conti testified, you found the fingerprints of three other people on the alleged murder weapon?"

"That's right."

"So that means, if Mr. Lyons actually was strangled by the Christmas lights, it's possible that one of the three sets of fingerprints you found on the lights could belong to the murderer."

Karpinen launched himself out of his chair. "Objection, Your Honor, that is sheer speculation."

"Sustained," Lindstrom said.

"I have no further questions." His point made, Burr walked to his chair with a victory, however fleeting.Karpinen marched up to Mueller as best he could with a bad knee. "Mr. Mueller, why did you leave the state police?"

"I retired."

"And how long had you worked there?"

"Twenty-nine years."

"Twenty-nine years," Karpinen repeated. "Isn't it customary to retire after thirty years?"

"I don't know what's customary."

"Mr. Mueller, isn't it true that you were forced to retire because of failing eyesight?"

"Objection," Burr said. "This isn't relevant to Mr. Mueller's qualifications."

"On the contrary, Mr. Lafayette, I would say that eyesight is fundamental to the qualifications of a fingerprint expert," Lindstrom said. "You may continue, Mr. Karpinen."

Karpinen straightened his tie. "Did your failing vision have anything to do with your retirement?"

"I don't remember."

"Mr. Mueller, how did you get all the way up here from, where is it, some place called Fish Point?"

"It's by Sebewaing."

"Wherever that is," Karpinen said.

Burr thought it the height of reverse snobbery for a Yooper to want to know where someplace in the Lower Peninsula was.

"How did you get here?"

"In a car."

"Let me make this painfully clear," Karpinen said, "did you drive your-self here?"

"No."

"How did you get here?"

"My sister dropped me off."

"Do you have a driver's license, Mr. Mueller?"

"No."

"You can't see well enough to drive but you can identify fingerprints. Is that right?"

"There's nothing wrong with my close-up vision."

Karpinen pressed on. "Mr. Mueller, did you lift the fingerprints you've told us about from the Christmas lights?"

"No."

"Did you personally examine the string of lights?"

"No."

"Then how, may I ask, could you possibly conclude that there were other fingerprints on the lights – much less whose they were?"

"I examined the fingerprints lifted by the sheriff's department."

"I see," Karpinen said. "The professionally trained Mackinac County Sheriff's Department couldn't identify any other prints. But you, who can't see well enough to drive a car, found three other sets of fingerprints."

"I don't think the sheriff's department knew what they were doing."

"I didn't ask for your opinion," Karpinen said.

"I thought that's what I was here for."

Bravo, Stanley.

"Mr. Mueller, if there were, in fact, fingerprints on the lights other than Mr. Halverson's, how many total fingerprints did you find?"

Watch yourself, Stanley.

"I don't know. Maybe eight or nine."

"Altogether?" Karpinen said.

Be careful, Stanley. He's going to come after you now.

Burr tried to get Mueller's attention, but his blind as a bat expert didn't see Burr waving.

"Yes," Mueller said.

"Damn it all," Burr said.

"Quiet," Lindstrom said to Burr.

Now it was Karpinen's turn to move in for the kill. "Mr. Mueller, if you were going to strangle someone with a string of lights, wouldn't you need to hold them with both hands?"

"I suppose so."

"And wouldn't that leave many fingerprints?"

"I told you I didn't look at the lights themselves, I looked at the prints taken from them."

"That's right," Karpinen said. "You were looking at second-generation evidence, which may well be corrupt."

"Objection, Your Honor," Burr said. "This is the very evidence the sheriff's department used. If you want to toss out all the fingerprint evidence, that's fine with me."

"Sustained," Lindstrom said.

This didn't seem to bother Karpinen. "Mr. Mueller, could you identify all of the fingerprints on the Christmas lights?"

"No."

"And why not?"

"Some of them were smudged," Mueller said.

"Smudged," Karpinen said. "Is it possible that you identified smudges as belonging to other people when, in fact, they were smudges and couldn't be identified at all.?"

"Objection, Your Honor."

"Please, Mr. Karpinen," Lindstrom said.

"I have no further questions."

* * *

Lindstrom adjourned them for the day. Burr was afraid he may have wasted all the time and money he'd spent on the fingerprint fiasco. This was the second time in as many murder trials that the judge had no idea what the law was.

Burr boarded the Star Line for the island, the only ferry still running this time of year. He had a date with Carole, but he needed her help more than her company, especially now. Twenty minutes later, they set off on bikes to find Toad. Burr still had Anne as his star witness, but he didn't think he could afford to leave anything to chance.

They climbed the hill behind the Grand and entered the woods in the twilight. Burr smelled the cedars and the fallen leaves.

Three-quarters of a mile later, the woods opened up to Stonecliffe, an early twentieth century Tudor, now a restaurant. Carole took his hand and led him and Zeke inside a paneled lobby, the paneling so dark it was almost black.

"What's Toad doing here?" Burr picked up a menu.

"We're not here to eat." Carole took his hand again, smiled at the *maître d'* and led Burr down a flight of stairs. There was a rumbling like thunder, a crashing sound, laughter, silence. And then it started over.

What's going on?

The stairs opened on a bar with shelving full of liquor behind it. Then the crashing sounds again. It was a bowling alley. A single lane in the basement of Stonecliffe. A bowling alley in a windowless basement where the noise bounced off the walls and echoed on itself.

An overly affectionate preppy couple was bowling, and there was Toad at the business end of the alley, setting the pins with three other college-age men.

That's about three too many pin-setters.

"Isn't it grand?" Carole clapped her hands.

How unlike her.

"It's the oldest bowling alley in the state, and the only one still with pin boys."

I don't have time for this.

Burr caught the sweet smell of burning hemp.

He's going to burn the place down.

Carole waved at Toad. He strolled up to her, smiling until he saw Burr. "What's he doing here?"

"We need your help."

"No, I'm going to set pins and Murdo's going to go to jail." Toad started back to the alley.

Carole snagged Toad by the hand and led him to the bar.

I'm here with Wendy, Peter Pan and the Lost Boys.

They climbed up on bar stools. A younger, pudgier version of Toad appeared behind the bar. Burr saw a Labatt tap and couldn't resist. Toad had a Coke. Carole passed.

"Was all the crew on the list you gave me?" Burr said.

"All the crew?" Toad said.

"Did you leave anyone off?"

"No." Then, "I don't remember."

Burr reached into his pocket and pulled out the reservation list from the Chippewa and passed it to Toad.

"These ten names. Is that it?"

"Yep, it is."

"What about Ronnie Cross? Jimmy reserved a room for him. But you didn't tell me about him."

"He's nobody," Toad said.

"Tell me who nobody is."

"He's nobody."

"I'll make it simple. Tell me who Ronnie Cross is now or you can tell me in court tomorrow."

"I don't know what you're talking about." Toad jumped down from the bar stool and hustled back to the bowling alley with the Lost Boys. Burr reached around to the bar and poured himself another Labatt. Carole joined him this time. Three beers later, Toad tapped him on the shoulder.

"He goes to U of M," Toad said.

Burr handed him two twenties.

CHAPTER TWENTY-ONE

Burr sat next to Murdo at the defense table and looked out the window. It was gray and cloudy. Most of the leaves on the tree had fallen off, and the branches looked like a spider web. Jacob had left for Ann Arbor early that morning in search of Ronnie Cross. He'd told Burr that this field trip was yet another of Burr's boondoggles. Burr hoped Jacob was wrong, but what if the third set of fingerprints did belong to Ronnie Cross and what if he was the murderer? What if elephants could fly, Jacob had said. Burr thought he might well be grasping at straws, but after Lindstrom had refused to let Mueller identify Jane's and Worthy's fingerprints, Burr wasn't feeling too good about his chances, Anne's alibi notwithstanding. And he still didn't have Buehler's prints.

Henry Crow called them to order.

Lindstrom entered and sat. "Mr. Lafayette, I believe you have more witnesses."

"The defense calls Jane Lyons," Burr said. He'd have been disappointed if Jane had looked any different than she did. She had pulled her hair back from her face and pinned it behind her head. No lipstick, her full, red lips gone. No makeup whatsoever. And, of course, a plain black dress, A-line, knee length. The only hint of fashion, a single string of pearls.

Burr wondered who dressed her. Karpinen? Worthy? Or was it do-it-yourself? No matter. The look was perfect.

The bailiff swore her in.

"Mrs. Lyons, how long were you and Mr. Lyons married?"

"Seven years."

"Children?"

"No. Unfortunately, no."

He'd have to be careful with her. She looked so sympathetic. "Mrs. Lyons, you were in The Pink Pony the night your husband died. Is that right?"

"Yes."

"And you were sitting with your husband and Mr. and Mrs. Halverson?"

"Yes."

"And you had a few drinks. Is that right?"

"Yes."

"More than a few?"

"I don't remember."

She's been well coached, but not by me.

"You didn't race with Mr. Lyons. You met him on the island. Is that right?"

"Yes."

"Where were you staying?"

"We had a room at the Chippewa."

"That's the hotel where The Pink Pony is located. Is that right?"

"That's right."

"Did you stay with your husband until the bar closed?"

"No."

"Why was that?"

"I was tired."

"What did you do?"

"I went up to bed."

"Did anyone see you go to your room?"

"I don't know."

"Did you see him again that night?"

"I never saw him again." She paused. "Alive."

"I'm sorry Mrs. Lyons."

She put her hands in her lap.

"Weren't you concerned when your husband never came up to bed?"

"I thought he went back to the boat."

"I see."

Here goes.

"After you drove all the way to the island, you left the celebration early because you were tired, but you stayed long enough to put your bra and panties on the Christmas tree. Isn't that true?"

"Objection, Your Honor," said the ever-vigilant Karpinen. "This is not necessary."

"Your Honor," Burr said. "Mrs. Lyons' lingerie has been identified as being on the Christmas tree. We can introduce it as evidence."

"I don't think that will be necessary, Mr. Lafayette," Lindstrom said, "but if you're going to continue with this, you must demonstrate how her lingerie is relevant."

"Yes, Your Honor."

The demure Mrs. Lyons has a little color in her cheeks.

"Mrs. Lyons, you had come to Mackinac Island to meet your husband and help him celebrate. You drank with him and the Halversons in The Pink Pony. You took off your lingerie in public and decorated the tree with it." Burr looked at the jury. They were mesmerized with the widow Lyons. "All in all, a jolly celebration." Burr turned back to Jane. She smoothed out the wrinkles in her dress and squeezed her knees together. "But then you left. Well before the party was over. Why was that?"

"I already told you. I was tired."

"You were tired," Burr said. "Could it be that you were jealous? Perhaps jealous of Mrs. Halverson? Because she sat on your husband's lap? Were you so jealous that you got mad and left? Were you so jealous that you came back down from your room later and murdered your husband?"

"Objection, Your Honor."

"I merely asked a question," Burr said.

"He's harassing the witness," Karpinen said.

"Stop it, Mr. Lafayette," Lindstrom said. His cheeks were redder than Jane's.

"I would like an answer to my question," Burr said.

"Mr. Lafayette, you have pushed the limits of decorum. If this continues, I will expel you from these proceedings," Lindstrom said. "I am sorry, Mrs. Lyons, but I am afraid you must answer the question."

She looked Burr right in the eyes. "No."

"Mrs. Lyons, would you say that you and Mr. Lyons were happily married?"

"Yes."

Burr turned around and walked to the defense table. He picked up a file and returned to the witness stand. "Mrs. Lyons, I have in my hand a complaint for divorce filed by your husband."

Jane lost the color in her face. She looked down at her hands, then at Burr. "I don't know anything about that."

"Your Honor, this is a divorce complaint filed by Mr. Lyons. He died before it could be served."

"Objection, Your Honor," Karpinen said. "This is inadmissible."

"It was filed in Oakland County Circuit Court and is, therefore, admissible," Burr said.

"Just because it was filed doesn't mean Mrs. Lyons knows about it," Karpinen said.

"Your Honor, I move to introduce this as Defense Exhibit One," Burr said.

"Mr. Lafayette," Lindstrom said, "I'm afraid that I must allow this to be admitted, but I find your methods despicable."

Thank you.

Burr handed the complaint to the court reporter. He'd considered bringing up the whole *Fujimo* business, but he thought that would be pushing it, even for him. He turned back to the widow Lyons. "Mrs. Lyons, let's assume that you didn't know about the complaint. Even so, how could you say you were happily married?"

"Jimmy and I were very happy."

Burr gave the jury a disapproving look. "Mrs. Lyons, you were aware of Mr. Lyons' financial difficulties?"

"No, I wasn't."

"You didn't know that he was being sued by a number of people and a number of companies?"

"No."

"I see," Burr said. "Mrs. Lyons, are you the beneficiary of a life insurance policy on your late husband's life?"

"Objection, Your Honor," Karpinen said. "Irrelevant."

"Your Honor, this is the most relevant question I've asked today."

"Please answer the question," Lindstrom said.

"Yes."

"Mrs. Lyons, is it possible that you knew your husband was going to divorce you? That you knew he was so broke you'd never get anything in a divorce?" Burr turned to the jury. "So you killed him for the life insurance."

"How dare you," she said.

Burr winked at her. "No further questions, Your Honor."

Karpinen limped to the witness stand. He looked at the jury, then at Jane. "Mrs. Lyons, I have but one question."

Jane looked at him sorrowfully.

"Mrs. Lyons," Karpinen said.

"Yes?" she said, still sorrowfully.

"Did you love your husband?"

She looked down at her lap, then at Karpinen. "Yes. Yes, I did love him."

"I have no further questions," Karpinen said.

* * *

Burr called Lionel Worthy. He didn't think he'd get much out of him, but it was worth a try. "Mr. Worthy, earlier you testified that you were Mr. Lyons' attorney. Is that right?"

"Yes."

"You were his personal attorney and the attorney for his company, New Method Screw Machine. Is that right?"

"Yes."

"Mr. Worthy, how much money did Mr. Lyons and company owe to his creditors?"

"I don't know."

"But you were his lawyer."

"I was his lawyer, not his accountant."

"Mr. Worthy, how many lawsuits had been filed against Mr. Lyons and his company?"

"In addition to Detroit Screw Machine?"

"Mr. Worthy, I asked a simple question. I would like a simple answer. How many lawsuits?"

"I don't remember."

"You're his lawyer but you don't remember."

"That's right."

"Isn't it your job to remember? Or are there so many lawsuits you don't remember?"

"Is that a question?"

"Your Honor, I request that Mr. Worthy be treated as a hostile witness."

"Objection, Your Honor," Karpinen said. "There is nothing in Mr. Worthy's answers to merit treating him as a hostile witness."

"Mr. Lafayette," Lindstrom said, "while the witness isn't being particularly cooperative, I'd hardly say that his behavior merits being deemed a hostile witness."

Burr paced back and forth in front of his uncooperative witness. Worthy hadn't told him anything of any importance, but at least he was on display to the jury as being unhelpful and unlikable, which was, in fact, helpful.

"Mr. Lyons and his company had a number of debts and a number of lawsuits, but you don't remember how much money or how many lawsuits. Is that right?"

"Yes."

"Mr. Worthy, does the estate of Mr. Lyons, or his company, owe you any money?"

"I don't know."

"Mr. Worthy, surely you must know if Mr. Lyons owed you money."

"Mr. Lyons is dead."

"Really? I had no idea." Burr took a step closer to Worthy, but the ashtray smell pushed him back again. "His estate then. Does his estate owe you money?"

"That's protected by attorney-client privilege."

"Nonsense. The privilege is extinguished on the death of the client and doesn't pass to the estate."

"I beg to differ," Worthy said.

"Your Honor," Karpinen said, "Mr. Worthy is correct."

"Lordy, Lordy, Lordy," Lindstrom said again. He chewed on his cheek. "The court agrees with the prosecution. Mr. Worthy, you need not answer that question. Surely you know that, Mr. Lafayette."

"Your Honor, please preserve my objection." Burr acted as outraged as he could. He knew attorney-client privilege applied, but he thought it was worth a shot. "Mr. Worthy, you crewed on Mr. Lyons' boat. Is that right?"

"Yes."

Burr clapped his hands. "You do remember something. And were you with Mr. and Mrs. Lyons and the Halversons at The Pink Pony the night Mr. Lyons died?"

"Yes."

"How long did you stay?"

"I don't remember."

"Of course you don't," Burr said. "Do you by any chance remember where you spent the night?"

"At the Chippewa Hotel."

"Do you remember if you spent the night with anyone?"

"I was alone."

"I see. And did you argue with Mr. Lyons about the money he owed you?"

"No."

Burr looked at the jury, then Worthy. "Mr. Worthy, I'm a bit concerned about your health. You seem to have a vivid memory of certain things but absolutely no memory of others. When someone has such a difficult time remembering even the simplest things, it can be a sign of injury. Have you been injured, Mr. Worthy?"

"No."

"Your symptoms indicate that you may be suffering from a closed head injury."

Burr's comment pretty much brought down the house not to mention the wrath of Lindstrom, who told him he was an inch from being thrown out. Again.

* * *

The band was just tuning their instruments when Burr and his merry band arrived at Horn's, not that a drum kit, an electric bass and a keyboard required much in the way of tuning. They sat next to the windows in the fading October daylight.

The island had virtually shut down for the season. The fort had closed. The Grand had shuttered some time ago. Stonecliffe would be next and there were only a few restaurants still open.

There were only a few locals, plus Burr and his merry little band in Horn's. Except they weren't so merry. Burr had ordered a Labatt and a plate of nachos. So far, no one had shown much interest in the nachos except Burr and Zeke.

Murdo looked spent. He'd just ordered his second Manhattan after pouring the first one down his throat. "Karpinen didn't paint a very favorable picture of us."

"That's his job, darling," Anne said. She squeezed his hand, waiting for her second Stoli on the rocks.

Burr peeled a jalapeno off a nacho and passed the nacho sans jalapeno to Zeke. Burr had insisted they meet after Lindstrom dismissed them. Anne was Burr's last, and far and away most important, witness, especially after the fingerprint debacle. He wanted to make sure she knew her part. He ordered a second Labatt and got right to the point. "Anne, you're the star of the show tomorrow. All you have to do is answer my questions, just like we've practiced."

"We were together the entire evening."

"So, you said." Burr chewed on a nacho. "I'm going to ask you very specific questions. Unless I ask you to tell me something, just answer *yes* or *no*."

"I know what happened and I know what to say."

Burr looked out the window. He watched a street cleaner pedal by, towing a manure cart with a shovel sticking out.

There can't be many of them left.

Burr looked at Anne, "This is the guts of our defense, and it's going to be even more important when Karpinen cross examines you. Because we know what he's going to ask about."

Anne started to say something but stopped when Jacob burst in to Horn's. "I found him," he said.

"Where was he?" Burr said.

"Room 206 of the U of M Engineering Building in Ann Arbor. At a lecture on displacement hulls or some such thing."

"Who'd you find?" Murdo said.

"Ronnie Cross," Jacob said. "I left him with Mueller. Mueller's taking his fingerprints, but he swears he was nowhere near The Pink Pony that night."

"Who is this Ronnie what's-his-name?" Martha said.

"He's the missing crew member," Jacob said.

"What's this all about?" Anne said.

"There's still one set of fingerprints on the Christmas lights that I can't identify," Burr said.

"What difference does it make? The judge won't let you admit them anyway," Anne said.

"He will if they're given voluntarily," Burr said.

"If this Ronnie Cross really is the murderer, he'll never let you take his fingerprints," Martha said.

Jacob picked an imaginary dog hair off his slacks.

CHAPTER TWENTY-TWO

Burr tapped his pencil. Murdo was next to him, then Jacob. All was as it should be. Henry Crow announced the entrance of the Honorable Arvid Lindstrom.

This is what we've all been waiting for.

Burr stood. He pulled the cuffs of his shirt down. "The defense calls Anne Halverson." Burr looked over at Anne, demure, just as he asked. She looked at him but didn't get up. "The defense calls Anne Halverson," he said again. Anne sat. Burr bent down to Murdo. "What the hell is going on?"

"I have no idea."

Burr stepped to the rail. "Anne, let's go." She looked at him again but made no effort to stand.

"Your Honor," said a voice from the gallery. "Roy Dahlberg here, counsel for Anne Halverson." Burr looked back at the voice, which now made its way to the bench.

Damn it all.

Dahlberg stopped next to Burr. Roy Dahlberg of Dahlberg and Langley. The Ford family's lawyers and the Halversons' lawyers as well. They knew all the judges, all the politicians, everyone worth knowing. Roy Dahlberg, the patrician's patrician. Mid-sixties. Medium build. Silver hair. Tan, lined face. Charcoal suit with a pencil-thin white pinstripe. White shirt. Gray silk tie. French cuffs and gold cufflinks. That's what you paid for when you hired him.

Burr had sparred with Dahlberg in his prior life. Many times. Burr had represented parts suppliers that Ford didn't want to pay. Burr won most of the time, but he'd certainly met his match with Roy Dahlberg.

"What is it?" Lindstrom said, annoyed.

"Your Honor, my client chooses not to testify," Dahlberg said.

"What are you talking about?" Burr said.

"My client chooses not to testify," Dahlberg said again.

What the hell is going on?

"Your client has been served a subpoena. She has no choice," Burr said.

"Mr. Lafayette, I am the judge here." Lindstrom looked at Dahlberg. "Having said that, Mr. Lafayette is quite right. She may avail herself of all her constitutional rights including the Fifth Amendment, but she must testify."

"May I approach the bench, Your Honor?" Dahlberg said.

Lindstrom sighed, "You might as well."

Dahlberg, flanked by Burr and Karpinen, stood in front of Lindstrom.

"Your Honor," Dahlberg said, "as you know, the law recognizes a privilege between a husband and a wife that, when asserted, permits them not to testify against each other."

"Mr. Dahlberg is quite right, Your Honor," Burr said, "but the privilege may be waived. My client, Mr. Halverson, waives the privilege and requests his wife to testify."

Lindstrom nodded. "For once, I agree with you. You may call Mrs. Halverson."

"Respectfully, Your Honor," Dahlberg said, "the privilege does not belong to Mr. Halverson. The privilege belongs to the witness. Mrs. Halverson is the witness and she claims the privilege."

"Mr. Dahlberg is correct, Your Honor," Karpinen said. "The privilege belongs to Mrs. Halverson."

"You have no idea what the law is. You just don't want Anne Halverson to be a witness and ruin your trumped-up case," Burr said.

"Mrs. Halverson has the puck," Karpinen said.

If he says one more thing about hockey, I'll be the one on trial for murder.

"Your Honor, the legislature thought this issue important enough that they codified it." The silk-stockinged lawyer just happened to have a certain brown, hardbound book right in his hand. "May I?" Lindstrom nodded.

"I quote from Subsection 2 of Section 2162 of the Revised Judicature Act." Dahlberg cleared his throat. "In a criminal prosecution, a husband shall not be examined as a witness for or against his wife without his consent or a wife for or against her husband without her consent." Dahlberg slammed the book shut. "It's clear from the statute that the privilege belongs to the witness. In this case, Mrs. Halverson."

"That is not what it says," Burr said.

"Of course that's what it says," Karpinen said.

"I wasn't aware you could read," Burr said.

"Do you have anything constructive to say, Mr. Lafayette?" Lindstrom said.

"Your Honor, the statute is clear," Burr said. "The privilege belongs to the defendant. In this case, Mr. Halverson. He's the one on trial. There is no reason for a witness to have the privilege."

Lindstrom nodded again. "Very good point, Mr. Lafayette. You may call Mrs. Halverson."

"Your Honor, that's not what the statute says. In fact, that is the opposite of what the statute says," Dahlberg said.

"Did you hear me, Mr. Dahlberg?" Lindstrom said.

"Your Honor," Karpinen said, "this is a matter of law and if, by chance, you are not correct, there could be a mistrial and we'd have to start all over again."

Lindstrom grimaced. "The court will take this matter under advisement. We will reconvene tomorrow at 10 a.m."

"Your Honor, tomorrow is Saturday," Karpinen said.

"Monday then. Monday at ten." Lindstrom held out his hand and Dahlberg passed him the book.

Lindstrom dismissed them. Dahlberg turned to leave, but Burr grabbed him by the arm, just above the elbow.

"I beg your pardon." He jerked his arm free.

"What the hell is going on?"

"I'm going to talk with my client."

"Anne's the reason I'm going to get Murdo acquitted. Without her, I don't have a prayer."

"Burr, you underestimate yourself. You've done a great job. Anne's testimony won't be necessary."

"That's not for you to say."

"It's not for me to say, but it is for my client to say."

"For God's sake, Dahlberg, I need her as a witness." Burr ran his hands through his hair. "What on earth is going on?

"If Lindstrom rules in your favor, you'll have Anne as a witness."

Burr looked over at Murdo, still sitting at his chair in the now empty courtroom. "Did you know about this?"

"Not until now," Murdo said.

"How could you do this? You've just guaranteed that Murdo will be convicted of murder." Burr looked at Murdo, then back at Dahlberg.

"Listen to me, Lafayette," Dahlberg said. "Let's assume that Anne does testify, and let's further assume that she does a bang-up job and gives Murdo an alibi. What then?"

"What then?" Burr said. "What then is, we win."

"Not necessarily. Because Karpinen is going to cross-examine her."

"Of course, he will. And all she has to do is tell the truth."

"Which is precisely the problem," Dahlberg said. "Because Karpinen will ask her about the affair. About the Townsend. About that night at The Pink Pony. And God knows what else. And that, my friend, will unravel your entire case. It's too big a risk."

"Anne doesn't have to answer those questions. She can take the Fifth."

"That will make it look worse."

"I'm Murdo's lawyer. It's my call."

"That's exactly what Anne said you'd say. That's why she hired me and why she didn't tell Murdo. He's upset enough as it is. Understandably so. You've done more than enough to establish reasonable doubt. All you need is a good closing argument." Dahlberg started to leave, then turned back to Burr. "Have a grand weekend."

* * *

Burr, Jacob and Eve took M-134 east from St. Ignace. About five miles out of town, Burr pulled into the Acorn, eight cabins more or less in a row, all equally rundown, across from Lake Huron in the middle of a stand of sixty-foot oaks. The Acorn's most important feature wasn't the view of the lake or the oak trees. It was next door to Art's Tavern.

Burr had told his myopic expert not to bring any of his glaucoma cigarettes across the bridge and into the less than progressive U.P., but he knew Mueller would need a nip so he'd put him up within walking distance of a bar.

Burr parked in front of cabin Number 4. An acorn fell on the hood of the Jeep. Burr got out and knocked on the door. Stanley Mueller answered.

"Aren't you supposed to be in court?" Mueller said, his eyes somewhere behind his glasses.

"I just lost my star witness."

"Don't look at me," Mueller went back inside. They followed him in. Mueller picked up the *St. Ignace News* off his bed, sat in a sagging easy chair and opened the paper.

"Why do you think I'm paying you to stay here?" Burr said.

"Because you don't have any money. This is the worst place ever." Mueller tossed the newspaper on the bed.

"It's next to Art's Tavern."

"True." Mueller stumbled over to a metal table with rusty legs next to the refrigerator and a hot plate. He had papers spread over the table. Mueller rummaged through them. "Come over here." Burr walked to the table. "These are from the lights." They were full of whirls, whorls and smudges. Mostly smudges.

Burr still didn't see how anyone could identify them, which was exactly Karpinen's point.

"These are the ones that match the widow and her lawyer." Muller picked up another piece of paper. "I still don't know who these belong to." He shuffled through the pile and picked up another one. "This one belongs to the kid next door, whatever his name is."

"Ronnie Cross," Jacob said.

"His prints don't match the prints on the lights," Mueller said.

"So, he wasn't there and he's not the killer," Eve said.

"All it means is that his prints aren't on the lights. He may have been there, and he may have killed Jimmy," Burr said.

Mueller went back to his newspaper. Burr and his entourage walked to cabin Number 5. Burr knocked on the door. No answer. He knocked again. "Are you sure this is his room?"

"This is where I left him," Jacob said.

Burr knocked again. The door opened a crack.

"Ronnie?" Burr said.

"Who are you?"

"Burr Lafayette." Silence. "The lawyer." More silence. "Jacob Wertheim's partner."

"Oh."

"Can we come in?"

"I'm sleeping."

"It's almost noon," Burr said.

"I'm in college."

"My client is on trial for murder."

"I'm not dressed."

"Ronnie, I'm going to count to three and then we're coming in. All three of us. One of whom is a woman." Ronnie walked away. He left the door open and in they went. Ronnie sat on the bed in a pair of plaid boxer shorts. He was at least six-three with broad shoulders, a small waist, and what was left of a tan.

Handsome. That was really all that was necessary to say about him. Big, strong and handsome. Wheat-colored hair and the same green eyes that Anne had. Eve couldn't keep her eyes off him. For that matter, neither could Jacob.

"Do you want to get dressed?"

"I'm good," Ronnie said.

"Your fingerprints don't match the lights," Burr said.

"I told him they wouldn't."

"You could still be the murderer," Burr said.

"I didn't have any reason to kill Jimmy. We were friends."

Burr was thinking that all this Ronnie Cross business had been a colossal waste of time. Not to mention money. But he thought he might as well keep going. "What was your job on *Fujimo*?"

"I did the pit some. Mostly I was a grinder."

Why is everyone keeping you such a secret?"

"I didn't know they were."

"Come on, Ronnie. You're the most top-secret grinder I ever met."

"I don't know why."

"How about this? You spend the weekend here in cabin Number 5 as my guest? Jacob will pick you up bright and early Monday morning and you can come to court and watch Murdoch Halverson be convicted of murder."

"I have class on Monday."

"I'll get you a tutor."

* * *

Saturday dawned crisp and clear, a stiff wind from the north.

It's a fine day for football.

Burr's bike had frost on the handlebars, but it had melted off by the time he reached Aerie. He walked up the sidewalk, past the garden that had the annuals, now replanted with mums in yellow, orange, purple and burnt red.

Anne answered Burr's knock, then tried to shut the door in his face. Burr stuck his foot in the door.

If I'm not careful, I'm going to lose another toenail.

"I don't have anything to say to you."

"What happened to Anne with an *e*?" Burr said to the formerly perky Anne of July.

"She's not here." Anne pushed on the door. "Take your foot out of the way."

Burr pushed the door open. He stood toe-to-toe with her in the foyer, but he still couldn't get all the way in. "You have to testify. We don't have a chance without you."

"Yes, you do. Roy says you do."

"Murdo's defense is based on your alibi. I need you to testify."

"Roy says it's too risky."

Murdo peered over Anne's shoulders. They wore matching maize and blue sweaters.

"Murdo agrees. Don't you, Murdo?"

Anne let go of the door and Burr literally fell into her arms. She pushed him away and shook her hair out of her face, like Murdo.

Burr looked at Murdo. "I need Anne to testify for you."

Murdo put his arm around Anne's waist. "She's not going to testify."

"Where's your mother?"

"She's the one who called Roy." He disappeared into the house, Anne at his heels.

* * *

At Horn's, Burr nursed a Labatt and watched the television over the bar. He'd just finished his second Bloody Mary, and the beer chaser took the edge off the Tabasco. The battle for the Paul Bunyan Trophy and the state of Michigan was going the Spartans' way. Then Michigan scored, giving them the lead at the end of the third quarter.

"Damn it all."

He looked out the window and watched a street cleaner shuffle by. He finished his beer and bolted out the door.

* * *

Burr found Chief Brandstatter at the jail, legs propped up on his desk, watching a black and white portable television with rabbit ears. A piece of aluminum foil was twisted around one of the ears.

"Don't bother me. This is the only peace I get."

"Chief, I only have one question."

"Come back after the game." Brandstatter turned back to the television. "Michigan's going to win this one. I can feel it."

Burr stood in front of the television.

"Get out of the way."

"One question," Burr said.

"Forget it." Brandstatter started to get up.

"How about if I just put my foot through it," Burr said.

"You do that, and I'll arrest you."

"You've been trying to do that for the past three months."

"What is it?"

* * *

Burr pedaled past the stables, the dump and into the Settlement, the only subdivision on the island, the houses modest, most of them less than modest, and where the year-round residents live.

He rang the doorbell of a small, white, single-story, painted over where the paint had peeled, been scraped, and painted over again. No one answered. He rang again. Still no answer. He started back down the sidewalk.

"The doorbell don't work." Burr turned around. A short, skinny man stood in the doorway. "You got to knock." Burr started back to the house. "Come back later. This is one helluva game."

"Burr Lafayette," he said, sticking his hand out. "Are you Sidney Ravenswood?"

He nodded. "I ain't told that sheriff nothin'. Not yet, anyways."

Ravenswood had an egg- shaped face with fine features, blond hair and clear blue eyes that, unfortunately for Burr, had seen too much.

"Are you a street cleaner?"

"It don't matter to me that you stole the pony. Happens all the time. Them sailors are the worst, and it's too expensive at The Pony. I can get a beer and a shot for two bucks at The Mustang." Sidney scratched his chin. "It was pretty damn funny when you hoisted it up that flagpole down at the docks." Sidney laughed. "I was just minding my own business, cleaning up after the horses, I ain't told Brandstatter nothin' yet, but he's got me on a couple of things. So, I don't know if I can keep mum forever. I got to finish up the game." He went back in the house. Burr followed him in.

* * *

"That was one helluva football game," Mueller said. He opened the door for Burr. "I got 'em, but it cost me a hundred bucks." Mueller went back into his room.

Burr followed him in. Mueller sat in the sagging easy chair. Burr pulled up a chair from the table. "What happened?"

"The janitor caught me, but he looked the other way for the hundred."

"Did you get a match?" Burr said.

"I did, and I'm passing the cost on to you."

I don't think I'll be able to put this on my bill.

* * *

Burr found Toad on *Fujimo*. He had a fire going in the charcoal fireplace. It was about the size of a toaster, but it took the chill off. Toad was tucked into a down-filled sleeping bag and not too happy to see Burr. Toad took a half-smoked joint out of an ashtray and lit up.

"Don't even think of passing that over here," Burr said, but if past was prologue, he was going to get a buzz just sitting there.

"I've done everything you wanted me to do. Leave me alone."

"There's just one more thing," Burr said.

"Whatever it is, the answer is no."

"Toad, why do all of you want to keep Ronnie out of this? What's the big deal?"

"It's not a big deal."

Burr looked out the porthole onto another beautiful fall day on Mackinac Island. "If it's no big deal, then why go to all the trouble? What are you protecting Jimmy from? He's dead."

"I know he's dead, but he was good to me."

"Are you willing to let Murdo get convicted of murder because Jimmy Lyons was good to you?"

"He paid me to race with him, watch his boat, and keep it clean."

"Come on, Toad."

Toad blew the joint back to life. Smoke filled the cabin. Burr opened the hatch.

"It's cold in here."

"You're in a down-filled sleeping bag. You can't possibly be cold." Burr stuck his head out the hatch and sucked in a breath of crisp October air. He sat on the bunk across from Toad. "Here's what I think. Jimmy lived large. He spent a lot of money. Money that he didn't have. So, he invited his creditors, including Murdo, on the race. To buy himself some time, smooth things out. Maybe make a deal. But you know what else? I think Jimmy was a man of large appetites. Very large appetites."

Toad didn't say anything.

"Let's say sexual appetites. And let's say that Jimmy was having an affair with Anne." Burr paused. "But you know what I think? I think Ronnie was, let's say, Ronnie was Jimmy's special friend."

Toad cringed.

"I've got it right, don't I? And let's say that maybe Murdo was also Jimmy's special friend. And maybe Jimmy's ego was big enough, and maybe he was a big enough fool to invite both of them on *Fujimo*. And let's just say Murdo's jealous. Jimmy blew him off in the bar. Murdo was drunk, and he killed him. That's what you think, isn't it? You don't care if Karpinen has the wrong reason as long as he has the right guy."

Toad pulled the sleeping bag over his head.

* * *

Burr sat across sat across from Carole at the Village Inn, the only restaurant still open that served wine with corks instead of screw-off caps. The candle-light picked up the highlights in her hair. She had on the fall version of the little black dress with a scoop neck and a gold necklace.

The waiter uncorked the second bottle of Bordeaux and poured them each a glass. The wine hadn't opened up and tasted like pennies. She reached under the table and put her hand on his knee.

"Did you see anything going on at Jimmy's table that night? Anything odd or peculiar?"

"I thought this was going to be a romantic dinner."

"It is," Burr said, although he knew it wasn't going to be.

Carole looked so good that he was afraid he'd lose his nerve. The waiter came back and started to tell them about the specials. Burr waved him off. Carole gave him a *what's going on?* look.

"I thought you said that, when you came in the morning after Jimmy was killed, that the doors were locked."

"What's all this about?"

"You did say that, didn't you?"

"Burr, please, we're having such a good time."

"We are, aren't we? You said the doors were locked, but they weren't, were they?" Burr took a sip of his wine. It was opening up nicely.

Here goes.

"Do you know who Sidney Ravenswood is?" She gave him a blank look. "Of course, you don't. Do you know what he saw that night?"

"Stop it." She looked into her glass but didn't drink.

"Of course, you don't," he said again. "He's a street cleaner. A lowly street cleaner. Do you know what he saw?"

"Is this some kind of a mystery?"

"That's what I'd like to know." He swirled the Bordeaux in his glass and took another sip. *Much better.*

"Sidney Ravenswood told me that he saw someone going into The Pink Pony from the street that night. After it closed. But if Karen Vander Voort locked the doors, how could that be?"

"She must have locked the doors after that." Carole picked up her glass but didn't drink.

"Carole, dear, what's really unfortunate for you is that you testified under oath that the doors were locked. But they weren't."

She set her glass down.

"So, Carole, you may be a suspect. At the very least you committed perjury."

"The doors were locked. I swear it."

Burr rolled his eyes. "You lied under oath, which could get you five years." Actually, he didn't think Carole could be charged with anything, but he didn't think she knew that. "Tell me what really happened. Then we can keep going with our wonderful evening."

Fat chance.

"The doors were locked when I came in."

"I love it when you lie."

"That's the truth. I swear it."

"I'm sure you didn't kill Jimmy, but if you don't tell me why you lied about the doors, I'm going to make it very painful." Burr put his hands on the table and folded them. Carole didn't say a word. Neither did Burr.

The first one who says something loses.

Carole drank. Burr drank. Again and again. Burr waved off the waiter twice.

Finally, Carole said, "After the bar closes, it's the bartender's job to lock up. But you know that. When I came in the next morning, the doors weren't locked." She brushed a hair off her forehead. "I went in the bar, and that's when I saw Jimmy."

"And?"

"And then I locked up."

"And?"

"And what?"

"And what about Karen Vander Voort? At the preliminary exam, she said she'd locked the doors."

"I didn't want her or the hotel to get in trouble, so I went along with it."

"That's a lot of trouble for a couple of doors that weren't locked."

"It sounds terrible now, but at the time it didn't seem like a big deal."

"So, you lied to me to protect Karen and the hotel."

"I didn't really lie."

"What exactly would you call it?"

"We have such a nice thing going."

"Who paid you to get rid of Karen?"

If he had her, she didn't let on.

She slapped him and walked out.

* * *

"I didn't expect to see you tonight," Eve said. "Lover's quarrel?"

"You could say that."

Eve had a fire going and was wrapped up in a blanket on the couch. She had a book for a date and didn't look especially glad to see him. Zeke, who had been napping in front of the fireplace, was glad to see him.

"What is it this time?"

Burr told her what happened.

Eve closed her book. "You're a fool for a pretty woman."

Burr sat down in a leather chair next to the fire. Zeke lay down at his feet.

"Is she telling the truth?"

"Not all of it."

CHAPTER TWENTY-THREE

"All rise," Henry Crow said.

"Counsel, approach the bench," Lindstrom said.

Burr, Dahlberg, and Karpinen stood in front of Lindstrom like ducks in a row.

"Mr. Lafayette, I trust you had a pleasant weekend," Lindstrom said, bright and shiny as a new penny.

"I did indeed, Your Honor."

"Really? In spite of the fact that your team lost?"

"My team won, Your Honor."

"I thought you were a Michigan lawyer."

"That's right, Your Honor, but I went to Michigan State for undergrad."

Lindstrom scowled at him, his penny tarnished. "Let me get right to the point. I've reviewed the statutes as they relate to privilege, and I find that Mr. Dahlberg is quite right. The privilege extends to the spouse who claims it. The court finds that the marital privilege extends to Anne Halverson, and she cannot be compelled to testify."

Karpinen looked at Burr. "Open-net goal."

Lindstrom peered over his glasses at Burr. "You may proceed."

Burr looked out in the gallery. He had asked Aunt Kitty to make sure she sat next to Martha for the grand finale. Then, "Your Honor, the defense calls Sidney Ravenswood."

Ravenswood looked like a street sweeper ready to go to church. The bailiff swore him in.

"Please tell us what you were doing at three a.m. on the morning after the first Port Huron boats came in."

Ravenswood fussed with his tie. "I was cleaning up after everybody. Like I always do."

"And where were you?"

"Just down the street from The Pink Pony. Across from the docks."

"Did you see anything happen at or near The Pink Pony?"

"Well, by that time of night, all the bars was closed and most of the drunks was gone. On race night, they're roaming around longer, but it was pretty quiet by then. But I seen this guy go in The Pony from the street door. Which isn't supposed to happen 'cause the bars was all closed by then. Then I got all caught up in the horse manure and I forgot all about it."

"Really?" Burr said.

"I already told you this."

Ravenswood wasn't much of a witness, but he was all Burr had, and Burr thought the street sweeper was believable. "Can you identify the man you saw go into The Pink Pony?"

"That's him over there, the guy with the hair all puffed out like a lion." Ravenswood pointed at Lionel Worthy. The courtroom went *aahh*.

"For the record," Burr said, "Mr. Ravenswood is pointing at Lionel Worthy."

"Have you seen him since then?"

"Not until today."

"Thank you, Mr. Ravenswood. I have no further questions." Burr looked at Karpinen on the way back to the defense table. "The puck is in your end."

Karpinen walked up to the street sweeper. "Mr. Ravenswood, do you have a drinking problem?"

"Not that I know of," Ravenswood said.

"I think we may have met before," Karpinen said. "In fact, I believe I was the prosecuting attorney when you pled guilty to public intoxication. Which means drunkenness. Three separate times."

Ravenswood didn't say a word.

"Were you drinking the night you said you saw Mr. Worthy?"

"I never drink on the job."

"Mr. Ravenswood, did you see Mr. Lafayette the night that you said you saw Mr. Worthy?"

"I did see that guy over there," Ravenswood pointed at Worthy again.

"So you said." Then Karpinen pointed at Burr. "Did you see Mr. Lafayette?"

"Yeah."

"What was he doing?"

Burr jumped up. "Your Honor, this is irrelevant. My whereabouts has nothing to do with anything."

"Your whereabouts are always of interest to me, Mr. Lafayette," Lindstrom said. "I'll allow it."

"Thank you, Your Honor," Karpinen said. "Mr. Ravenswood, did you see Mr. Lafayette outside The Pink Pony on the night you say you saw Mr. Worthy?"

"Yeah, I guess so."

"And what was he doing?"

"He was walking around."

"Mr. Ravenswood, we need to get beyond the faceoff."

"What's all this hockey business about?"

Karpinen stood up as straight as his bum leg would allow. "Hockey is a metaphor for life."

Ravenswood looked at Karpinen like the prosecutor was the one with the drinking problem.

"Never mind," Karpinen said. "Mr. Ravenswood, did you see Mr. Lafayette steal the pink pony that was hanging in front of the bar?"

"I saw him take it down, if that's what you mean."

"And what did he do with it?"

"He took it down to the docks and hoisted it up the flagpole." Ravenswood snickered. The courtroom roared. Burr groaned. Brandstatter smiled like the Cheshire cat.

How could a murder trial get to this point?

"Quiet." Lindstrom banged his gavel. "Mr. Ravenswood, there is nothing funny about stealing."

"It looked pretty funny to me," Sidney Ravenswood said. He snickered again, as did the gallery. Karpinen turned around and glared at the courtroom. "I have no further questions, Your Honor."

"The defense calls Carole Hennessey," Burr said. Lindstrom reminded her that she was still under oath. The late morning sun from the window highlighted the blond highlights in her auburn hair. Burr went right for the kill. "How much did Mr. Worthy pay you to send Karen Vander Voort away?"

Carole looked at him, but she didn't say anything.

"Ms. Hennessey, I asked you a question."

Carole looked down at her hands.

"Ms. Hennessey, how much did Mr. Worthy pay you to send Karen Vander Voort away?"

"He didn't pay me."

"I see." Burr put his hands in his pants pockets. "You are aware that you could go to jail for lying under oath?"

"Objection, Your Honor. Counsel is threatening the witness," Karpinen said.

Burr started in again before Lindstrom could rule. "It will be a simple matter to find out, Ms. Hennessey."

"Stop it, counsel," Lindstrom said.

"How much?" he said.

Carole didn't say anything. Neither did Burr. He looked out the window at the maple tree. There were still a few leaves hanging on for dear life. He looked back at Carole. "Ms. Hennessey, why would Mr. Worthy pay you to get rid of Ms. Vander Voort?"

"I didn't say he did."

"No, you didn't, but if he did pay you, why would he?"

"I object, Your Honor. This is sheer speculation," Karpinen said.

"Sustained," Lindstrom said. "Mr. Lafayette, you are treading on thin ice."

"Yes, Your Honor," Burr said. "Ms. Hennessey, let me review the bidding. You said Mr. Worthy didn't pay you and you don't know why he would. Am I right so far?" Carole still didn't say anything. "The silence is deafening."

If I didn't ruin it last night, I am now.

"Ms. Hennessey, if you don't tell me how much Mr. Worthy paid you, I am going to subpoena your bank records."

Karpinen jumped to his feet. "Objection, Your Honor."

Burr kept going. "How much?"

"Objection." Karpinen jumped up and down.

"How much?" Burr said again.

"Five-thousand dollars."

"I have no further questions," Burr said.

Karpinen asked Carole a few questions, but the damage had been done.

Burr called Lionel Worthy.

I'm going to win or lose right here.

"Mr. Worthy, on the night of July 17th, why did you go into The Pink Pony after it closed?"

"I didn't go into The Pink Pony," Worthy said.

He's awfully matter of fact.

"Mr. Ravenswood said he saw you go in after it closed. How do you explain that?"

"He's mistaken."

"Mr. Ravenswood testified under oath that he saw you go into The Pink Pony." Burr looked behind him at Ravenswood, then back at Worthy. "Which one of you is lying?" Worthy didn't say a word. "I asked you a question."

"Objection, Your Honor," Karpinen said. "Asked and answered."

"Sustained," Lindstrom said.

"Mr. Worthy, how do you explain the fact that your fingerprints were found on the Christmas lights?"

Karpinen bolted to his feet. "Objection, Your Honor," Karpinen said. "That evidence has already been ruled inadmissible."

"Lafayette, this is an outrage." Lindstrom wagged his gavel at him. "If you bring this up one more time, I will eject you once and for all. Is that clear?"

Burr did his best to look contrite. "Yes, Your Honor."

Lindstrom addressed the jury. "You will disregard Mr. Lafayette's last question."

"Mr. Worthy, how much did you pay Ms. Hennessey to send Karen Vander Voort away?" Worthy flinched, not much, but he flinched.

"I didn't pay her anything."

"About five minutes ago, Ms. Hennessey testified that you paid her five-thousand dollars to send her away."

"I did no such thing," Worthy said.

"Mr. Worthy," Burr put his hands in his pockets and rocked back and forth, heel to toe. "Mr. Ravenswood testified that he saw you go into The Pink Pony after it closed. At about the time Mr. Lyons was killed." Burr stopped rocking and glared at Worthy. "And Ms. Hennessey has testified that you paid her five-thousand dollars to send Karen Vander Voort away. What do you say to that?"

"I did no such thing," Worthy said again. He flinched again. Still not much of a flinch but enough for the jury to notice.

This is it.

"Mr. Worthy, you're now between a rock and a hard place." Worthy sat there like the rock. "The way I see it, you're either guilty of perjury or murder." Burr looked over at the jury. They didn't much care for Worthy. "Either way, you go to jail. Which is it? Perjury or murder?"

Worthy reached in his jacket pocket and took out his cigarettes. He studied the red and white pack of Pall Malls. He turned it over in his hand. Then he put it back in his pocket. He turned red but didn't say boo. But he was clearly rattled.

"Which is it, Mr. Worthy? Perjury or murder?"

Silence.

"I'm going to ask you one more time. Did you pay Carole Hennessy to send Karen Vander Voort away?"

More silence.

"Your Honor, please compel Mr. Worthy to answer the question."

Lindstrom looked down at Worthy. "Answer the question."

Worthy sat. And sat. And sat. Finally, "I exercise my Fifth Amendment rights."

"And why is that?" Burr looked at the jury, then back at Worthy. "Because answering the question might incriminate you?"

"No," Worthy said.

"No, what, Mr. Worthy?"

"No, I did not commit perjury or murder."

Worthy was regaining his composure. Burr knew he had to finish before Worthy put himself back together. "Mr. Worthy, did you do these things on your own or did someone pay you to do them?"

"All of my actions are protected by attorney-client privilege."

"So, someone did pay you?"

"No one paid me."

"So, you did these things on your own."

"I didn't say that."

"I'm sorry, Mr. Worthy, but I thought that was exactly what you said." Burr turned to Lindstrom. "Your Honor, I believe that Mr. Worthy strangled Mr. Lyons in The Pink Pony during the early morning hours of July 18th. I request the court order that Mr. Worthy's fingerprints be taken."

"Objection, Your Honor," Karpinen said. "Mr. Worthy is not on trial here."

"He's about to be," Burr said.

Lindstrom pointed his gavel at Burr. "Mr. Lafayette, you are without a doubt the most combative attorney I have ever had the misfortune to have in my courtroom." Lindstrom pointed his gavel at Worthy. "And you, sir, are the most belligerent witness I have ever had." Lindstrom pointed his gavel back at Burr. "Mr. Lafayette, in the interest of justice, I am inclined to grant your request."

Burr exhaled. "Thank you, Your Honor." He turned to Worthy. "Just to review, you have claimed attorney-client privilege. You have taken the Fifth Amendment. And your fingerprints are about to be taken. Let me ask you one more question. Were you with anyone after the bar closed that night?" Worthy didn't say anything. "Mr. Worthy, were you with anyone after the bar closed?"

"I don't remember."

Bingo.

"Mr. Worthy, why did you kill Mr. Lyons?"

"I didn't kill him. I swear I didn't. I was outside on the street after the bar closed and I saw Anne Halverson go into the bar from the sidewalk. I waited for a few minutes. Then I went in."

Burr thought this was all going a little too fast, but he decided to let Worthy finish.

"When I got inside the bar, I saw Jimmy sitting on a chair with the Christmas lights wrapped around his neck. She was strangling him." Worthy pointed at Anne.

* * *

Karpinen didn't question Worthy, not that Worthy would have said anything anyway. Lindstrom called for closing arguments. Karpinen laid out his proofs. He did his best to discredit Worthy's testimony as unreliable. He outlined the elements of murder and called for the jury to convict Murdo of first-degree murder.

Burr told the jury that there were any number of possible murderers, each of whom had a motive. All of Jimmy's creditors. Jane and, of course, the villain *du jour*, Lionel Worthy. Burr didn't use Worthy's testimony to incriminate Anne but rather to show that Worthy was lying to save his own skin. He said that there wasn't enough to convict Murdo beyond a reasonable doubt. It wasn't even close.

Lindstrom instructed the jury on the ins and outs of murder and sent them off to deliberate.

After Lindstrom dismissed them, Burr and company met with the Halversons underneath Burr's maple tree. Burr looked up through the branches. He counted seven leaves hanging on for dear life.

Murdo flipped his hair off his face. "I can't fathom how any juror in their right mind could convict me, but did you have to do it at Anne's expense?"

Burr watched one of the leaves fall off the tree. He looked at Murdo. "I had no idea that Worthy would say that. He was desperate to save himself."

"We were together the whole night," Anne said.

Of course, you were.

"Carole, Ravenswood and Worthy wouldn't have been necessary if you would have let me call you as a witness."

"I don't want to be the next one tried for murder."

"I don't think anyone thinks you killed Jimmy, and I'm sure Karpinen doesn't," Burr said.

"You didn't have to humiliate me."

"Jimmy Lyons is dead. Murdo is as good as acquitted and you're worried about being humiliated?"

"What do we do now?" said Martha.

"Now we wait," Burr said.

CHAPTER TWENTY-FOUR

Burr, Jacob, Eve and Aunt Kitty sat in front of a fire at Windward. Zeke lay in front of the fireplace. They were all drinking martinis, except for Jacob, who was drinking tea. Burr wasn't celebrating yet. As far as he was concerned, this was just another cocktail hour.

Martha Halverson arrived by carriage twenty minutes later, unannounced. Burr answered the door.

"May we speak alone?" she said.

"Come join us in the living room."

"I should fire you on the spot," she said, hissing.

"You could, but your precious Murdo hasn't been acquitted yet." He led her into the living room and seated her in one of the wingback chairs. It was the most throne-like chair he could find. "A martini? Cognac?"

"Cognac," she said.

"I'd like one, too," Aunt Kitty said.

Burr poured their cognacs. Martha set hers on the table beside her.

I wonder what the queen of screw machines has on her mind?

Martha raised her glass. "To justice."

Burr raised his glass. "To an acquittal."

"You've certainly done enough to acquit my son. In spite of what you did to Anne." She looked at Aunt Kitty, then at Burr. "I hired you to prove my son didn't kill Jimmy Lyons. I didn't hire you to find out who did. There is a difference."

There surely is.

Martha stood. "Would you mind terribly coming over for a few minutes. We'd like to have a private conversation."

"How about tomorrow?"

"There's a check waiting for you."

"We haven't heard the verdict yet," Burr said, immediately wishing he hadn't.

It's never too soon to get paid.

"We have confidence in you." Martha started to the door. "You can ride with me."

* * *

Burr pedaled on the trail that ran through the woods to the fort, Zeke just behind him. Riding in a carriage with Martha was more than he could stand, but if there was a check waiting for him at Aerie, he could put up with whatever they had to say.

The moon ducked in and out of the clouds, but there was just enough light to see the trail. The leaves crunched under his tires. He smelled the cedars. He saw the water below him through the trees. "Zeke, we may have to take Main Street back."

"I have a flashlight you can use."

He skidded to a stop.

"Anne, how nice to see you. I was just on my way to Aerie."

"I know."

"I was expecting you. But not here."

"I thought we might talk about what happened at The Pink Pony."

Burr climbed off his bike. Anne shined the flashlight in his eyes.

"You've done all you needed to do to acquit Murdo."

Burr took a step to his right, but Anne kept the light in his eyes.

"It was a great performance on your part, but you went too far. I didn't hire that awful Lionel Worthy to do anything."

"You didn't hire him. He blackmailed you."

"He did no such thing."

"Jimmy and Murdo were lovers. I think Worthy was blackmailing Jimmy, but he needed a new client once Jimmy was killed. That's where you came in."

"Nonsense." She kept the light on his eyes.

He took a step toward her. "Worthy didn't care who killed Jimmy. He just wanted a new fish. Maybe he saw you standing over Jimmy. Maybe he didn't. I think he thought Murdo killed Jimmy and you found him after he was dead."

"That's exactly what happened."

Burr took a step. "That's not how it happened. You saw Jimmy and Murdo making eyes at each other in the bar and it made you wild. That's why you sat on his lap. You loved Jimmy, too. God knows why. You were jealous because Jimmy liked Murdo more than he liked you. It was Murdo and Jimmy at the Townsend. Not you and Jimmy." Burr tried to see the expression on Anne's face, but the flashlight was still in his eyes.

He took another step.

"The two of them snuck back into the bar after it closed. Buehler was right about that. Is that when you decided not to testify? After you heard what he said? Because you thought Buehler might have seen you? Is that when you panicked?"

Another step.

"Because Karen Vander Voort, wherever she is, forgot to lock the door."

One more step.

"Did you catch them, Anne? Is that when Murdo ran out the back door? Did Jimmy make fun of you? Or was he just not interested?"

He could almost reach the flashlight.

"Murdo didn't kill Jimmy because he was jealous of you. You killed Jimmy because you were jealous of Murdo."

One more step and he could take the flashlight from her.

"That's why you wouldn't testify. I was getting too close to the truth. So, you decided to sacrifice Murdo. You're such a loving wife."

Burr lunged for the flashlight. Anne jumped away from him, but at least the flashlight wasn't in his eyes.

"You can't prove it."

"Your fingerprints are on the lights."

"No, they're not."

"Stanley Mueller says they are."

"So are everyone else's on Mackinac Island."

"Mueller got them from the courtroom yesterday. Where you always sit."

She pulled a pistol out of her jacket and pointed it at him.

"Come on, Anne. Isn't this a bit dramatic? Does Martha know? I'm sure she's suspicious."

"Keep this between us, and I'll make it worth your while."

"Put the gun away. I'm on my way to Aerie. But you knew that. Is

Martha in on this? How about your husband? My guess is he's your husband in name only."

Burr edged closer.

"If you take another step, I'll kill you."

"Just like Jimmy?"

"He shouldn't have made fun of me. We were just playing around until he made fun of me."

"So, you strangled him."

"I didn't mean to. At first." She kept the pistol on him. "There were so many people who had a reason to kill Jimmy. No one will ever believe it was me."

Clouds passed in front of the moon, and what little light there was in the woods was gone.

"Don't move," Anne said.

"You're not going to shoot me. You're in the clear. Why get caught now?"

"I won't get caught. This is Worthy's gun."

"Your fingerprints are on it. Just like the lights."

"I think I'll start with your dog." She pointed the pistol at Zeke and fired. Burr lunged at her, but she ducked underneath him. She turned and fired again, at Burr this time. He leapt at her but missed. The moon peeked out from behind the clouds. She was holding the gun with both hands, pointing it at him. "This could all have been so easy."

"Anne, that's quite enough." Anne turned to the sound of the voice. Burr jumped at her and knocked the pistol out of her hands.

* * *

"All rise," Henry Crow said. Lindstrom entered from his chambers. "Be seated," the bailiff said.

Lindstrom addressed the jury. "Have you reached a verdict?"

"We have," Mrs. Gunthorpe, the foreman, said.

"The defendant will stand," Lindstrom said. Murdo stood and faced his twelve peers. He had on a winter-weight black suit with red and white pinstripes, a starched white shirt and a royal-blue tie with red diamonds. Anne, eye-popping in a belted, black wool dress with a scoop neck and a silver necklace. A stunning, if unhappy, couple.

I guess the dress code doesn't matter anymore.

Lindstrom looked at Mrs. Gunthorpe. "How do you find?"

"We find the defendant not guilty."

The courtroom didn't erupt. Pandemonium didn't break loose. No one seemed particularly surprised or particularly relieved. This is what they all thought was going to happen. At least since yesterday.

Murdo looked at Anne. She nodded at him and left. He turned to Burr. "Thank you," he said. Martha handed Burr a check and left with her son.

Karpinen limped over. "Sudden death goal in overtime."

"I find that hockey is a metaphor for life," Burr said.

"It is, isn't it," Karpinen said.

"Anne Halverson's fingerprints are on the lights," Burr said.

"So are everyone else's on Mackinac Island," Karpinen said.

"Worthy said he saw Anne strangle Jimmy," Burr said.

"I've had enough of Mackinac Island." The prosecutor limped out.

* * *

Jacob, Eve and Aunt Kitty walked down the sidewalk and climbed into the carriage. Aunt Kitty waited on the sidewalk. Burr turned the key in the lock. He looked at the porch swing one last time. He and Zeke started to the carriage. They stopped next to Aunt Kitty.

"Nephew, you did it again. I don't know how, but you did."

"Well, it was …"

"Don't say a word. Not a word. You and Zeke are both lucky that the Cognac upset my stomach. Otherwise, I'd have never tried to walk it off, and if I hadn't heard those two shots, you might both be dead."

"Thank God she missed us both," Burr said.

"I'm not finished, Burr. When it comes to women, you're a fool. A complete fool. But you're brilliant in a courtroom." She started to the carriage, then turned back to him. "You're the idiot savant of law."

Burr helped his aunt into the carriage and climbed in. He and Zeke sat next to her.

"Does he ever stop shedding?" Jacob said.

"How did you figure it out?" Eve said.

"There was something cold about their marriage. Even by Grosse Pointe standards," Burr said.

"That's hardly cause for murder," Jacob said.

"Toad started me wondering. I couldn't figure out why Ronnie Cross was such a big secret. But it was Sidney Ravenswood that really got it going for me."

"All because you stole the pink pony," Eve said.

The carriage rolled down the hill to Main Street.

"All this for a blasted hobby horse," Jacob said.

"When Ravenswood told me he saw a fat man lower it from the flagpole, I knew it was Stubby. My guess is it's hanging in the Bayview Yacht Club."

"Do you think Martha knows about Murdo?" Eve said.

"I'm sure she does," Aunt Kitty said.

"Do you think that Murdo and Anne wanted to have a baby?" Eve said.

"Only if it was an immaculate conception," Burr said.

They passed the marina. *Fujimo* was gone.

"But then things got too close for her. When I asked her about Ronnie Cross, she decided to sacrifice Murdo. That's when she hired Dahlberg, and that's why she wouldn't testify."

"Do you think Dahlberg knew what was going on?" Eve said.

"No. He was all wrapped in the legal ins and outs, not what really happened," Burr said.

Eve turned to Burr. "So, Jimmy was having affairs with Anne and with Murdo."

"Not to mention Ronnie Cross," Burr said.

They went by The Pink Pony one last time. The chains swung in the breeze.

There'll be a new one next year.

"I guess Karpinen's going to be busy with Anne, Worthy, and Carole," Eve said.

"Somehow I don't think so," Burr said.

"Why not?' Eve said.

"I think Karpinen has had enough of Mackinac Island, and there just isn't enough proof." The carriage stopped at the ferry dock. They all got out. Burr paid the driver and they walked across the dock to the ferry.

"Where's the justice in that?" Eve said.

"They all had a part to play, and they're all going to have to live with it. Especially Murdo and Anne. I think that's about as much justice as we're going to get." Burr helped Aunt Kitty up the gangway.

"At least we'll be off this terrible island," Jacob said.

"After one more boat ride," Eve said.

Jacob shuddered.

"I love Mackinac Island," Burr said.

The engines fired. The deckhand cast off. Burr and Zeke sat in the stern. The wind blew in their faces.

A flock of canvasbacks flew just above the waves.

"Zeke, there's still some duck season left."

THE END

Acknowledgements

Thanks to:

Jim Buehler, Dave Irish and Frank Shumway for their expertise on sailboats, sailboat racing and the Port Huron to Mackinac race.

Bob Stocker for his advice about the intricacies of Michigan law.

Carole Erbel for her knowledge and insights about Mackinac Island.

 Ellen Jones for her copy editing, sage advice, encouragement ... and deciphering the yellow-pad scratchings that were my first draft.

Mark Lewison for his copy editing, story editing, unflagging attention to detail, and especially for his enthusiasm.

John Wickham for the cover design.

Bob Deck at Mission Point Press for the book's interior design.

Heather Shaw and Jodee Taylor at Mission Point Press for all their help with publicity and marketing.

Doug Weaver at Mission Point Press for his calming voice and for keeping everything on schedule.

Finally, and most importantly, thanks to my wife, Christi, for encouragement, support, tolerance, patience, and most of all, her love.

They all made *The Pink Pony* a much better work than it otherwise would have been. Whatever shortcomings remain are my own.

About the Author

Reviewers are calling Charles Cutter a master of the courtroom drama and the next Erle Stanley Gardner, author of the Perry Mason series. Although Mr. Cutter has years of legal experience, he is now a "recovering attorney" writing full-time. In addition to the Burr Lafayette series, he has written literary fiction, screenplays, short stories and a one-act play. He is currently working on the next book in the Burr Lafayette series. He lives in East Lansing, Michigan, with his wife, two dogs and four cats. He has a leaky sailboat on Little Traverse Bay and a leakier duck boat on Saginaw Bay.

His books are available on Amazon and at your local bookstore.

For additional information, please go to www.CharlesCutter.com.

Also by Charles Cutter

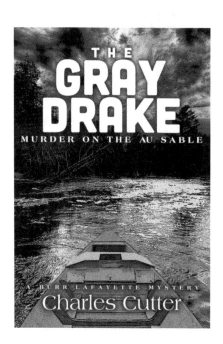

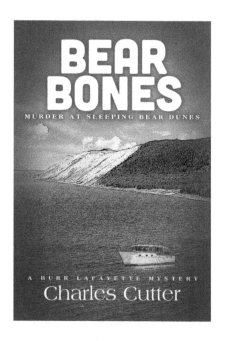

CPSIA information can be obtained
at www.ICGtesting.com
Printed in the USA
LVHW022317270121
677708LV00038B/934

9 781950 659630